Married in Michigan

JASINDA
WILDER

Married in Michigan

1

I HAVEN'T EVEN CLOCKED IN BEFORE TANYA, MY IMMEDIATE superior, is hovering behind me. I try to ignore her, but I can tell she's a little bit stressed. I clock in, change into my uniform—a classic maid outfit: black knee-length shirtwaist dress and white apron, modest and sensible. I examine myself in the little mirror on the inside of my locker: my explosively curly brown hair is braided back into a tight, neat fishtail, the wispies around my temples clipped back with bobby pins. My blue-green eyes look right back at me, friendly and open, and I take a quick peek at my skin—the color of caramel and milk chocolate. No makeup at work because the last thing my employers want, or I want, is to be noticed while I'm cleaning rooms—it's a contracted part of the job, as a matter of fact.

I'm a housekeeper at Beach by deBraun, a boutique hotel in Petoskey, Michigan—owned by none other than the deBrauns; a sprawling family of billionaires. The deBrauns have investments in shipping, technology, hotels, politics, and real estate. This particular hotel is a favorite of the deBrauns, personally over-seen by Camilla deBraun, the matriarch of the family, as her pet project. She's here frequently, and person-ally decorated every room, chose every wall color, lighting sconce, tablecloth, and piece of silverware. Every member of the staff, from housekeeping to desk clerks, are interviewed and hired and fired by Camilla. Front desk clerks are hired as much for their beauty as their skill and experience, and are taught diction by Hollywood voice coaches so as to articulate each syl-lable perfectly, without accent, with perfect elocution. Chefs are Michelin-starred, and even room service dishes are prepared and presented with five-star flair and elegance. Housekeepers are trained to the same exacting standards as the housekeepers at Buckingham Palace, and I am not exaggerating—Tanya's job, as a matter of fact, is to inspect each room before it is as-signed to a new guest, and she does so literally wear-ing white gloves. From toilets to tubs, nightstands to windowsills, every corner and crevice must be dusted to perfection, the beds turned down without a single wrinkle in the freshly laundered sheets and comforters. And we, as the housekeeping staff, are to be seen and not heard, and preferably not seen—"invisible and ef-ficient!" is the motto Camilla insists we live by. Even the shoes we wear are checked for squeaks and creaks. Cart wheels are oiled regularly, vacuums are custom designed by Dyson for deBraun hotels in order to be as silent as possible.

Mine is a very demanding job, and one for which I am well paid.

I finish my preparations for my shift, and finally turn to face my boss. "Let me guess, someone trashed a room and no one else wants to touch it?" I ask, tying the apron around my waist.

Tanya, on the older side of middle age, with graying brown hair in a severe bun, carrying more than a few extra pounds in the usual locations, huffs. "I wish it was that easy," she says.

I stifle a groan. "Bachelor party in one of the suites?"

"Worse," Tanya says.

I blink. "Worse than a bachelor party…a bachelor-ette party then?"

She cackles. "You wish it was a simple matter of penis-shaped glitter balloons." She eyes me with sympathy. "Let's just put it this way—Camilla herself assigned this job to you, and she has authorized me to pay you time and a half for the work. This assignment is your sole job for today."

I raise my eyebrows. "Time and a half? What could have happened that she's assigning me for a full shift at time and a half?"

"Two words—Paxton deBraun."

I groan out loud, "Shit."

Paxton deBraun is a notorious playboy—a twenty-first-century Jay Gatsby, complete with the aura of dark, dramatic mystique, and Paxton is infamous for throwing absolutely wild parties. And by wild, I can truthfully say the stories I've heard make my housekeeper's blood run cold. It seems that until last night, his mother has succeeded in keeping him away from her precious boutique hotel, but it sounds as if that run of good luck is over. I've spoken to other deBraun hotel employees, and they've cleaned up after Paxton bashes in the past, at some of the other hotels, and it was not pretty.

I shudder all over. "You're kidding."

Tanya sighs, patting me on the shoulder. "Nope. He threw a party in the penthouse last night."

"Of course he did."

The penthouse—the entire top floor of the building, with a private elevator, also comes with a private floor of the parking garage, both a private chef and a concierge available twenty-four hours a day, and a Mercedes S-Class with a private driver also available at all hours.

Let's review a few housekeeping facts: the penthouse is an entire floor in the hotel. It takes a team of eight women working in concert for four hours to clean an entire floor's worth of rooms. But this is just me, in a single shift, and I'm cleaning up after a Paxton deBraun party.

"Can I give up the extra pay to get someone to help me?" I ask.

Tanya shakes her head. "No. Camilla was adamant—one person, my best cleaner, my most trustworthy and reliable." She glances around to make sure we're alone in the room. "I guess this was a pretty wild one, and Camilla wants it to stay…quiet." Her eyes fix on mine, giving me a meaningful look, and she lowers her voice. "Cleaning up after these parties of Paxton's is supposed to be…lucrative. I worked with a woman who did one at the deBraun Chicago, and Camilla gave her a big enough bonus afterward that Lucy paid off her mortgage with it." Tanya's eyes widen. "It's not common knowledge, and Lucy had to sign some of kind nondisclosure agreement that she'd keep quiet, both about the bonus and whatever she saw during cleanup."

"Jesus," I mutter. "What did she see?"

Tanya shakes her head. "She wouldn't say, nor would she say how much she got paid, just that she was able to take out her mortgage note with it."

I blow out a breath, stiffen my spine, and lift my chin. "Fine. Let me stock my cart and I'll head up."

Tanya nods. "Bring extra garbage bags, extra gloves, a lot of bleach, and call Rick in maintenance directly when you need something fixed or garbage taken away."

Rick is head of maintenance, which means he's probably being given similar marching orders.

I stock my cart, loading it with extras of pretty much everything I can think of, and then roll it to the service elevator, transfer to the penthouse elevator and take it up the top floor. The doors open directly into the foyer of the penthouse, and my breath halts in my chest—I've never cleaned the penthouse before, so I've never been up here; the view is absolutely breathtaking. Floor-to-ceiling windows frame the foyer, looking out over Lake Michigan, the water rippling with the glittering flash of a billion diamonds in the early morning sun. Seagulls wheel on wingtips, sailboats carve across the bay with white sails, and the sky is endless and blue.

The view of the bay, however, is not what takes my breath away—it's the mess.

I stand in the foyer and try to figure out where I'm even going to start.

I've been to my share of keggers and house parties gone awry, cleaned up after bachelor and bachelorette parties gone crazy, and in the process seen some colossal messes. I have an iron stomach, and an ability to look at a disastrous mess, stay calm, and take on the cleanup one step at a time without getting overwhelmed. It's why Tanya assigned this to me, after all.

But this?

Holy shit.

This mess…I need a bulldozer, and a flamethrower. A hazmat suit, at least.

I look at my contractor-grade garbage bag hanging open off the side of my cart, and realize it's not going to be anywhere near sufficient. I take my walkie-talkie from the cart, switch it to the maintenance channel, and thumb the mic.

"Rick?"

A gruff, smoker's voice answers. "This is Rick."

"This is Makalya, up in the penthouse."

"You just clocked in, and you're already calling me?"

I sigh. "I'm going to need, like, a dumpster. Or a garbage can, or something. And maybe a shovel."

A puzzled silence. "You what?"

"My little garbage bag isn't going to cut the mess I have in front of me, Rick. I need something bigger, or I won't get this done by the end of my shift."

"That bad?"

I sigh into the mic. "That bad."

I replace the walkie-talkie on the cart, stick my hand into a pair of gloves, and then a second pair, and then, with a deep breath, start cleaning.

Trash covers every surface. In order to get past the foyer, I have to wade through a pile of beer bottles, red plastic cups, chip bags, pizza boxes...god knows what else. The trash is too much and too jumbled to make sense of it all. I take a roll of garbage bags, rip one free and shake it open, and start cramming handfuls of trash into it. Within ten minutes, I've filled six bags, and I've barely made a dent in the area directly in front of the foyer.

Rick comes by with a big round gray trashcan on wheels. "Let me know if you need anything else," he says, shaking his head at the mess. "I'm guessing you will, and soon."

I shrug. "I have no idea. Just the garbage is going to take forever."

And, indeed, it does. The kitchen and dining room are just beyond the foyer, and it was clearly ground zero for the party. The counters are cluttered to capacity with empty liquor bottles by the dozen, and beer bottles by the hundred, not to mentions stacks of Solo cups and empty two liters, soda cans, tonic bottles, lime and lemon rinds...I haven't even begun to assess the mess beyond just TRASH.

I fill the garbage can, heave the bag out, replace it with a new liner, and keep going.

I'm finally making a dent in the hundreds of empty liquor bottles—a rough estimate so far would be around a hundred and thirty empty fifths, mostly Grey Goose, Johnnie Walker Blue Label, and Patrón, as well as Dom Perignon, and what I assume are very expensive white and red wines. The amount of money represented here just in liquor is absolutely staggering.

I'm dragging a trash bag to the foyer when I hear an odd honking noise from somewhere in the penthouse—I was so overwhelmed by the mess in here that I hadn't even looked through the rest of the space. I leave the bag near the others in the foyer and head out in search of the noise. Beyond the kitchen and eating area is an open-plan living room, with a huge set of glass doors which open onto a massive roof-top deck, and then beyond the living room and outdoor area is a hallway leading to two guest bedrooms, a full bathroom, and the master suite. I round the back end of the sectional couch that divides the dining room from the living room, and I stop in my tracks, boggled, speechless.

There's a donkey. In the living room. They used the coffee table and part of the sectional to create a little makeshift stall, and the donkey is lying down in a pile of hay. Actual hay, for an actual donkey. There's an empty ice bucket on the ground near the donkey, and the creature is licking at the bottom of the bucket, making a mournful donkey honking sound.

"Now, what the hell?" I mutter to myself.

The donkey hears me, turns its head to face me, and its long ears lay back on its head, it opens its mouth and bares its teeth, and makes a long, low, drawn-out *heeeeee-HAWWWWWWW* sound. The donkey is very clearly displeased. It stands up, tail swishing, and kicks the ice bucket with a front hoof.

I've never been on a farm, never seen a horse or a sheep or a goat or any farm creature any closer than at a petting zoo, but that seems like a pretty obvious gesture—*I'm thirsty.*

"You want some water, huh?" I say, edging slowly toward the coffee table separating me from the donkey. "All right, I'll get you some. Just…you know, don't kick me."

I slide over the coffee table, and the donkey trots toward me with the bucket in its mouth. Now, I'm no coward. I'm a kickboxer, and I'm no slouch with a pair of Kali-Silat sticks, either. I've faced down muggers, date rapists, and just generally nasty people. But animals? Nuh-uh. No way. Not my thing. A cat is about my speed, and that's because you don't have to do anything but give it food and water now and then, and change the litter box. I always thought of donkeys as small, for some reason, but the creature trotting toward me stands almost as big as a horse, and is clearly male—the tackle swinging between its legs is unmissable.

"Heee-haw," the donkey says.

I scream, back away over the coffee table, and press my spine to the window behind me. "You can't come at me like that, donkey. We're not friends, you know."

"Hee-haw-haw—HAWWWW." He drops the bucket on the table, and bobs his head at me.

Are donkeys supposed to be this smart? He's obviously begging me for water.

"Fine, fine." I summon my courage and tiptoe back to the coffee table, which stands knee-height, a four-foot square of thick, raw wood and twisted metal legs. I grab the bucket without getting too close, and fill it at the kitchen sink.

Bringing it back to the donkey, I set it on the coffee table—or that was the plan. The donkey has other ideas, namely shoving his muzzle into the bucket as soon as I'm within reach, splashing water everywhere. But he's so thirsty, drinking so greedily, that I don't dare take it away, or move. This close, the donkey is even bigger than I first thought, and he smells pungently of farm animal.

I'm stuck holding the bucket as he slurps and slurps

until finally he lifts his muzzle, dripping water everywhere, and walks away to stand near his hay. Looking right at me, he lifts his tail and drops a massive pile of shit, in the form of smelly brown balls of nastiness.

"Really?" I shout. "Really?"

"HEEE-haw…hee-hee-HAW."

"Thanks," I mutter. "Thanks a lot."

"Heee-haw."

Better see what other surprises there are waiting for me, I suppose. Leaving the donkey to his hay and his poop, I round his makeshift stall, treading through more Solo cups and beer cans and bottles and empty liquor bottles. The rooftop deck seems to be fairly normal—general party mess, no living animals or strange surprises.

I move into the hallway, and into the first guest bedroom. Aha, yep. Here's the fun: a king bed, two naked men, and four naked women. Not a stitch of clothing between them, bodies and limbs everywhere. Condoms on the floor, on the nightstands, on the dresser—used, I might add. Yuck. More liquor bottles, mostly Grey Goose in here. All the clothing seems to be in the bathroom, for some reason—bras hanging from the showerhead, thongs from the doorknob, suit coats and slacks in the sink, a baggie of cocaine on the counter, more in lines next to it. I back out of the bathroom, wondering what I'm supposed to do with the lines of coke. The next bedroom is more or less the same—this one has just one man, two women, all three naked, drugs, condoms…and a live boa constrictor coiled in the corner of the bathtub.

Not touching that one—no way; I'll have to have Rick call animal control.

What the hell kind of party was this? Donkeys? Snakes? I shake my head as I prepare to enter the master suite. I mentally brace myself for the worst.

I PUSH OPEN THE DOOR TO THE MASTER SUITE, ALREADY cringing at what I'm prepared to find—but, instead of more evidence of total debauchery, the room is clean, empty of trash, and the bed is occupied by a single body. I check the bathroom, but that too is clean and empty—no animals, no hookers or strippers, nothing weird, just an average luxe penthouse bathroom, with miles of marble and acres of shower space and fluffy white towels on towel warming racks...

Back in the bedroom it is evident the person in the bed is clearly a male...the sheet is tangled low around his waist, revealing the fact that the sleeping man is in fact naked—and immaculately, perfectly, deliciously, incredibly gorgeous. Even from halfway across the room, it's obvious he's a perfect male specimen—broad shoulders, tanned skin, a smattering of body hair on a hard chest and a thin trail down between rippling abs...the sheet doesn't quite cover the evidence that he's experiencing...*ahem*...what I suppose is the natural physical process of male anatomy common in the morning. By which I mean he's got morning wood the sheet cannot contain, and holy hell and almighty heaven, the man is hung like a freaking elephant.

I turn away immediately—well, *almost* immediately. Sort of. I mean, good grief, how can a girl *not* take a second look at that? Or a third? God, get out of the room, Makayla.

Okay, okay. Moving on.

Nothing to clean up in here, clearly, so no reason to be in the master suite.

But damn, the man is perfect—one last look: dark brown, nearly black hair, jaw stubbled with a days' worth or so of beard growth. I assume the occupant of the master suite is Paxton deBraun himself—so my assumption is that he's as arrogant and awful as he is beautiful.

None of my business, though. My job is to clean this room.

Which I assume doesn't include evicting the occupants, as they're guests of Mr. deBraun, which means check out times do not apply.

Clean the mess, Makayla.

I return to the public living spaces—to where the worst of the mess is. First things first, the animals.

I click my walkie-talkie. "Rick?"

"Yeah."

"I'm going to need animal control up here."

A long, significant pause. "Animal control?"

"Yeah."

"Should I even ask?"

I sigh. "There's a donkey in the living room, and giant-ass boa constrictor in one of the bathrooms."

"Haha. Yes, Paxton deBraun is an ass, and no, I don't want to know how hung he is."

I swallow hard to keep from laughing somewhat hysterically at that. "Um, no. I mean, there's a literal, actual, real-life donkey in the living room, and a literal, actual, real-life snake in the tub."

"Shit. For real?" At that moment, the donkey lets out a deafening *HEE-HEE-HAW-HAW-HAWWW*. Rick cackles abruptly. "Holy mother of shit. That was a donkey."

"Told you."

"And a snake, you say?"

"A big, giant-ass snake. It was all coiled up in the tub so I couldn't guess at a length, but what I could see was thick as my thigh. So unless you know how to handle donkeys and snakes, call animal control."

"Yeah, I'm on it."

I pause. "Is there an animal control for naked hookers?" I ask.

Rick snickers on the other end. "I volunteer my services."

"Judging by the number of used condoms I'm gonna have to clean up, I'm guessing they've been very well… serviced."

"Yeah, well…still my services are still available. Assuming they ain't ugly, and being that deBraun hired 'em, I'm guessing they ain't."

I sigh. "Men."

He laughs. "Just remember, we're all the same, deep down. When you think you've found Prince Charming? Just remember he's still a dude."

My turn to cackle. "Yeah, right—I've come to the conclusion that Prince Charming has never existed, and never will."

"Listen, I got a bathroom with a leaky faucet to fix, and now animal control to call."

"Over and out," I say.

Another laugh. "Exactly. Try not to need me for anything else, yeah?"

"I'd love nothing more."

That conversation over, I go back to the mess in the kitchen, and it takes me more than two hours just to bag up all the trash, at which point the foyer is filled with piles of bulging contractor-grade garbage bags. And that's just the kitchen. Another hour to collect the trash elsewhere—I don't exactly tiptoe in the guest rooms, but the naked occupants are clearly down for the count and don't stir.

I turn the walkie to the housekeeping channel. "Tanya? This is Makayla. I need some…directions."

After a minute, the walkie crackles. "Channel nine."

I change to the correct channel. "Tanya?"

"What's up?"

"What do I do about the beds?"

"Change them?" Tanya answers, somewhat testily.

"There are people in them. Several people per bed, passed out."

"Oh." A hesitation. "I guess do everything but the beds, and hope they wake up and leave before your shift is over."

"Okay. Thanks."

I huff, annoyed, and go back to cleaning—wipe down the counters and cabinets, scrub the sink to gleaming, empty out the refrigerator, clean it, and replace the items; sweep and mop the kitchen floor; vacuum the area I've cleaned. Animal control still hasn't shown up, so the donkey is still here, which makes trying to clean the living room pointless. Argh. Bedrooms, then. I can clean the bathrooms and vacuum the floors, just not make the bed, and I'm not touching the tub with the snake in it.

The first bedroom, then. Ugh, so many naked people—penises, butts, and boobs galore. Condoms everywhere, used and unused. I put a third pair of rubber gloves on, and start picking up. Throw out no less than eight used condoms and their attendant ripped-open wrappers, shove the strings of unused condoms in the box and set the box on the nightstand, trying to keep my eyes on my work rather than the two dicks and eight sets of silicone tits immediately to my left.

"Unnngh—" a female voice moans.

The sounds of imminent vomiting can be heard—I leap with alacrity to grab my garbage bag. The woman nearest the edge of the bed is rolling to the side, mascara and eye shadow and lipstick smeared beyond all recognition, making her look like a cartoon clown. She's groaning, holding her hand over her mouth. I hold the garbage bag under her mouth just in time to catch a long, splattering stream of vomit..., which turns my stomach, but I've dealt with worse, so this doesn't entirely faze me. Babysitting alcohol-poisoned prostitutes isn't in my job description, but it's better to catch the hork in a bag rather than have to clean it off the floor.

She blinks at me blearily, clearly still drunk. "Water."

I restrain the urge to snap, knowing Mrs. deBraun would expect me to go out of my way to care for the hotel's guests, no matter who they are, no matter the request.

I find a cold bottle of water, and even an industrial-sized bottle of off-brand acetaminophen, and bring both to the bedroom. Upon my return with water and painkillers, I find the rest of the bed's occupants waking up in various stages of illness. Sighing under my breath, I provide them each with wastepaper can-sized garbage bags and bottles of water.

One of the men—hugely muscled and well-padded with fat, covered in body hair, with a receding hairline and a Rolex still on his wrist—eyes me as he spits bile into the bag. "Paxton sure knows how to party—even provides wake-up drunk services."

I can't quite stop myself from glaring at him. "I'm with the hotel housekeeping, actually. Giving you bags to puke in just makes my job of cleaning up after you easier."

His head wobbles on his neck. "Ohhh." His bleary eyes go to the naked women in the bed with him. "Oooh—nothin' better than waking up to hot naked bitches in the bed."

One of the aforementioned women gives him a death glare. "Our contract was through six this morning." She glances at the digital clock on the nightstand, which reads well past ten in the morning. "Which means I don't have to listen to you talk to me that way."

"How about I hire you for the morning, then?"

"How about you fuck off?"

"How about I talk to your madam about your attitude?"

I huff in disgust as I push my cleaning cart out of the room, leaving them to hash it out. Donning my backpack vacuum, I reenter the room and make quick work of vacuuming, ignoring the bickering. I pile the various items of clothing on the couch under the window.

I scurry through scrubbing the toilet, cleaning the mirror, the floors, and the shower, even as I realize I'll just have to do the bathroom again since the occupants will likely use the bathroom before leaving. But maybe if I make a nuisance of myself, they'll leave sooner. I leave the cocaine where it is, cleaning around it.

I finish the bathroom and head for the next bedroom. A quick check in the living room says animal control still hasn't shown up, as the donkey is still braying noisily and shitting everywhere.

The occupants of the second guest room stay passed out as I clean—once more piling clothing on the couch, vacuuming, cleaning the bathroom and not touching the drugs on the bathroom counter.

Once the guest rooms are clean, I grab the walkie-talkie again. "Tanya?"

"Yes?" she asks, a minute later.

"Two questions." I hesitate. "Wait, this is a private line, yes? And you're alone?"

"Hold on—" a silence, and then the walkie crackles. "Okay, go."

"First, there's cocaine in both guest bathrooms—bags of it, and lines. I cleaned around it, but I wasn't about to touch it, and I'm not sure what you want me to do with it. Second, I told Rick to call animal control, but they're not here yet, and I can't clean until they come take care of the donkey and the snake."

A silence. "The what?"

"A live donkey in the living room, and a live boa in one of the tubs."

"I really don't want to know," Tanya says.

"Me either," I say. "I just want them gone so I can clean up and go home."

"A *donkey*?"

"Yep."

"What the hell?" Tanya mutters. "Fuckin' weird-ass rich people."

"No kidding," I answer.

"Okay, I'll call them and see what's up."

"Thanks."

"Don't touch the drugs. Leave it for the deBrauns to handle, especially since I'm guessing our guest of honor is still there."

"That's what I was thinking, just had to be sure." I sigh. "And yes, he's here, as well as a few others."

"I don't want to know. The less I know, the better."

"Lucky," I mutter into the walkie. "Okay, back to work."

"I'll let you know what animal control says."

"Great."

And…back to work.

The master suite is last, and the room I want least to enter again. But, it's my job. At least there are no weird surprises in here. I go in, clean the bathroom, even though it's mostly clean already and doesn't really need much besides a little shine and polish. I ignore the figure in the bed—now more covered, thank god—and start the vacuum.

"Shut that fucking thing off, goddammit," I hear a deep, angry, sleepy male voice growl.

"Sorry, sir," I say. "Housekeeping."

"Well housekeep somewhere fucking else."

I dare a glance at him: he's upright in the bed with the sheet pooled around his waist—seems like his morning issue has subsided, thank god. Mussed dark brown hair that's entirely too sexy for someone waking up drunk, and deep, wild, irritated, sleepy brown eyes—although brown is nowhere near descriptive enough. Golden—not quite tan, not quite khaki, not quite brown. A pure animal golden-brown.

I decide the better part of valor is to simply listen, so I take the vacuum and my cart and head for the door.

"Coffee."

I pause, summoning every ounce of self-control I possess. "I'm housekeeping, sir, but I'd be glad to call room service for you, if you like."

"My family owns this hotel and I'm telling you to make some damn coffee. There's a pot and a bag of grounds in the kitchen." He waves a hand at me. "I'm not asking you to serve it to me, just...fuck. My head is pounding."

"Well, you brought it on yourself, you know." A new voice startles us both—female, crisp, authoritative, brusque, and impatient; I turn to see Camilla deBraun waiting on the other side of my cart. "Excuse me please, I need to speak with my son."

Tall, at least five-ten, with raven black hair pulled up in a sleek, elegant chignon, dressed in what I'm guessing is a custom-made designer sheath dress; she's slender, beautiful, elegant, and exudes authority.

I pull the cart backward out of the room and wheel it aside. "Sorry, ma'am."

She waves a hand, sparing me a quick glance. "I know it's not your job, dear, but please start the coffee maker. He's ever so much more tractable once he's had caffeine."

"Yes, ma'am."

I leave the cart, slip the vacuum off my shoulders and set it on the floor near the cart, heading for the kitchen.

I hear Camilla as I walk away: "Now, Paxton. I'd like you to explain, if you can, why there is a donkey in my penthouse."

I can't help myself—I poke my head back in. "Sorry to interrupt, but, um…there's also a giant boa constrictor in the second guest bathroom." I pause. "Animal control should be on the way to handle it, ma'am."

She stares at me. "A boa constrictor." Her voice is flat. "You're joking."

I shake my head, eyes wide—Mrs. deBraun is intimidating under the best of circumstances, and I'm far from easily intimidated. "No, ma'am."

Her eyes narrow at her son. "A snake?"

He shrugs. "I dunno, Mom. It was a party. People do weird shit."

I head for the kitchen, dump grounds into a filter, add water to the reservoir of the coffee maker, and press start—within seconds, there's a gurgle of hot water percolating through the system; a few moments later, coffee trickles into the carafe. The coffee maker is sleek and expensive-looking, a clear plastic reservoir, carafe, and a basket for the filter. No extras, no timer or auto-start or fancy buttons, but the coffee is made within minutes. God, I want one. I have been using Mom's ancient Mr. Coffee machine from what I imagine is the 1970s, and it takes forever to make coffee, the hot plate doesn't work, and it only makes three small mugs worth of lukewarm, weak coffee.

This thing? Probably costs more than my car.

Sigh. Rich people.

When there's enough coffee in the carafe, I pour some into a mug and grab a bottle of water from the fridge—I snag the bottle of painkillers from the guest room, where the occupants seem to have come to some sort of arrangement, as there's moaning under the covers; I hurry out and close the door, but the moaning—faked female screams—gets louder and louder by the moment.

I bring the coffee, water, and pill bottle into the master suite and set them on the nightstand. Without a word of thanks to me, Paxton deBraun tosses back three pills with a swallow of water, and then settles back against a nest of pillows, the sheet once again draped low over his waist; no erection this time, thankfully.

A voice calls from foyer: "Animal control!"

Camilla shoots me a glance. "Deal with that, will you, dear? Thank you." She suddenly looks to one side, at the adjoining wall from which comes ever-louder screaming. "And that too, please."

I widen my eyes. "Um, that's...that's Mr. deBraun's...guests, ma'am."

She narrows her eyes at me. "By guests, you mean his degenerate friends and their gaggle of prostitutes?"

I nod. "I...yes, ma'am. As far as I can tell, ma'am."

She sighs. "Fine. You deal with the animal control situation, and I'll deal with the prostitutes and degenerates." She stands, sniffing. "Honestly, I have no problem with the prostitutes. It's your so-called friends I cannot abide."

"They're not degenerates, Mom," Paxton growls. "They just like a good time."

"We'll discuss that in a moment, Paxton."

"Whatever."

Camilla stalks toward the bedroom door and rolls her eyes at me, as if commiserating. "You're a grown man, Paxton, and one with several Ivy League degrees. Let's graduate beyond monosyllabic grunts, shall we?"

I head to the foyer and find two animal control officers looking a bit out of their element. I show them the donkey, and then the snake. Of course, to get to the snake, they have to go past the occupants of the second room, who have woken up at this point, and who are now engaged in a rather acrobatically flexible display of oral sexual three-way exchange. They don't seem to notice us as I show the officer the giant snake—the officer is a female, and she has a large plastic crate with a lid containing air holes, and one of those long-handled poles with the adjustable loops at the end. She makes easy work of snagging the head of the snake with the pole, and then heaves the bulk of the massive snake into the crate—the snake seems to not care a whit, and even complies by tucking its head down into the corner of the crate so she can close the lid. The crate now containing the snake is so heavy that she has to drag it by one end, but even so the orgy in the bed doesn't stop. I shake my head, following her out. The other officer, at this point, has the donkey somewhat under control, with a halter around its muzzle and a leash attached to the halter, and he's struggling to lead the recalcitrant animal out of the living room and onto the elevator. The donkey is less inclined to cooperate than the snake was, however, and fights all the way onto the elevator. Eventually, the officer, a large man with graying blond hair and a wispy goatee, gets the loudly braying creature onto the elevator, and the second officer drags the snake crate after her and, with a quick thank you to me, they're gone.

I sigh, then.

Turning, I find Camilla loudly shooing people out of the first bedroom. "Enough, all of you. Ladies, if you haven't been paid, you can rest assured that my son always pays his debts. Gentlemen, the party is over. Please leave."

There's grumbling, but two men hobble out, hurriedly hopping into pants and carrying the rest of their clothing. Rightly afraid of Mrs. deBraun, they're gone within minutes. The women are slower to leave, taking their time to dress.

"We were paid up front," one of them says to Camilla. "But after the way this party went, if he calls us again, we're doubling our rates." She snorts. "We didn't get paid anywhere near enough for what they wanted us to do."

Camilla shakes her head and holds up her hands. "No, no, no. Please, spare me the details. Charge him whatever you wish, I don't care, I'm not paying for it anymore. Just please be on your way. There's coffee made, if you want some." She's oddly solicitous of them, I'm noticing, as I go about the nasty business of cleaning up after the donkey; her next words make clear why. "Did my son have you sign a nondisclosure agreement with your contract?"

I focus on using the dustpan to scoop donkey shit into a bag, but I'm definitely eavesdropping.

The spokeswoman of the prostitutes nods. "Yeah, we all signed one. No talking about him, or this party, or any of his friends, or anything that happened. We sell the story, we get sued."

Mrs. deBraun nods, somehow managing to seem both pleased and nonplussed at the same time. "At least he had that much sense." A noise from the second room draws her attention, and she glances at me. "Are there more?"

I nod. "Yes, ma'am."

She sighs. "The snake is gone, I hope?"

"Yes, ma'am."

She eyes the mess I'm cleaning up. "That is positively vile." A disgusted sigh. "Will the rug be salvageable, do you think?"

I shrug. "I don't know yet, ma'am. I should have a better idea in a few minutes, though. I'm nearly done cleaning up the poop."

She glances at the bedroom, from which male grunts can be heard. "Yes, as am I."

I snicker at that, and then go back to work. Once the piles of shit and garbage are bagged and set with the rest in the foyer, it's obvious immediately that the rug—an expensive hand-woven import, by the looks of it—is beyond salvage. I slide the furniture off it and move the rug aside—the hardwood floors underneath are stained, and I go to work trying to fix the situation. I remain focused as Camilla finishes ushering the last of Paxton's guests out of the penthouse, and then she floats serenely over to the couch, settling to sit down on it.

I wince. "I, um…I wouldn't sit there, ma'am. The couch was part of what Mr. deBraun's friends used to contain the donkey, and I don't know how clean the couch is."

She shoots up, swiping at the seat of her dress with both hands, which come away covered in slobber, hay, and who knows what else. "Oh my, how disgusting." She wiggles her hands, and then rushes to the kitchen sink to wash her hands, and then sighs at me. "So, the rug?"

I wince again and shake my head. "I'm sorry, ma'am. I'll bring it downstairs and work on it, but I'm honestly not hopeful. It's pretty stained."

Another long-suffering sigh, French-manicured fingers dimpling against her delicate temples. "That rug was a personal gift to me from the Sultan of Brunei."

I blink. "Sounds like it was expensive."

A slant-wise look at me, smacking of disbelief. "Have you heard the term 'priceless', Miss Poe?"

Yes, she knows us all by name, from housekeeping to janitorial staff to chef to clerk. "Oh," I say. "In that case, you may want to have someone who's an expert in priceless rugs try to fix it. I would just be spraying it with Resolve, scrubbing, and hoping for the best."

This earns me a faint ghost of a smile. "Yes, an expert would be best, I believe." She pours herself a mug of coffee, leaning her backside against the edge of the kitchen counter, and eyes me speculatively. "I think you'll have earned quite a bonus for this cleanup, Miss Poe. Paxton has thrown some wild parties in his day, but this one takes the cake." She snorts. "A live donkey. Someone's idea of a joke, probably."

I'm not certain what response if any is required from me, so I just smile, shrug, and keep working on the stained hardwood with a hardwood floor cleaning and polishing agent and a rag.

"More coffee?" I hear Camilla say, which is answered by a single grunt. I risk a quick glance to see Paxton with a towel wrapped around his waist, hair a gloriously beautiful mess, desperately sipping at a fresh mug of coffee; the pot is empty, which means in five... four...three...two...one...

"Miss Poe?" Camilla says.

"Yes ma'am. I'm on it." I toss my rag over my shoulder and head into the kitchen to make more.

Which means brushing past Paxton. He smells... good. How can he smell good? He's been partying all night. He probably screwed one or all of those hookers. He's still drunk. He has no right to smell like expensive cologne.

I make a fresh pot of coffee, and as I brush past him once more, I catch his eyes on me. A quick glance, and I'm dismissed.

Nothing special.

Nothing to see here.

That's my job—to be invisible, unnoticeable. Sometimes, though, a girl wants to be noticed, especially by a gorgeous, naked man who I know for a fact has a monster...*ahem*.

Work, Makayla. Work. He's an arrogant, lazy, spoiled, entitled rich white asshole.

He'll never even look at me again.

And, as I go back to scrubbing the hardwood floors, he indeed doesn't spare me a second glance. As a housekeeper, I'm little more than furniture to someone like him.

I keep working, ignore the brooding, beautiful, silent man in the kitchen, and his mother, who is visibly displeased—the entire penthouse seethes with her displeasure.

I don't envy the tongue-lashing I'm certain is coming his way.

A subtle glance at Paxton tells me he knows it as well as I do—his shoulders are hunched, and he's curled in around his coffee mug like it can protect him from his mother.

"It's time we had a serious talk about your lifestyle, Paxton."

Oh boy, here we go. Front row seats.

3

"NO THANKS, MOM," PAXTON DRAWLS. "I'LL pass.

A snort. "I'm sure you'd like to. But unfortunately for you, this one isn't negotiable."

A groan. "Must we, Mother? Now?"

Her voice raises just a little to impinge on his hangover headache, I'm certain. "Yes, Paxton, now. We've allowed you your dalliance, up until now, your father and I have."

"Can this wait until I've eaten something?" Paxton mutters.

She huffs, whips out a cell phone and dials a number. "Good morning, Julius. An egg white omelet with spinach, whole wheat toast, and a side of sweet potato hash. To the penthouse, thank you."

Julius is the chef assigned to the penthouse when it's occupied, and he's a wizard with eggs—if he likes you, and you ask him nicely, he'll make you an omelet after your shift, and god, the things the man can do with eggs and cheese are simply sinful.

Paxton groans. "Egg whites, Mother? Do I look like I need to watch my weight?"

I suppress a snicker at that, because he clearly can afford to eat a less-than-healthy breakfast. He's ripped, without an ounce of extra fat anywhere on his body.

"Honestly, how you've managed to retain your physique with the way you live your life is beyond me."

Paxton growls. "I work my ass off, actually. I'm in the gym ninety minutes a day, four days a week, and I run five miles the other three days."

"And yet you drink your body weight in alcohol most nights."

"Less than you'd think, actually. I host the parties, but I don't get hammered at all of them."

Camilla snorts. "You're still drunk, Paxton. I'm not stupid."

"Yes, I am. This was one of the rare nights I cut loose." He sighs. "I'm not as irresponsible as you seem to think."

"The media sees you as irresponsible and untrustworthy, Paxton. There have been articles in the *Huffington Post*, Vox, *Variety*, *People*, and *Time* about how you're essentially a good-for-nothing playboy, less relevant and useful than even a reality TV star."

"Who cares what the media has to say?" Paxton snarls. "I sure as hell don't."

"You sure as hell *should*, as a matter of fact." A heavy, significant pause. "Unless you've changed your mind regarding your political career."

"I'm one of the youngest members of the House of Representatives, Mother."

"And if you want to continue past the House, you need to clean up your image, Son." Another of those somewhat sad, long-suffering, condescending, mothering sighs. "We've discussed this before, Paxton, but it's reached critical mass. This latest party of yours is proof. A donkey, Paxton? Really?"

"A practical joke by Robert, Mother."

"Well, I admire the fact that you have friends across the aisle, and we'll need to leverage your bipartisan reputation certainly, but your Republican friend's practical joke ruined a Persian rug hand-woven two hundred years ago, a rug which was a personal gift to me from the Sultan of Brunei himself."

"Oh. Well. I'll pay to have it replaced."

"It cannot be *replaced*, Paxton," Camilla snarls. "It was *priceless* and *irreplaceable*."

"I'm sorry, Mother."

"There was also a snake in the tub, I'm told?"

A groan. "Crap, I forgot about that stupid snake. I told Drake not to bring it."

"Well, animal control has it, now."

"That's Drake's problem, not mine."

"The point is, this has gone on long enough. It's time to stop behaving like a careless frat boy. It's time to settle down."

During this exchange I've done my best on the hardwood floor, and have moved on to cleaning the furniture—vacuuming the donkey hair off the couches, polishing the coffee table, stain removal from various parts of the furniture—and all the while I've been listening to Camilla's tirade, and a few stolen glances tell me Paxton is pretty much tuning her out.

"If you want to make the move to senator, and especially if you want to put yourself in position for Speaker or Majority Whip, you need a much cleaner image." Camilla pauses. "You need a wife, Paxton."

"I don't want one." Paxton sips coffee, as if this declaration is all he needs to say on the matter.

"You need a wife," Camilla repeats. "You need a woman to soften your image, to give you the appearance of someone who has sowed his wild oats, making you relatable to the younger voters, but who has gotten serious and has the maturity to look at the issues clearly and responsibly."

"I can do that without getting married."

"Well, our staff of political advisors think differently."

"Your staff of political advisors just want to make more work for themselves. Grooming my image means they stay employed."

"You've been photographed with a different woman every weekend for the last four years, Paxton."

"So?"

"And there are the photos from your vacation to Santorini."

"Which is why everyone signs NDAs now. Nonissue."

"It *is* an issue. Every time your name is brought up in the news cycle, those photos come out."

"I don't care about the news cycle."

"Then you don't understand politics, Paxton."

"I took my seat in the House when I was twenty-nine—I was single, I was in the news, and I attracted trouble. Yet I still got voted in."

"The Senate is different, Paxton. The stakes are higher, and so are the expectations."

"I'm not playing the game your advisors want me to play, Mother." He sips coffee again, clutching at the towel; I turn away before he catches me staring.

Camilla sighs, and lets the silence build.

"What, Mother?" I hear the impatience in his voice. "I know you have something else to say."

"It's time to settle down, Paxton."

"You've said this already." Paxton grunts. "I'll tone back the parties, okay? And I'm sorry about your rug. For real."

Another pause, and even I can tell her silence is that of a loaded gun preparing to fire. "We've made a decision on your behalf, Paxton."

This gets his attention. "You have, have you?" Amused, more than anything. "And what might that be?"

"In one hundred and twenty days from today, there will be a wedding." This time, the pause is positively explosive. "St. Patrick's Cathedral in Manhattan—and you don't want to know what I had to do to get that slot—with a reception at the Plaza. The invites have gone out already, and to a who's who of politics, music, and Hollywood."

I detect a faint note of rising panic in his flat, modulated voice. "Who's the lucky couple?"

Another, longer, tenser, thicker pause. "You, Paxton."

"But I'm not getting married, Mother."

I can't help but pause in my cleaning of a window in the living room, ears pricked, doing my best to not stop and outright listen.

"Ah, see, that's where you're wrong, my son." Her voice is…somewhere between crackling with icy cold, and razor-sharp. "You are. The wedding is yours—and it is nonnegotiable."

He's caught speechless. "I…but…" A sharp inhalation. "I am *not* getting married. I'm not dating anyone, because I don't date. So who, pray tell, would I be getting married to, in this theoretical wedding of yours?"

Camilla's sigh is soft and slow, but no less somehow audibly threatening for all that. "Paxton. Dear boy. Allow me to be crystal clear." I dare a peek: she's cupping one of his stubble-scruffy cheeks in a manicured hand, a condescending smile on her perfect face; I immediately turn back to wiping down the window. "You will be at the altar of St. Patrick's Cathedral in one hundred and twenty days from today. You will say 'I do', you will exchange vows, and you will become a married man. If you wish to continue receiving the support, both personal, political, and financial, of the deBraun family trust and board of advisors, you will take a wife, and you will cease your philandering, and clean up your playboy-every day is a party-devil may care mess of a life and image. As far as the world is concerned, you will become a family man. Your wife will appear on your arm, in photographs, on the town whether in DC, New York, LA, or anywhere on this planet. You will not be seen with any other women, you will not be *connected* in any way to any other woman ever again. There will be no scandals of any kind attached to the name Paxton deBraun."

"Mom—"

"I'm not finished, Paxton." A sharp snap of her voice. "You *do* have a choice in this matter, so don't try to paint this as being left without a choice. Your choice is to get married and *stay* married, and remain in the good graces of this family's considerable support, or if you wish, you may make your own way in this world, using the resources, influence, and finances you've made for yourself."

"Are you fucking kidding me right now?"

"Do I sound like I'm kidding?"

"Fuck." He snarls under his breath, a vicious, feral, curse-laden sound. "How am I supposed to find someone to marry me in four months?"

"We've arranged a...fallback."

"Oh no. No way."

"Yes."

"*Hell* no."

"Cecily Amador-Richards is a beautiful, successful, intelligent young woman of impeccable breeding. She would make an excellent wife to an up-and-coming senator…and an invaluable asset for someone considering an eventual run for…say…the Oval Office."

"Mother." His voice is venomous. "I wouldn't marry that fucking snake of an ice-cold bitch if she were the last woman on earth."

"That's a little excessive, Paxton."

"It's nowhere even close to capturing how much I despise her, Mother."

"You're harboring a grudge, Paxton. Let bygones be bygones."

"You don't know what you're talking about. You have no idea what happened, and I'm not about to tell you, but let's just say I wouldn't touch her with a twenty-nine-and-a-half-foot pole. And I would wager a case of Rolexes that she feels the same way."

"Then you owe me a case of Rolexes." I hear a rustling of paper, and risk another quick glance to see Camilla withdrawing a folded letter from her purse. "In her own hand, signed, sealed, and delivered."

"No one seals letters anymore."

Yet, another stolen glance tells me the letter is indeed sealed with wax. I've finished the window, and move on to the next one—farther away, so I have to listen even harder; this is better entertainment than *Real Housewives*.

There are a few moments of silence as Paxton reads.

"Un-fucking-believable."

"Must you be so vulgar, Paxton? I know I raised you better than that."

"Oh please, Mother. Boarding academy and military school raised me, not you."

"Now, now, Paxton, let's not bring up that old warhorse of an argument."

"How the hell did you all convince Cecily to agree to this?"

"It's a perfect match, that's all. Anyone can see how you two are made for each other."

"Meaning, her family is holding her inheritance over her head, too."

"I'm sure I have no idea what agreement she's made with her parents. I know she was...reticent, at first, but she's come around." A significant pause. "As will you."

"You make a good case for a vow of poverty, if not celibacy, Mother."

"Oh, come now, Paxton. It can't be *that* bad."

"She fucked my best friend in *my* bed on *my* boat, on *our* three-year anniversary."

"You cannot claim innocence on that score, Paxton. I know this for a fact."

"Yeah, but I didn't sleep with her best friend, and I didn't do it for all-access passes to Coachella."

"You're making that up."

"Harry confirmed it, after I knocked his fucking veneers down his fake-tanned throat."

"He was just trying to pass the buck, Paxton."

"She'll suck as many dicks as it takes to get her fifteen minutes of fame, Mom. She'd trade her soul for likes on Instagram. She'd send her entire family to a mass grave if it meant being more relevant than Kim Kardashian."

"Paxton!" A whip of a command. "Enough. There may be bad blood between you, but that's going too far."

"Okay, fine—she'd sell her *parents*. Maybe not the entire family."

"Paxton!"

"I'm not doing it, Mother! I'll live under an underpass before I'll go near her." His voice is hard as steel, and as icy as his mother's. "Trust me on this one: I *will not* marry Cecily—no matter the cost."

"Then you'd better bring your own girl, Paxton, because this is nonnegotiable. Cecily, a Kardashian, a hooker from one of your parties, I don't care. As long as she toes the line and plays the game *our* way. You *will* get married, or you *will* be cut out of the will, the trust, everything. We won't disown you, in the sense of never speaking to you again—you're our son and we love you. But we *will* cut you off. This is hardball, Paxton."

"Goddammit."

"Look, Son...just between you and me? I don't really like her either. But she knows how to play the game, and well. You get married, you pose for photos, play husband and wife, have a couple of kids, make it look real for the press. In private, as long as you're discreet, you can do what you want. You and Cecily can live your own lives, have your tawdry little affairs, and no one will know or care, if you're smart and discreet about it."

This makes me snort—I can't help it. It just...erupts out of me. What a crock of bullshit!

Both Camilla and Paxton fix identical stares at me.

"Something to say, Miss Poe?" Camilla's voice could put frost on a hot grill.

I fake a cough. "No, ma'am. Allergies, ma'am, my apologies."

A tense silence. "The bed in the master suite needs turning over, Miss Poe," she says. "Perhaps you could see to that?"

"Certainly, ma'am."

I head into the master bedroom, strip the bed, clean the bathroom, vacuum the rug under the bed and the hardwoods around it, dust, replace the bedding with fresh, clean sheets and a new comforter—unlike most hotels, we replace the blankets and comforter after every guest with freshly dry-cleaned linens.

Once the master bedroom is turned over, I finish the other bedrooms because Camilla is still arguing with Paxton about the marriage idea, and if I want to keep my job it's best I stay away or my mouth will get the better of me—and I'll get fired.

I'm nearly finished with the bedrooms when I hear Camilla's voice, Rick's voice, and then the sound of trash bags being removed from the foyer. All that's left now is to put the finishing touches on the kitchen, figure out the imported rug situation, and then I'm done and I can go home.

Hopefully with a tidy little bonus, on top of time and a half.

Upon my emergence into the living area, I find Paxton at the table, picking at his egg-white omelet, looking morose.

Rick is still carting away the many, many bags of garbage, and Camilla is gone, so I'm free to finish the kitchen.

I hesitate, however. "Mr. deBraun? I need to finish the kitchen, sir. Will you need anything else in here?"

He waves a hand. "Just the coffee."

The pot is empty again, and I realize he's had two full pots already. "Should I make another pot?"

He glances at the coffee maker. "Oh. It's gone again." He sighs, poking at the omelet with his fork. "No, it's fine."

"Then I'll just clean it out, sir."

"Fine. Whatever."

I clean out the coffee maker, which includes running a cycle with white vinegar.

"God, what the hell is that smell?" Paxton snaps. "Vinegar?"

"Yes sir." I gesture at the pot. "Coffee pots get run with vinegar after every guest."

He frowns at me. "Why?"

"It kills any mold or mildew and removes calcification. So each guest who makes coffee gets as clean and new a coffee maker as possible."

He watches as I wipe down the counters again, and then use glass cleaner on the refrigerator shelves. "You're pretty fucking thorough, aren't you?"

"Yes, sir. I'm paid to be as thorough as humanly possible."

His gaze is speculative, those lion-golden eyes fixed on me with an interest that makes my girl parts sit up and beg, and my heart and mind retreat behind my walls. "Are you paid to eavesdrop on conversations, too?"

"No, that's just a perk of the job," I hear myself say, before my professional filter can stop it.

He snorts. "Allergies, huh?"

I fake another cough. "Yeah, allergies. Bad this year." I sniffle, for good measure.

His eye roll is a pretty good indicator he's not buying it.

The coffee maker finishes burbling the last of the vinegar, so I dump the pot, rinse it until the scent of vinegar is gone, and then run the machine again with fresh cold water to rinse the vinegar out of the machine.

"Why the snort? For real?"

I hesitate. "I told you. Allergies."

I'm keeping busy just to keep away from him and

his eyes and his scent and his heat and that stupid shredded body of his—I'm sweeping the kitchen even though it can't get much cleaner.

I'm not even aware that he's moved from his place at the table, but his hand latches onto the broom, halting it. I flinch, my eyes floating slowly and reticently upward to his.

"Why did you snort, Miss Poe?" His voice is commanding.

I blink, chewing on my tongue to keep a salty retort from getting me fired. "I...I have to get the rug to the cleaners."

"Mom's got that handled. The janitor guy is taking it to a specialist."

"You mean Rick, head of maintenance?" I say, and immediately wince at the sass in my voice.

Paxton waves a hand. "Whoever. The guy, he's handling it." He doesn't let go of the broom, which somehow prevents me from going anywhere. "Why did you snort, Miss Poe?"

I bite down hard on my lip. "Because sometimes my attitude gets the better of me. I apologize, Mr. deBraun."

"Answer the question." He's closer to me, standing face to face, towering over me, golden-brown eyes commanding and demanding.

"I'm not supposed to converse with guests like this, sir," I say, edging for the exit, ducking my head to escape those damned sexy, predatory golden eyes.

"I'm not a guest, I'm your boss."

"With all due respect, sir, your mother is my boss."

He smirks. "Yes sir, no sir. I like that." He's looking at me. *Into* me.

I only just restrain the urge to smack him across the face. "I have to go, *sir*."

"You don't."

I blink. "I. Um. Yes—I do, as a matter of fact. Once I'm finished cleaning this unit, I'm done…and I'm done. So, I have to go."

"You have to answer my question, Miss Poe."

"Stop calling me that, please," I say, mostly managing to sound decently polite and respectful.

"I don't know your name."

"Makayla."

Shit. Why did I tell him that? He doesn't need to know my name. As if he'll remember it anyway.

"Makayla. Very pretty." He tilts his head to one side. "Like you."

I don't know whether to be insulted that I'm merely *very pretty* to him, or complimented that Paxton deBraun thinks I'm pretty at all—that he's noticed me that much.

Both, I suspect—which is a complicated set of emotions.

"Why did you snort while eavesdropping on my conversation with my mother, Makayla?"

"Why do you care so much?" I ask in return.

"It felt like you were mocking me, and I don't

like that. It's not a feeling I'm familiar with, so I'm curious."

"Not a feeling you're familiar with," I echo. "Incredible."

"Nor is being refused."

I cackle—it's an eruption of disbelief I have no control over. "You are something else, Paxton. Seriously."

"I don't remember giving you permission to address me by name, Miss Poe."

I turn away, shaking my head and laughing still. The hubris of the man was breathtaking. "Good day to you, *Mr. deBraun.*"

"I didn't dismiss you."

"I don't work for you, I work for your mother. And I'm finished my shift. I've completed the turning over of this unit, which means I'm now on *my* time, *sir*, and I won't be spoken to the way you're speaking to me." I glare at him, my gut roiling and my heart hammering, knowing each word is another nail in the coffin of my employment at any deBraun hotel, assuming they don't completely blacklist me across the industry, which I know for a fact Camilla can do, will do, and has done.

"You've got a big ol' set of balls, don't you, sweetheart?"

I don't dignify that with a response. Instead I punch the elevator call button, and face the polished wood-paneled door, staring a hole in the wood rather than risk eye contact with the unbelievably arrogant man behind me.

"Makayla." His voice is surprisingly gentle, this time.

Thus, I reward him with actual eye contact. "Yes?"

"Thank you."

I'm rocked back on my heels. "For what?"

He gestures with a huge hand and thick forearm at the penthouse. "For cleaning up after my degenerate friends."

"Time and a half and a hefty bonus from your mother is thanks enough."

"Meaning, it was a big job."

"Yes."

He swaggers across the room, towel slung low across his hips. I lick my lips, an involuntary flashback of what I'd seen under the sheet—what's under the towel—haunting me. His broad chest fills my vision, rippling abs drawing my gaze, a sharp V-cut disappearing under the towel. I close my eyes, shake away the lust, and then open my eyes and force my gaze to his.

"One last time, Makayla. Why'd you snort at me?"

"It wasn't at you, it was at your mother."

His eyes widen. "You *do* have balls of titanium if you're willing to snort at my mother."

"It's just so ridiculous," I say, the words tumbling out unbidden. *"We're forcing you to marry some fluffy trol-lop for the sake of appearances, but don't worry, you can still fuck around all you want, just be discreet about it."*

Two slow blinks of his eyelids, and then Paxton is

guffawing uproariously. "Oh my god, I would give up my Ferrari to see Mom's reaction to hearing you say that," he says, wiping a tear of mirth away from his eye. "Fluffy trollop. You called Cecily Amador-Richards a fluffy trollop. God, that's amazing."

I frown. "It feels like you're making fun of me."

"No, not at all." He shakes his head. "You clearly have no idea who Cecily is if that's your description of her."

"Shallow, vapid, selfish, cruel, thoughtless, and obnoxious—if I had to pick descriptors off the top of my head without having met her." I literally bite down on my lip until it hurts. "I can't believe I just said that out loud."

He shrugs. "You're not wrong. But you forgot cunning, devious, vicious, manipulative, slutty, gold digging…"

I can't help but laugh. "Sounds like she's a real piece of work."

"You mispronounced 'shit'."

"Well, I'm sorry for your circumstances, Mr. deBraun," I say. "Good luck with the marriage."

"I'm not getting married."

"Will your mother really cut you off?"

He nods, no humor on his face now. "Yes, she will. She controls the purse strings, really. Dad's sole focus is his company—day-to-day affairs are of no concern to him. I doubt my mother has even consulted him on this, to be honest."

"So you really do have to marry this Cecily woman, or suffer the life of a common peon, laboring for a paycheck."

"I'll survive," he says, wryly. "I've made quite a bit of my own money. It's the political connections I'd lose that worry me, not to mention the clout that comes with the backing of the deBraun family come election cycle."

The pause, then, is…fraught. His eyes are on me, and now the speculation and curiosity are replaced by something else. Something devious. Sly. There's all but a light bulb over his head, lighting up and going *ding*.

A grin curls across his lips. "Oh man. That would be something."

I frown. "What?"

He shakes his head. "No, no way. I can't. I couldn't." He laughs. "What a way to stick it to her, though."

I have a sinking feeling in my gut. "What? What are you thinking?"

He shakes his head. "It's of no consequence, Miss Poe. An idea with no real merit." Yet despite his words, his eyes remain on mine, probing, searching.

The elevator door has long since opened, and I push my cart onto it, and then turn to press the button for the service level. As the door begins to slide closed, Paxton's voice rings out.

"Are you single, Miss Poe?"

"Yes," I hear myself answer, and wish I'd lied. Wish I'd had a snarky retort—the one time I really need a witty, sassy, nasty comment to avoid the question, I don't have one.

Just the truth.

I'm alone on the elevator, but I still feel Paxton's brooding, thoughtful silence as if he were here in the elevator with me.

I don't want to know what he was thinking. I really, really don't.

4

"Hi, Mom." I lean down and wrap my arms around her.

She leans her head against me and her eyes smile, but the rest of her cannot.

"I've missed you," I say, setting my purse on the counter and taking my usual seat on the couch in the corner of her room at the hospice care facility. "You haven't watched without me, have you?"

She shakes her head, rolling her eyes at me. *Of course not,* I can almost hear her saying. *Oughta know better than that.*

Today's a bad day—she's still in bed, and for Mom, the most vital and active and strong and unstoppable person I know, staying in bed is anathema. But advanced MS doesn't care. It lays you low, and there's nothing anyone can do about it.

I find the remote and turn on our favorite show—*Vanderpump Rules*. Mom loves the drama, the vapid nonsense, and the arguments...and if she were to admit the truth to me, the boys. But she won't admit to it, so we both pretend like it's just for the mindless over-the-top enjoyment. A guilty pleasure we both love because it's a chance to get out of our own lives for a while.

My spot on the couch is as close to Mom as I can get without being in the bed with her—I can reach out and hold her hand, which I do.

She squeezes, and I turn to look at her—a squeeze means she has something to say.

I can interpret her many expressions, and this one is one I know all too well. "No, Mom, I haven't met anyone."

Another squeeze, and her eyes bore into mine. "Truth," she whispers.

I sigh. "Fine. But I wouldn't call it meeting someone. The owner of the hotel where I work, Camilla deBraun, she has a son, Paxton. We spoke briefly. But don't get your hopes up—he's not just out of my league, he's in a league I don't want any part of. He's rude, arrogant, spoiled, and far too good-looking to be real."

"Pax...Jax." Mom smirks, referencing her favorite character from *Vanderpump Rules*.

"Actually, there's a resemblance. Except Paxton has more money than God and he's twice as arrogant and twice as sexy."

Mom's eyebrows go up. "New page."

I translate, and shake my head. "Tigers don't change their stripes, Mom, you told me that. Just because Jax is a little nicer and more self-aware now that he's met Brittany doesn't mean he's any different, deep down. And Paxton…well, I only spoke to him for a few minutes, but he's the world's most unapologetic playboy. And anyway, his mom is making him marry some rich bitch."

Her eyes narrow at me. "Judge not."

"Lest ye be judged. Yes, Mom, but Paxton himself said she's basically the worst human being on the planet."

"Why marry?"

I shake my head. "It's a rich person thing. Appearances, basically, from what I gather. They were talking about it while I was working. He's a politician, in the House of Representatives, and she wants him to clean up his image so he can run for Senate. Which means getting married to spin things away from his life as a playboy. He does nothing but throw extravagant parties and prance around with expensive hookers." I hiss. "Worst part of it all is that his mom doesn't even care if it's a real marriage—she said, in so many words, that as long as he's *discreet*, as she put it, he can keep sleeping around as much as he wants, just don't let it make the media."

Mom's eyes are on me, and I'd give anything for her to be able to just talk to me. She has to gather her strength, visibly rallying to find the energy and focus for what she wants to say. "Gone soon. Then…you're… you're free."

Tears fill my eyes, and I know Mom hates it more than anything when I cry about this, so I shake them away. "Stop that, Mom. You're not going anywhere. I won't let you. I'll take care of you the way you took care of me. Forever and ever, Mom. So...I don't want to hear you talking like that or I'll—"

Her hand squeezes mine as hard as she can. "Or... what?"

"Or I'll watch it without you."

She snorts, the same sound that caused me so much trouble last week. "Not."

"I will too!"

"Punk."

I laugh, and squeeze her hand. "Fine, I wouldn't. But for real. No more of that. Okay? Please?"

Her eyes fix on mine, and as she does occasionally, she shields her thoughts from me. Normally I can translate her expressions and guess what she's thinking, but sometimes, like now, she gives me a long, hard stare than contains too much for me to untangle, too much to read.

"You should be...free. Young. Beautiful. Smart." She thumps the bed with her hand. "Not...this. Old hag. Sick...no future."

I choke. "Mom, stop. There's nowhere I'd rather be, and no one I'd rather spend my time with."

"I cost...too much...money."

"I'm boring anyway. I wouldn't go out even if I had friends or anywhere to go, or money to spend." I squeeze her hand. "You're my friend. And this is where I'll be, every night. No matter what."

"Gettin'…bored…of your nonsense." Mom hates emotional scenes like this, always has. Bad days like this, though…they're hard on both of us.

We watch our show, and partway through, Mom squeezes my hand three times.

I don't look at her, don't dare. "I love you, too."

I'm fresh out of the gym, dripping sweat, hair a loosely-braided frizz-bomb of kinky black curls, no makeup, wearing purple spandex booty shorts and a white tank top, the tightest one I've got to keep the girls in check while doing far too many barbell cleans than is sane. Sipping from my Hydroflask, Justin Timberlake bumping in my earbuds, I head home on foot to shower and get ready for my shift.

My carriage-house apartment is a good twenty-minute walk from the gym, which is usually just enough time to cool off and let my heart rate settle. I'm walking briskly, minding my own business, head bobbing to "Tunnel Vision", not really thinking of anyone or anything in particular—a few precious minutes of Zen, which I only really get post-workout, when I'm sweaty and out of breath and sore and pleasantly shaky from the high-intensity exercise.

Thus, I'm not really paying attention to the world around me—in Petoskey in the summertime, you tend to get a lot of wealthy tourists driving fancy cars, and a lot of them aren't exactly the most polite or thoughtful. So I'm not entirely surprised when a sleek, low-slung, absurdly expensive-looking sports car zips up the hill behind me, engine revving loudly enough to be obnoxious even over my music. I snort, watching the stupid thing with its stupid driver swerving around slower-moving traffic, darting and weaving as if the driver owns the entire road—nay, the world.

I mentally dismiss the car and its driver, trying desperately to regain my moments of Zen.

I'm about to cross a side street, on the other side of which I'll turn left into the neighborhood behind downtown. A quick glance either way, and then I cross the street, head bobbing, singing under my breath.

"Tunnel vision…for you…"

Squeeeeeeal.

Tires howl, an engine revs, and I trip over myself to stop from being run over by the same red sports car as it darts around the corner and jams on the brakes, squealing to an abrupt halt directly in front of me.

I kick the tire. "Hey, watch it, asshole!"

"Get in, Makayla." A familiar voice, one I'd hoped to never hear again; or rather, which I assumed I would never hear again, and one which a tiny, teeny, and very stupid part of me deep down did sort of hope to hear again.

I duck to peer in through the half-lowered passenger side window—the car is so low slung I have to bend and duck quite a lot to see in. And yes, my ears did not deceive me: the driver is, unsurprisingly, none other than Paxton deBraun.

"Figures it would be you in this ridiculous car, driving like an entitled dick." I'm off duty, and I'm annoyed, so my filter is...not entirely engaged.

"Get in," he repeats.

I frown. "Um, no thanks. I have work in less than two hours, and I have to shower still. And, besides, I don't get in strange cars with strange men."

Those damned eyes of his—they're what get me. They're...pleading, almost. Desperate, nearly. Along with that voice, which somehow manages to growl in annoyance while still being somehow soft, if not quite tender.

"Please."

I blink, because it wasn't just evidence of actual manners, but the tone in his voice. "I beg your pardon?"

He snarls, a sound somewhere between a sigh and groan. "Makayla, please. Get in the car."

"Why?"

"Are you always this difficult to deal with?"

I laugh. "Yes."

"I need to talk to you. Please, get in the car."

"Paxton. I'm dripping sweat, I stink, I'm in workout gear, and I have to work soon. What could you possibly want to talk to *me* about, and so urgently?"

His strong, elegant hands release the death grip he has on the steering wheel and rake backward through his fine, artfully messy dark brown hair. "Goddammit, you're so impossible." He lifts a buttock and slides a phone out of from the back pocket of his dark-wash jeans. Unlocks it, taps a contact from his favorites list. It rings twice and I hear a tinny, distant answer. "Mom. I'm having a dinner for some friends from DC—no, not *those* friends, this is work. I need to borrow Makayla. She's scheduled to work today and I need her to get my condo here ready. Okay, thanks."

I'm speechless—for a moment. "I'm not cleaning your house for you."

"No, you're not. But now you have the day off. Get in, we need to talk."

"I can't afford a day off, Paxton. I have bills to pay."

"How much will you make today?"

"I…I don't know, I don't have it broken down by day. I just know I can't afford a day off."

"What's your monthly take home?"

"Four thousand, usually," I answer, not knowing why answers just come out for this man when I'm normally disinclined to answer personal questions for anyone.

He's wearing a blazer over a white T-shirt, and digs into an inner pocket of the blazer, pulls out the fattest wad of cash I've ever seen in my life. Peels off hundred-dollar bills with blinding speed, until there's a stack of hundreds that makes my head spin. He hands it to me. "There. Two grand. Covers half the month, should cover an hour of your time today."

I feel my fingers twitching—two grand would mean I could breathe this month. Pay Mom's hospice bill, rent, utilities, *and* go grocery shopping all in the same month.

Pride, however, is stronger. "I'm not taking your money."

"Mom's already covered your shift."

He has me over a barrelhead. I can't not work, but now my shift is covered. Which means I have to call Camilla and beg for an extra shift, which means explaining whatever the hell is happening right now. Granted, I did get paid handsomely for cleaning the penthouse, but that's not enough extra to make *all* the ends meet, and if Camilla is planning to give me a bonus, I haven't seen it yet and can't afford to assume it's coming.

I glance at the interior of the car, which is a kind I've never seen before, and which looks like it costs more than all the cars parked on this street combined. The seat alone probably costs more than my entire life. "I'm covered in sweat. I'll ruin the seat."

"Don't care. I can get it fixed."

I sigh. "You really do know how to get your way, don't you?"

He doesn't even respond to that, just waits until I'm in the seat, which is more comfortable than any car seat has a right to be. There's open air over my head, and the suede under my thighs is so supple and soft it seems almost fake, a charcoal color that shifts when I subtly stroke it with one careful fingertip. Every surface of the interior of the car is carbon fiber, luxurious and soft to the touch. There's a fire extinguisher in front of my seat, wrapped in suede to match the seat. The steering wheel is squared, more of a *squircle* than a wheel. There are dials and gauges, and the display is more of a heads-up display from a high-tech fighter jet than an automobile.

"What kind of car is this?" I ask, because curiosity is a diabolical weakness of mine.

"Ferrari LaFerrari."

"What an original name," I quip, my voice droll.

He shoots me an annoyed look. "For most hypercars, you have to put your name on a list and pay a hefty deposit to even be eligible to buy one. For a LaFerrari, you have to be *invited* by Ferrari to buy one."

"Do I want to know how much it cost?" I ask.

"Tricky question. There's how much I paid, and how much it's worth. Which are not the same."

I shake my head. "Forget I asked. Either one is a number I'll have no way of comprehending."

He nods. "Probably true." There's no sense that he's even aware of the insult in that. "I'm not even really supposed to be driving this on public streets, but fuck it, right?"

I shouldn't ask. But I do anyway. "What's the point of a car you can't drive?"

He taps the accelerator and the car launches

forward, pressing me back in my seat; a jerk of the wheel, and we're around a corner, and then seconds later we're on US-31 heading for the McMansionville that is Bay Harbor.

"This is a track car," Paxton says, his eyes and head in constant motion, as are his hands and right foot, as he guides the rocket ship that is this ridiculous vehicle at insane and illegal and unsafe speeds around traffic, sometimes crossing the centerline into oncoming traffic.

"Holy shit slowthefuckdown!" I manage, biting the words out past a barely restrained scream. "And what's a track car?"

He snorts. "A car you only drive at a racetrack."

"So you're a race car driver?"

"No, Makayla," he says, with exaggerated patience. "I own a race car. And it's not a race car, per se. It's a car designed to be driven very, very fast, which you can only legally and safely do at a designated track."

"And yet you're driving this on the streets."

"Yes. Which is highly irresponsible of me, considering this is one of two hundred ever made, and worth upwards of five million dollars, minimum."

"Five...*million* dollars? For a *car*?"

"For a Ferrari LaFerrari Aperta? Yes."

"I guess I'm not sophisticated enough to understand how that's possible."

"It has a hand-built V-12 making 950 horsepower, weighs less than three thousand pounds, has a removable carbon-fiber hardtop, goes from standstill to sixty-two miles per hour in two-point-four seconds, and there will never be any more of them ever made."

I roll my eyes, make my voice deep and cartoonishly gruff. "Oook oook. Me man. Me have big car, because me have small penis."

His eyes cut to mine. "I saw the way you were looking at me yesterday. I think you know very well that's not true."

I shift in the seat, keep my eyes on the road outside the passenger window, and then cast a glance upward to the sky overhead, visible through the car's removed hard-top—which, apparently, is one of the reasons this car is so expensive. Finally, I find my grit.

"I wasn't looking at you any kind of way." I huff. "And besides, you're so self-absorbed it's a wonder you even know I exist."

"I may be self-absorbed," he says, his voice a low growl that somehow matches the snarl of the massive engine, "but I noticed you."

I snort. Keep my eyes trained out the window. "Right."

A fingertip brushes a droplet of sweat off the back of my neck. "I noticed you enough to know you're a hell of a lot sexier out of that dumbass maid outfit."

I shiver at the delicate touch of his finger at my nape. Shift away, lifting a shoulder to dislodge his touch, and the memory of it—though the latter seems nearly impossible. "Stop."

"Stop what, Makayla? Touching you? Or telling you you're sexy?"

"Both."

"What woman doesn't want to be told she's sexy?" His voice is a purr, and I refuse to make another comparison to the engine of this stupid vehicle.

"This one," I lie.

He sniffs a laugh. "Yeah, okay. Pull the other one, Makayla."

I don't respond to that. "Where the hell are you taking me, anyway? And do you have to go a hundred and thirty miles an hour—HOLYSHITWATCHOUT!"

"I'm going ninety, not a hundred and thirty, for one thing," Paxton says, breezy and casual, as if he hadn't just swerved a half-second and millimeters away from smashing into the back end of a semi. "And for another, I've been through several exhaustive advanced driver's training courses by the world's foremost racing and evasive driving instructors. So just fucking relax, would you? I've got this."

I scrabble at the handle and the seat belt—you'd think for a track car, this would have oh-shit bars for the passenger, but no. Too fancy for that.

"Aren't you worried about getting a ticket?" I ask.

Another dismissive snort. "Cops around here know my cars, and they know who butters their bread."

"Meaning they're paid off?"

"Not paid off. But our family makes hefty donations every year to the department and I, in turn, miraculously never seem to get a ticket. Mostly because I may drive fast and seemingly recklessly but I'm an excellent driver, and I never endanger the other drivers. *They* don't always appreciate that fact, but such things are often lost on plebeians."

"Plebeians?" I echo. "Really?"

"They were a member of the lower socioeconomic class in Ancient Rome," he explains, with dismissive loftiness dripping from his voice.

"Yes," I say, drily. "I'm aware of what a plebeian is."

He catches the tone in my voice this time, amazingly. But he doesn't apologize or try to backtrack. Just shrugs, grins.

"Where are you taking me?" I ask again.

"Home."

5

EVEN THOUGH HE'S GOING RELATIVELY SLOWLY AT THIS point, the turn onto the wide, winding driveway still somehow manages to feel effortlessly reckless. We're approaching one of the homes in the area that routinely appears on national lists of "most expensive homes." Sprawling, with columns and walls of glass, multilevel decks facing Lake Michigan and several hundred feet of private lake frontage, with a built-in boathouse and enough garage space for a fleet. A large house is a mansion; *this* is an estate, in the sense of the word used by aristocrats in eighteenth-century England.

I always figured this place belonged to Camilla's family, but I never knew for certain—it's one you can see from US-31, but only from a distance, and you get the sense that you're only seeing a fraction of it, and that the interior would be even more impressive than the outside.

Of course, knowing the wealth of the deBraun family, they may very well own more than one house in the area.

"This isn't my home," I say, helplessly pointing out the obvious.

"I said home, not your home." He doesn't look at me, but his attention is nonetheless focused on me. "Although—" he cuts himself off, starts over. "But let's not get ahead of ourselves."

"What does that mean?" I ask, panic tingeing my voice.

"Nothing."

The driveway winds around aimlessly through acres of manicured, richly green lawn for a quarter of a mile or so before coming to an end at a bank of garage doors…I count six doors, each one wide enough to admit two cars abreast. He touches a button somewhere near where the missing panel of the roof would fasten in, and a garage door slides open. The home towers above us as we wait for the door to silently open, stretching away in both directions as well as upward. Behind us, the lawn arches away, with a few stands of elegant birch and towering pine here and there to diffuse the view of endless grass. The door now open, Paxton gently nudges the gas so the car moves just above an idle through the door and into a cavernous garage filled with row after row of gleaming metal and glass. There's an obvious gap where this car is parked, front and center in the collection, which is so vast as to make even me—a complete neophyte when it comes to cars—dizzy with the collective value in this garage.

This car, obviously, is one of the Crown Jewels.

Parking it perfectly in the space, Paxton unfolds himself from the driver's seat and makes a quick circuit of the glittering, sleek, red hypercar, examining it for imperfections. A slender man in a black and white suit, wearing actual white gloves, waits off to one side—he's buttoned up, stern, serious, and polished.

Paxton addresses him. "Hey, John." He tosses something large and black and red over, and John, the suited man, catches it, a look of horror on his face.

"Please, Mr. deBraun. One doesn't *toss* the key to a LaFerrari." John's voice is smooth and cultured and vaguely English, and clearly disapproving.

"Like you'd drop it?" Paxton says, a wave of his hand dismissing the topic. "Give it a polish and gas it up, would you? And replace the top." He grins easily. "Thanks, Johnny."

With an actual half bow of his upper body, John turns away. "Sir."

I snort at the absurdity, gaining me two looks of bemusement and disapproval. Paxton grabs me by the hand and hauls me through the rows of cars—I see several logos I recognize: Porsche, Ferrari, and Lamborghini, as well as others I don't recognize. Paxton pauses in his march through the cars, gesturing with a sweep of his arm at a section of the garage— mostly red and yellow cars with similar lines as the Ferrari. In fact, an entire quadrant of the massive garage is dedicated entirely to Ferraris.

"That right there is why we got an invitation to buy

the LaFerrari," he says. "Several of those are one-of-one ever made, and all of them are rarities in the car world, and even more rare in the Ferrari-owner world."

Dozens, at least. Some old, some new, some in between.

I roll my eyes and yank my hand away from his. "Congratulations."

He catches the sarcasm, miraculously. "There are people who would pay a fortune just to get a *look* at the contents of this garage. This is one of the greatest car collections in the world."

"I don't even own a car, Paxton. So if you're thinking I'm going to, like, swoon over you because your dad owns some fancy cars, think again."

"Well, to be fair, it's not just Dad. Some are Grandpa's, some are Uncle Nicholas's, and a couple are mine."

"Which are yours?" I ask, curiosity once again getting the better of me.

Oh boy—judging by the way his eyes light up, that question was a mistake. He makes an about-face and wades through row after row of polished metal and chrome to the far back corner. He stops at a small, old hunk of metal—it's rounded and cute and quick looking, rather than sleek and sexy.

Paxton runs a hand over the curved, rounded hood. "1956 Porsche 356 Speedster, matching numbers, all original exterior and interior."

I sigh. "In English?"

He laughs, and sighs. "It means old car go zoom zoom." He opens a hatch in the rear where a trunk should be and I see the engine, looking the worse for age. "It means this car looks and runs exactly as it did when it came off the line in 1956, that the engine, transmission, and exhaust system are all original to the car as manufactured, as well as the paint, body, seats, everything. Makes it rare and valuable. This is one of the most desirable of the classic Porsches." He says it *Porshuh,* two syllables rather than one.

"Just looks like an old car to me."

He sighs, shakes his head. "It's anything but just an old car, Makayla. I'll take you out for a drive in it someday, and you'll see what I mean."

I wonder at that, why he thinks I would go for another drive with him, and why it would a someday thing. I don't ask, though, because he's off and running on another old car.

"Dad, Grandpa, and Uncle Joe all have a hard-on for the newer hypercars and supercars—all the McLarens and Lambos and such. They're both in the garage in New York, but Dad has a Koenigsegg One-to-One, and Uncle Joe has a Bugatti Chiron." He gestures at the car next to the Porsche. "This is a 1964 Shelby 289 Competition, fully restored." He looks at me expectantly.

I shrug, and he glances at the ceiling as if uttering a plea for help from heaven, or for patience with the very dull. "Okay. This one looks a little nicer than the Porsche."

"A little nicer—?" he sputters, nearly apoplectic. "Clearly this is wasted on you."

I smirk, pat his arm—which is a bit like patting a brick wall. My girl bits sit up and take notice. "Yep. Sure is." I shrug. "Show me a vintage Hermès handbag and I may be slightly more impressed."

"You'd have to talk to Aunt Evelyn about that. She's got a purse collection valued at several million dollars. She hosts a yearly viewing of her purse gallery, and tickets to the event go for thousands of dollars. Proceeds to charity obviously."

"Obviously," I echo, feeling faint. "What is a purse gallery? And why would anyone pay thousands of dollars to see it?"

He shakes his head. "You said you'd be impressed if you saw a vintage Hermès. Aunt Evelyn has a—well, it's hard to explain. Basically, half of her house is dedicated to their bedroom, and of that entire wing of the house, most of it is closet. I'd say, oh…five thousand square feet or so of the house is just closet. Of that closet, most of it is her purse gallery. Which is exactly what it sounds like—a gallery of museum-quality purses, displayed like the artwork they are. In temperature-controlled, biometrically locked, fire, water , and shatter-proof, lighted, all that."

I blink for a few minutes. "I don't even know how to process any of that."

He laughs, shakes his head, and gestures. "Come on."

This time, I let him lead me out of the garage. He doesn't take my hand, and I'm an odd mixture of relieved and disappointed. The doorway from the garage to the inside of the house is, anticlimactically, just a normal door; I'd half expected some kind of Star Trek-like automatic sliding door with a disembodied voice. The anticlimax stops as soon as I'm through the door: acres of polished hardwood, floor-to-ceiling glass overlooking Lake Michigan with a view that beats even the view from the penthouse at the hotel. Everywhere you turn, you're overwhelmed by the view, stunned breathless. And then, once you've gathered your senses, you start to look around, and you see the house itself—windows everywhere you turn, the floors so polished you can see your reflection in them, the marble counters, the glass-fronted floating cabinets in the kitchen and the massive range and the...the everything. This is a home to which the phrase "money is no object" was taken to its upper extreme.

Paxton stands beside me where I've stopped dead in my tracks two steps beyond the door to the garage. "Yeah, gets you every time."

I glance at him. "Didn't you grow up here, though?"

He laughs. "No. They built this when I was in middle school."

"But I mean, from then on, though."

"Well, still no. I went to boarding school."

I frown at him. "That's still a thing?"

He laughs again. "Very much so."

I remember bits of the conversation I overheard. "You went to military school too, didn't you?"

He chuckles. "You *were* eavesdropping."

I shrug. "Told you—perks of the job."

He moves into the kitchen. "Yes, I did, and thank you very much for the reminder."

"'Thanks so much for bringing up such a painful subject. Why don't you give me a nice paper cut and pour lemon juice on it while you're at it?'" I eye him as I quote *Princess Bride*, wondering if he'll catch it. Probably not.

He snickers, grinning at me. "'Whoo-hoo, look who knows so much! This man is only *mostly* dead. See, there's a difference between *mostly* dead and *all* dead.'"

I raise an eyebrow at him. "I didn't think you'd catch the reference."

"Part of the reason I ended up in military school was because I kept getting other guys in trouble. One of my favorite pastimes was convincing kids to sneak out of the dorms at night. I'd...found, shall we say...a movie projector, and a buddy and I hooked it up in a nice little out-of-the-way spot in a corner of the school grounds so it was playing up against the back of an old shed, and we'd watch movies and drink booze and smoke dope and shit. One of our favorite movies was *Princess Bride*. Oh man, we must've watched that a hundred times."

"Well, we have that movie in common, at least," I say. He's looking at me expectantly again. "What?"

"What's your story with it?"

"With what? *Princess Bride*?" I laugh. "My mom. She worked a lot when I was growing up, but no matter what, she always had Sunday evenings off, and we'd watch a movie together. Usually, that one. *Girls Just Wanna Have Fun*, *Footloose*, *Sixteen Candles*." I sigh, remembering. "But mostly, *Princess Bride*."

"For us it was that one, *Roadhouse*, *Big Trouble in Little China*, *Escape From New York*, *Terminator*, guy stuff like that." He chuckles again. "The thing that got us caught was when Freddie stole his stepdad's collection of 70s porn. Our little group of kids sneaking out to watch movies went from half a dozen, to a dozen or so guys, to half the school, because of porn."

I laugh. "That'll do it. But…70s porn? Really?"

He shrugs. "I mean, for a bunch of high school boys locked in a boys-only school, where our every move was watched and judged and criticized, that was a major score."

I shake my head. "Why am I here, Paxton?"

He hesitates. "I thought you could use a day off."

I snort. "Hardly. What was it you said earlier? Pull the other one?"

He rubs the back of his neck, suddenly seeming hesitant. You said you needed a shower. We have seven full bathrooms, so…pick one."

I laugh outright at that. "Thanks for the offer, sort of."

He frowns. "Sort of?"

I wave a hand around my head. "You see this? Taming *this* takes a lot of products I guarantee you don't have here." I pluck at the strap of my sports bra—which, now that I'm alone with him in this decadent, extravagant house, I'm starting to feel self-conscious about being clad in nothing but a sports bra and booty shorts. "Then there's the fact that I don't have clean clothes here. And no, there's nothing of your *mother's* which I would either wear or fit in, assuming I'd feel comfortable borrowing clothing from my boss—not just my *boss*, but the owner of the entire hotel." I gesture with both hands, at the house around us. "Then there's the fact that there's no chance in *hell* I'm gonna take a shower when I'm alone in a strange house with a man I don't know."

He opens his mouth to get a word in, but I bulldoze over him.

"So, Paxton. You nearly hit me with your five-million-dollar Ferrari, force me into a day off which I neither wanted nor needed nor could afford, and then you bring me to your parents' house when I'm just out of the gym, half-naked, sweaty, tired, thirsty, hungry, and want nothing but a shower and few minutes alone. I say again—*what...do...you...want?*"

He scratches his head. "What I want—what I need, what I'm hoping you'll agree to, is something I can't just come out with. So, how about I make us some lunch, fix us a drink, and then we'll get down to business."

I cross my arms under my breasts, which was a mistake, because it plumps them up and draws his eyes to them, and even in this tight-as-hell sports bra, there's no hiding what Mama gave me in the breasticular region. Which is…a *lot*.

His eyes rake over my plumped breasts, over my dark caramel skin swooping down in a deep *V* into the white fabric of the bra, down my flat belly to my bell-curve hips. And then back up to my eyes, in a valiant attempt to pretend like he wasn't brazenly ogling me.

I narrow my eyes. "How about you just tell me what you want so I can tell you no, and then you take me home. Or better yet, call me an Uber."

He groans, head tipping back as his hands rake through his hair. "You are *so* fucking difficult, you know that?"

"You basically kidnapped me, Paxton. I'm supposed to be easy-going and cooperative?"

"Kidnapped you? Really?" He turns away, stalks angrily across the kitchen to a side table along the wall opposite a huge white sectional couch; he pours a couple fingers of what I assume is hideously expensive scotch or whiskey, turns back to me with the glass in hand.

I wait, but no offer is forthcoming. I fake a cough, and arch an eyebrow at him, pretending to drink from a nonexistent tumbler. "No, that's okay. I'll just have this nice glass of nothing."

He makes a puzzled face. "You drink scotch?'

I shrug. "Yeah? Is that weird or something?"

"Yeah, it is. I mean, I was about to get you some wine. I wasn't going to leave you hanging."

I shake my head. "Presumptions, Mr. deBraun. They'll get you every time."

He hands me the glass in his hand, pours another, and then gestures at the wall of glass. "Would you like to sit on the deck with me?"

I shrug. "I'd rather be at home with my pineapple curls conditioner and my spongy-poof, but I guess."

He blinks at me, and I'm guessing I probably don't want to know what went through his head at that moment. Something inappropriate that would put me off my game, and right now, my game is all that's keeping me sane. I'm *way* out of my element right now, in this place with this man.

He shakes his head to clear it of the presumably scandalous thoughts he was having about me, and slides open a section of the floor-to-ceiling glass, leading the way out onto a multitiered deck—stairs lead up to sections of deck on the two stories above this one, and another set of stairs lead in a winding descent down to the beach below. This part, though, off the kitchen and living room, is the main attraction. There's no railing, just sections of glass, creating an unbroken view of Grand Traverse Bay. The wind blows, bringing the scree of seagulls.

Paxton sits at a wrought iron table, slumping to sprawl with kingly elegance in a throne-like wrought iron chair padded with a thick cushion, one leg hanging over the armrest, an elbow on the table, crystal tumbler of expensive-smelling whisky clutched lazily in one hand.

His eyes search mine, no lust or lecherous thoughts, now. Rather, it's apparent he's very carefully considering what he's about to say. So, I wait. He sips, swallows; I do the same. I, however, cough and wheeze, staring with amazement at the liquid in the glass.

"What is *this*?"

He waves a hand, rubs his brow with the effort of recall. "Balvenie, I think. "

"It's incredible."

A slow smile crosses his face. "Show you a garage valued in the tens of millions, you don't blink an eye. Give you a glass of whiskey, and you're impressed."

I take another sip, savoring it. "My first serious boyfriend was a few years older than me. Like, ten or so. He, um…he liked whiskey, and since I was young and trying to impress him, I got into it too. Developed a taste for it on my own." I shrug. "Of course, my idea of a treat on a night out is a glass of Red Label on the rocks, because that's all I can afford."

"Red Label." His snort of derision is no less arrogant and dismissive than I expect; he wiggles his glass slightly. "This is Balvenie Fifty Year. Thirty-seven grand a bottle, extremely rare."

I cough in shock, slowly lowering the glass to the table. "I'm drinking the equivalent of a month's rent, then, at least."

He shrugs. "I wouldn't know. I read somewhere that a hotel got a bottle once, and charged twenty-six hundred per glass."

I shake my head; push the glass back to him. "You'd better keep that."

He shakes his head, pushes it back. "It's just whisky, Makayla, for god's sake. There's a whole cask of twenty-year-old Dalmore in the fucking basement. Don't make this weirder than it already is."

I blink at him and take a careful, measured sip of the amber liquid, which burns like velvet sunfire, the expansive taste exploding on my tongue and in my throat and blossoming in my belly. "Why's it already weird?"

"Do you deny that this is an unusual situation?"

I shrug. "I've never been kidnapped by a rich asshole before, so I wouldn't know if it's unusual. It's certainly out of the ordinary for me."

He sighs. "Goddammit, Makayla, for the last time, I didn't *kidnap* you."

"You may not have, like, tossed me in the back of a van and hogtied me, but you certainly didn't leave me many options."

He groans, sitting forward. "If I'd left you an option, would you have given me the time of day?"

I snort, shake my head. "Nope."

He gestures with a hand. "Well, there you go."

I frown. "What does that mean, 'well, there you go?' Like it's the obvious solution to a woman not wanting to talk to you."

"You're not making this easy." He pinches the bridge of his nose.

"Am I supposed to be?" I take another sip, but I know I have to be careful because this shit is potent and I have a feeling I'm going to need my wits about me.

"It would be nice if you did." He's earnest, genuine, and that makes it all the funnier.

I laugh, shaking my head at his clueless hubris. "Seeing as I still have no idea what it is you want, or why I'm here, I'm not even sure how to make it easier on you, or what I'm even supposed to be making easier."

He groans again, rakes a hand through his hair, and takes a long sip of his scotch, then sets it aside and turns to face me, elbows on his knees, eyes on mine. Laser focus, all business, no humor, no arrogance, this a Paxton deBraun I think few ever see: open, showing his emotions.

Namely, nerves, if not outright fear.

Yet, he takes a deep breath, reaches forward and takes my hands in his. Both of them, holding my hands in his gently, his eyes piercing and deep.

"I want you to marry me, Makayla."

6

THERE IS A LONG, STUNNED SILENCE.

I stare at him, unable to breathe or to blink or think or move. When I'm certain he's not being funny, I carefully set the tumbler on the table, extract my hands from his, and stand up.

"And we're done here. I'll walk home." I head for the door, and make it as far as putting my hands on the handle of the sliding glass door.

"Makayla, wait. Please, just...hear me out." His voice is low, barely audible over the wind. But it cuts through me, every syllable landing on my ears like explosions; he's not begging, but he *really* doesn't want me to leave.

I turn back. Spine stiff, I pull my chair away from his, sit bolt upright, legs crossed. "I don't know what you're playing at, Paxton, but that's not funny."

"I am in no way trying to be funny." His eyes are certainly serious. "You heard my mother's ultimatum."

I nod. "I did. I don't see how it's my problem, or why you think *this* is some kind of solution."

He leans back, rests an ankle on his knee. "I don't know what else to do, to be perfectly honest."

"What else to do other than proposition a maid from your mom's hotel?" I stare at him in disbelief. "Wait, go back—you don't know what to do other than nearly hit me with your dumb car, coerce me into coming here when I'm in a vulnerable state, and then ask me to *marry* you? Just like that?" I shake my head. "What else could you do? Literally anything. Get one of your hookers to marry you—offer her a boatload of cash, jewelry, some nice cars and a fancy condo and I guarantee you'll find one who'll play the arm candy dutiful wife for your family's political shenanigans." I pause for breath, and then keep going. "Or, just spit-balling here, you could just *not* marry and take the consequences. Or you could marry that Cecily woman."

He shudders, and it is not a faked gesture for the sake of drama. "Death first," he says, once again quoting *Princess Bride*, but this time it seems to encapsulate his real feelings on the subject.

"Is she really that bad?" I ask, unable to get the better of my curiosity. "If you've basically got free reign to sleep around as long as you play the game for the public, how bad could it really be?"

He wipes his face with both hands. "You don't get it. Yes, I could marry her and have as many side pieces as I wanted, as long as I was quiet about it and played the game for the public, and she'd do the same. But I'd have to produce children with her, and that's the problem—I'd have to *procreate* with her and I'd honestly rather fuck a cactus."

I can't help a snort of laughter. "Wow. She must be pretty awful."

"Don't get me wrong, she's attractive...in a Barbie sort of way."

"So, perfect blonde hair, perfect big boobs, perfect slender waist?"

He nods. "Exactly."

I tilt my head. "So, what's not to like about that? Sounds like every man's dream girl."

He shudders again. "Yeah, great hair, great tits, great ass...and it's all attached to a vicious, shrieking, evil harpy of a bitch who doesn't give a single shit about anyone or anything but herself, and that's coming from *me*." He shakes his head. "No thanks. Been there, done that, and I'd rather take a bath in hydrochloric acid than let that gold-digging whore get within twenty feet of me or my dick."

My eyes widen. "Damn, you really hate her, don't you?"

"Is there a word stronger than hate?"

"Love?"

A snort from him. "Wrong direction, babe."

"Oh. Not sure. I've never had feelings that strong for anyone before."

He sighs. "Don't start psychoanalyzing me, Makayla. It's really not complicated—we grew up together, everyone expected we'd get married and have the perfect life together, and I thought so too, until she betrayed me in the most public and humiliating and painful way possible, and so yes, I absolutely hate her with every particle of my being, and I will absolutely take the consequences of not marrying her if that's the only option." His eyes lock on mine. "That being said, I'm going to explore all other possible options before I accept being cut out of the will and family trust, simply for not being willing to sell my soul."

I frown. "Seems to me your family takes a pretty loose view of marriage, so how dearly would you really be selling your soul settling for a sham marriage? I'm not saying *her*, but one of your hookers."

He growls, takes a big swallow of scotch. "If I have your opinion of me pinned down with any accuracy, I'm not sure you'd believe my answer to that."

I can't stop my hand from reaching for my glass of whisky, because it's the most expensive thing I've ever tasted, and probably ever will taste. "Can't say you're wrong, but also can't hurt to try, right?"

He takes another careful sip, moving the mouthful around before swallowing. "They're not my hookers."

I snort. "Yeah, you were right."

"That snort of yours—you sure do manage to pack a lot of expression into it." He narrows his eyes. "Did you see anyone in my bed with me?"

"Snorting is a family trait. You should hear my mom snort. It could take your hide straight off." I frown, tilting my head. "And as far as having a bed partner, I figured you just kicked her out when you were done."

"No. I don't even pay for them. My friends do. I just allow them at the parties."

"Why?"

He shrugs. "Honestly, I'm not sure."

"So you're telling me you don't...partake, shall we say?"

He lifts a shoulder. "Can't truthfully say I *never* have, but it's not my scene."

"What is your scene?"

He sips, licks his lips after swallowing, and sets his glass down. "I wasn't joking before, Makayla. There is a rhyme and reason to asking you in particular to marry me."

I groan and laugh all at the same time. "This again?" I shake my head, still laughing. "Let me put it in simple, easily understandable terms, Paxton: No. There's no rhyme or reason you could possibly give that would convince me to marry you."

He sighs, rubs his jaw. "Can you at least pretend to have an open mind?"

I cackle. "It would be pretending, Paxton. Not gonna lie to you."

He runs a fingertip around the trace work design in the wrought iron of the table, eyes now flitting from me to the table, from me to the water, and then finally finds whatever is necessary to keep his gaze locked on mine. "I'm not accustomed to asking for things, or being at someone's mercy, or having to explain myself. And you're not making this easy on me. But I'll try to explain my thinking as clearly as I can and, in return, all I ask is that you truly, honestly listen to me and promise, at the very least, to give it a single moment of consideration."

I hold his gaze. "This is serious for you."

He nods. "If my mom cuts me off because I won't play along with her stupid political games, I can't see myself being able to face her." He drops his eyes. "If she's willing to cut me off for not getting married when I'm not ready…" He shakes his head, leaving the rest unsaid.

"She said she wouldn't disown you in an emotional sense," I point out.

"But I would, though. And it's not about the money," he says, finding my eyes again. "I swear it's not."

"I'll hear you out, but that's all I can promise."

A seagull screeches in the distance, and a thin shroud of clouds briefly occludes the sun. I'm chilled, the sweat now dry, and I feel more aware than ever that I'm more than a little undressed in front of a man I don't know at all. Dressed like this, working out in the gym, I have my headphones on and I'm in the zone, totally focused; there's no one else around, and if they're looking I don't really give a shit. This is different, somehow.

He nods. "That's all I can ask for, I suppose. I know it sounds crazy."

I laugh, nodding. "I wouldn't even call our first

interaction a *meeting*. The second time I lay eyes on you, you ask me to marry you. Even knowing the backstory of what your mom is expecting of you, it's still crazy."

He nods. "There are a lot of issues to this. A lot of angles. So I'm not entirely certain where to start."

"How about with why me?" I suggest, and take a tiny sip of scotch, to fortify my nerves.

"Nothing about this is simple. It's really not. You'd have to understand the expectations behind what a marriage means to my parents—to my mom, really, because, as I said, my dad doesn't give a shit about much of anything but his company and his work and his cars. For Mom, everything is about appearances. Everything. Every outfit, every purse, every stitch of makeup, every appearance, every article in every magazine, every TV appearance, she takes it all into consideration. Not just herself, but me, Dad, my aunt and uncle, her brother and sister-in-law, my dad's sister and brother-in-law—which would be Evelyn who has the purses, and Nicholas who owns some of the cars in the garage. My cousins, my grandparents, all of us, the entire deBraun clan—everything we do and say is scrutinized under a magnifying glass. We're not just your average family, we're the deBrauns. Dad owns MagnaCom, as I'm sure you're aware—the third-largest telecommunications corporation in the world. I guess I probably don't have to list my family's various enterprises, as it's fairly common knowledge at this point."

I wave a hand. "You guys own football teams, basketball teams, telecom companies, hospitals…"

"My brother-in-law is president of a university, my grandparents founded the deBraun family of hotels, blah blah blah. It's all boring. Point is, here, that we're high profile. And no one takes that more seriously than Mom. She's obsessed with relevance, and spin, and how things *look* for the *family.*" His annoyance, as he emphasizes these words, is a physical force. "Sara, my sister, was engaged to Lyle Burnett, as in the eldest son of the guy who owns one of the biggest pharmaceutical research companies in the world, but Mom forced her to end it because Lyle wasn't 'the right look'"—and here he uses air quotes and heavy emphasis—"for the family. So, Sara, being the dutiful daughter she is, broke it off with Lyle, who by the way was a pretty cool guy, real stand-up sort of dude."

"And now she's married to Miller Frances Conroy, right?" I say, racking my brain for deBraun family facts, as learned from Buzzfeed and *People* magazine. "As you said, president of Calbright College, and his family are all bigwigs too, I think."

"Yeah, his dad is CEO of a security firm, and his brother is a high-profile venture capitalist." He waves a hand. "You want a family tree, I can draw you one some time. Our family net worth isn't relevant. It's about the fact that Sara really did love Lyle, and he loved her. It was the real deal. But Mom said no dice, so Sara broke it off, because losing the connections and support of our combined family is a big deal, and she knew Mom was as good as her word—she plays hardball, and she plays for keeps."

"And then there's you," I say.

He scrapes out a slow breath. "Yeah, then there's me. The bad boy of the family. Kicked out of Yates Academy for, and I quote, 'routine and excess delinquency.' Barely made it through military school. Mom bought me a slot at Princeton despite my somewhat less-than-impressive educational record, and I managed to find a niche in the political science program. I liked the scheming, the debates, the research, the art of compromising in a way that still benefits you more than the other person...it let me put my personality quirks to good use. At Yates, I was always working deals with people, putting groups together for various reasons. Like the kid who always has a pet cause, except my causes were always somewhat more nefarious than civic-minded. I learned to toe the line enough to survive in military school, and the value of keeping quiet and listening when necessary, and I guess that helped me more than anything." He laughs. "Listen to me, yammering on like a tool. You don't want a personal history. You want to know why the hell I thought asking you to marry me was a good idea."

I wasn't about to admit this to him, but I *was* curious—his personal, private history was something he kept under wraps. You knew the name Paxton deBraun, you knew he had a seat in Congress, and that he had a reputation as a player, a party boy, that he was photographed leaving the hottest clubs around the country with the most glamorous and gorgeous and most exclusive and unavailable women, and that somehow despite this reputation, he was considered a shoe-in for a second term in the House.

I kept quiet and let Paxton talk.

"God, I really don't know how to make sense of this. I had it straight in my head, but putting it into words is a hell of a lot harder." His golden eyes skim my skin, land on my eyes. "Another thing I suppose you should know is that a lot of my family is…I wouldn't say *racist* per se, but definitely classicist, and subtly, quietly not approving of dalliances outside the accepted… zone. Which is something that's never put into words, but is just somehow made clear."

I chew on what he's saying, and put it in context of what I know from the media—Lyle Burnett, for example, isn't white; his father is, but his mother is from some Caribbean island, as I understand it. She's exotically beautiful, and was a very successful model in her day.

"So when your mom shot down your sister's engagement to Lyle Burnett…" I prompt.

"It's not appropriate, was Mom's verbiage," Paxton says. "His skin color was never brought up, and she'd throw a hairy conniption if you were to suggest such a thing, but more because being racist is more passé at this point than any kind of actual conviction. She made some kind of excuses about his laundry list of exes, his lack of formal education, how he's just not polished enough for the deBraun family."

I laugh outright at that. "Not polished enough? Isn't Lyle the lead singer of a wildly successful rock band?"

Paxton nods. "Yes, he is. Vein. They have, like, eight or ten number one hits and three platinum albums. Rich on his own terms, successful, and like I said, just a good, solid dude. Not a rock star in the traditional sense of the word. I liked him."

I let the silence breathe as I consider what he's saying. "So she made it about his…god, I don't know, not pedigree, because his parents are both wealthy and successful." I hunt for the right word. "The appearance, I guess. Like, a rock star isn't right for *this* family," I say, affecting a snooty, hoity-toity tone of voice.

Paxton jabs a finger at me. "Exactly! It's never one thing, never anything you can take exception to, except for the snobbery of it."

"But what you're saying is, his skin color was definitely a factor, just not a spoken one."

He shrugs. "I have no hard evidence for that, but I was on the receiving end of it myself, more than once."

I tilt my head. "Oh?"

He hisses a slow breath, scratching at his scalp. "I dated Monique Thompson for a few months."

Supermodel, actress, climate change activist, and black.

I nod. "I remember the tabloid coverage."

"Well, most of that's bullshit, you know. I really liked her. I wouldn't say there was a chance of it being anything permanent, because neither of us were in a place where we were thinking of it, but we had a good time together and there was real affection between us." He pauses. "Mom shot it down, hard."

I frown. "What could she possibly have against someone like Monique? Beautiful, classy, successful, and doesn't she have an Ivy League degree in humanity or something?"

Paxton laughs, but it's bitter. "Yeah. She has a BA in anthropology from Columbia. Smart as hell; just fell into modeling sort of by accident. And you said it, she's classy, a really elegant sort of girl. But Mom made her usual excuses. Not the right angle for the family, you know you're not pursuing anything serious so why drag it out, your lives are taking vastly different trajectories so you may as well end it before either of you get hurt. That kind of thing. She made it seem like she wasn't opposed to Monique as a person, but...there was this underlying sense of disapproval." He hesitates. "I overheard her talking to a friend on the phone later, and she said something like, 'that girl was entirely too *ethnic* for my son.'"

I draw back, disgusted. "She said that?"

He nods, shrugs. "Yeah."

I'm struggling with how to react, how to feel. "I can't say I'm shocked, but...still. What the fuck?"

"Right. That was my thought. And that's what I

said to her. I made it clear I heard her and that I was pissed about it."

"But you didn't get back together with Monique."

"No, but she was ready to move on anyway, and Mom was right in that it wasn't going to be anything serious, so we just let it lie. I never told Monique about Mom's comment, but I sure as hell haven't forgotten." He waves a hand. "I also dated Vera Collins for a while, and Mom pulled the same card, but was much more careful in her reasoning, but I knew full well why she disapproved. I broke that one off myself, though, but only because Vera's schedule was too crazy for us to ever be together, and her career was her priority."

Vera Collins—musician, aspiring actress, and daughter of a famous musician-turned-actor, and also black.

I stare Paxton down. "So I'm a 'fuck you' to your mother."

He shrugs. "That's an element, yes."

I snort. "Are you sure I'm *ethnic* enough to really insult her, though?"

Paxton laughs. "I know nothing about you other than what you look like and your name, so I don't know the answer to that."

"Well, you said yourself it's all about appearances, and I do look like my mother, just with slightly lighter skin."

He nods, tracing a line down my forearm with a fingertip. "There's more to it than skin color, though."

"Such as?"

"The racial thing is mostly my mom. The rest of my family is openly classicist, though."

"And I'm poor—a maid in your mom's hotel, barely making ends meet."

He nods. "Dad, my sister, all of them—you're not allowed past the front door if you're not *someone*. Sara collects famous friends, Uncle Nicholas plays golf with A-list celebrities, Dad is always flying to Germany and Italy to get all smarmy with the heads of the VW Group and Ferrari and Lamborghini and guys like that, Mom is heavy into the political scene in DC…we don't do nobodies."

I cock an eyebrow. "I know you said the tabloids are mostly bullshit, but it seems like you're guilty of that too."

He nods. "Sure. It's part of the gig. I grew up around rich, famous people, grew up with my parents' rich, famous friends' kids. And it's just easier to stick with people who…I dunno, get it, I guess."

"Who also know what it's like to grow up rich and famous, you mean?"

He nods again. "Yeah. It's got its tricky aspects, and those are things you can't understand if you didn't grow up with it."

"Poor you," I say, droll.

He snorts. "Not my point, Makayla. I can't help who I was born to any more than you can, and I can no more pretend to understand your circumstances than you can mine."

"Fair enough." I'm scared of the fact that there's a certain part of me that's not just hearing him out, but actually *listening*, and…considering. "Go on."

He shrugs. "You're the last thing Mom would expect, on every level there is. Not just Mom, but everyone. They're all complicit—they all play the game, to one degree or another, and I'm fucking sick of it. Sara dumped a really good guy who had real feelings for her on my mom's say-so, and she didn't back me up when I fought with Mom over Monique. I was pissed about that, and it was a big, big fight. Uncle Nicholas got pulled into it, and that Christmas was a pretty damned tense affair, I'll tell you. I expected Sara to have my back, considering, but she took Mom's side. Acted all disapproving, and like I should know better and shit."

I spend a few seconds thinking. "So, I get why me, now—a poor, biracial nobody brown chick who works in your mom's hotel—the most objectionable possible choice for what is essentially a forced marriage. The real question, then, is why in the hell would I agree to it? Why would I marry you, knowing your mom won't approve, and neither will the rest of your family. She'll say she doesn't care who you marry, as long as she plays the game—but do I know how to the play game, Paxton? If all I'd have to do is look pretty on your arm, I could probably pull it off, assuming you even think I'm anything but *very pretty*." I put venom into those words, because it still rankles. "But something tells me there's more to it than just being arm candy. And I'll tell you one thing for free about me, Paxton—I'm not an arm candy kind of girl. I don't like wearing heels, I hate heavy jewelry, I don't like parties, and I don't dance except for at the club with my friends."

Paxton opens his mouth, but I'm not done.

"I'm not arm candy. I don't look the part, for one thing. And I'm not getting plastic surgery to look the part, either. You'd take me as I am, or not at all." I can't believe these words coming out of my mouth—it almost sounds as if I'm considering his crazy-ass plan. "I don't know shit about your world, about how to behave at the events I'm sure you'd drag me to. I don't have it in me to play pretend for very long, if at all, so the whole fake marriage, knowing you're cheating on me thing? That don't fly with this chick, Paxton." I gesture with a hand. "So…what makes you think I'm a good choice for your little game? And more to the point? What's in it for me?"

Paxton, to his credit, doesn't offer me a flippant, off-the-cuff answer. He takes his time, mulling over his answer. "I'm not sure how to put this without insulting you, or in such a way that you wouldn't assume I'm saying something I'm not."

"Well, with that caveat in place, you may as well just come out with it."

He blows out a breath. "Okay, but…fuck. You're gonna assume the worst anyway, so fuck it." He sits forward. "You said it yourself, you're a poor, biracial nobody brown chick. I can offer you a lifestyle you really can't even fathom, and I don't say that to be a dick about your life or cocky about mine." He pauses, considering his next words, and I give him the space to think. "It would be a chance for you to…I don't know. Get a break from the struggle, I guess you could say. No responsibilities, no boss. It would be temporary, I'm assuming. We do the marriage thing for a while, a few months, a couple years at most, and then we put it out there that it's not working, irreconcilable differences, blah blah blah, we get a divorce, and you're set for life once the dust settles."

I suck in a long breath, hold it, and let it out slowly. "Paxton…"

"I don't want you to think I'm offering you, like, a financial contract to be my fake wife. But I'm not ready to concede to my mom's bullshit games, and I'm also not willing to marry someone I don't like. For whatever reason, even though we don't know shit about each other and we're vastly different people, I feel like I could actually like you. I've enjoyed this time together this morning, and I really don't often truly *enjoy* hanging out with many people. It would be fake, yes, as in we're not getting married for love, and we're both going into it knowing it's fake and will end." He eyes me with disconcerting openness. "It can be fun for you, if nothing else. Some vacations to the Caribbean, fill a closet with fancy shit from Fifth Avenue and Rodeo Drive, fly private, live in a mansion, all that. Or a condo in New York, if that's your gig. In return, we do our best to make it look to my mom like we gave it a shot. It buys me time to figure out what I'm going to do about her in a more long-term sense. Perhaps get myself settled in a position where I can really afford to tell her to fuck off."

I don't know what to say. I'd thought—and said—that there was no possible way he could tempt with this bullshit crazy idea.

But he has.

Six words in particular tempt me more than any others: *Get a break from the struggle.*

It'd be temporary.

Have some fun playing rich girl.

I have visions of lying on a beach somewhere in a teeny bikini, without a care in the world.

Except...I do have a care. Something no amount of money or finery or luxury can change.

She lives in a nursing home here in Petoskey, and she has advanced multiple sclerosis, and I've never spent more than a weekend away from her.

I couldn't.

I couldn't leave her for a fake marriage to some spoiled rich white boy.

I couldn't, wouldn't—*will not*—ask or expect Paxton to take care of her expenses, because she's my mother and it's nobody's responsibility but mine. But what if I could leverage this, somehow, in such a way that I can get ahead on her nursing home expenses?

Maybe there'd be some kind of weekly or monthly allowance, and I could pretend to spend it but really send it to the nursing home. Or buy expensive stuff, wear it once or twice, and then pawn it for cash.

Something.

I have to at least consider it, because this could be a chance, my one chance, to get Mom taken care of without working my ass to the bone twelve hours a day, seven days a week. Marry this guy, play the game, and then I get a nice little divorce settlement that will hopefully allow me to take care of Mom.

The middle part gives me more than a little pause.

"I'd have to quit my job," I point out.

"I'd make sure you were well taken care of in the divorce," Paxton says. "Or if you don't want the divorce on your back, we could even get an annulment and have an agreement where I make sure you're taken care of. Either way, quitting your job won't be an issue, because you'd be in a position to choose what you want to do with your life, instead of having to...you know..." He waves a hand vaguely.

I quirk an eyebrow. "Work?" I fill in.

He narrows his eyes at me. "A seat in Congress isn't exactly all tea and crumpets, you know," he says. "And despite my reputation, I do take my responsibilities as a representative very seriously."

I watch the lake in silence for a long time, and this time Paxton is the one to sit and wait and let me have my silence.

"I need to think," I say. "This isn't something I can just go, 'oh sure. Why not?'"

Paxton sits forward, blinking at me. "Wait—you're considering it?"

"I can't believe I'm saying this, but…yes. I am."

He blows out a breath, rubs his face with both hands. "Wow. Not what I was expecting. It was a long shot, and I really did just expect you to tell me to go fuck myself."

I laugh. "That makes two of us."

"I'll take you home." He stands up, grabs his glass of scotch, and holds it out to me. "A toast."

I stand up with my own glass, but arch an eyebrow at him. "Don't get ahead of yourself, Moneybags. I haven't agreed to anything. I said I'd *think* about it."

"Which is more than I was expecting, to which I say, let's toast." He holds out his glass. "To thinking about this crazy-ass idea."

I shake my head, snorting a disbelieving laugh, and clink my glass against his. "To thinking about this crazy-ass idea."

7

I HAVEN'T SLEPT MORE THAN THREE HOURS AT A TIME IN the four days since my conversation with Paxton.

My brain is operating in turbo, hyper, super mega overdrive. Constantly trying to make sense of why I'm even remotely tempted by the idea. Why it doesn't seem as crazy as it should seem. Why there's a part of me that wants to be a part of his fuck-you to Camilla deBraun and the rest of his bizarro hyper-rich family.

Is it about the money? About the chance to see what the one percent live like? And honestly, the deBrauns are in the one percent of the one percent, and that's a whole different level of wacky-rich. As I've said before, I suffer from a debilitating case of curiosity— what is Paxton like, day to day? What are the deBrauns like? What is it like to never ever worry about money, or bills? What is it like to just go out and buy things just because you feel like it?

Is it more than that? Is it about *him*? That's dangerous thinking, girl.

Whatever it's about, I'm curious, and very little can make me ignore something as obviously stupid as the need to satiate my curiosity.

Which is a really, really, *really* stupid reason to marry a man—any man, let alone one like Paxton deBraun.

I go over it in my head again and again—while I'm working, while I'm at the gym, while I'm in the shower, while I'm trying to fall asleep. I go over all the reasons I shouldn't even think about it anymore, all the reasons why even considering it makes me the single dumbest human being on the planet—past, present, or future. I go over and over and over all the reasons against considering Paxton's crazy-ass idea.

Yet despite the heavy list of reasons against it, I can't shake the burning curiosity. I can't dull the sharp edge of what-if.

I know the most logical reason in the "for" column is that it will, one way or another, put me in a position to take care of Mom. And that's worth a few weeks, months, or even years of a fake marriage to an arrogant, self-absorbed, egotistical narcissist rich white boy.

I once got an offer to be a high-end escort making serious bank, and I nearly went with it. I also have had several offers to be an exotic dancer, and I actually accepted one of them, and showed up for my first day—this was before Mom was completely wheelchair and bedbound. She showed up and hauled me home, verbally berating me the entire way.

"You will *not* whore yourself out for me, child,"

she'd shouted. "I'll die before I see you strip or whore yourself out to pay for my care. I'll die anyway, but I'll kill myself before I let you do that."

She hadn't been kidding, and that was one of the worst fights we'd ever had—me screaming at her about how she can't talk like that, that's not an issue, and her screaming back about how I don't know what it's like to live with MS, and how she knows she's a burden on me and she hates that more than anything. When we both ran out of energy to scream, we collapsed into sobbing on each other, ate a gallon of ice cream between the two of us, and came to an agreement: I wouldn't sell my body in any way to pay for Mom's care, and she would in turn fight as hard as she could against the incurable, degenerative disease.

I'm not sure if this scheme of Paxton's counts as whoring myself out—I certainly have no intention of sleeping with him just because we got married. Sure, he's attractive, and sure, I feel the weight of his incomparable beauty every moment I'm near him, but I know for a fact I can hold my libido in check indefinitely.

I have needs, obviously, and those needs are powerful, and sometimes I find myself with no choice but to find a willing partner for a night to sate them. Those hookups serve to temporarily dull the edge of my needs, physically, but emotionally they do nothing. I'm not really emotionally built to be a one-night stand sort of girl. It's not what I want from a sexual partner, and I dream of finding someone who sweeps me off my feet—what woman doesn't? But my life is just not... there.

Taking care of Mom is a full-time job, and once that became more than I could handle and we knew it was time for her to start getting round-the-clock hospice care, I had to work overtime to pay for that care—full-time at the hotel during the week, plus I work week-ends—waiting tables early at a breakfast place, and as a cocktail waitress at a late-night pub. So there's just no time for dating, let alone a boyfriend.

See? Thinking about it is a rabbit hole. Down, down, down I go.

If I take the offer and fake-but-for-real marry Paxton, how will I visit Mom? I'm assuming he'll expect me to live with him wherever it is he lives year-round.

I know I have to talk to Mom about this.

I've avoided it, so far, even though I visit her nearly every day, but I can tell she's sniffing out the fact that I've got something on my mind.

So, five days after the discussion with Paxton, I'm sitting with Mom and we're watching *Beaches*, because it's one of Mom's favorites, and a go-to when we're caught up on our shows and don't know what to watch.

We're holding hands, as we always do. I'm trying to figure out how to broach the subject when I feel Mom's hand squeeze mine.

I look at her, and she gives me a long, penetrating glare. "Out...with it," she says. Today is a better day.

I sigh. "I don't know even know where to start."

"Beginning." This, with a Mom smirk, teasing.

"So, I told you I met someone, but not really." Mom squeezes my hand twice, which means *go on*. "This is hard. I want to tell you everything, but I'm scared to."

"Tell me."

I shake my head. "I can't." I have to look away from her, at the TV. "There's a decision I have to make. I have this…opportunity. Not really a job, per se. But it would mean I'd be able to take care of you better, without having to work three jobs seven days a week." I chew on my thoughts, deciding how much to tell her. "It's crazy. It doesn't make any sense. But I…I kind of want to do it. Not just for the money aspect of it, which is in itself kinda tricky. I just…on paper, it's really crazy. You'd probably tell me not to do it. I know I probably shouldn't. But I think—I think I'm going to. Not just for you."

Mom stares at me a long, long time. "Mack." Her private nickname for me, which no other human being is allowed to call me. "Nothing for me."

"I just said, it's not entirely for you. It'd be for me, too."

"Is there…" She has to pause, hunting through the speech/cognitive impediment for the right words. "Is there a man…in it?"

I nod. "Yeah."

"You like him?"

I shrug. "Honestly, I don't know. Yes, and no. It's complicated."

Her eyes narrow at me. "Sugar baby?"

"No, Mom." I mean, it's not that, is it? It's not. It's something else. Not sure what, but something else.

"Rules are...are rules, Mack."

Meaning, the agreement stands. I'm not allowed to use my body or my sexuality to pay for her care. Which this isn't. It's using my entire self, my life, my person. Which somehow seems more intimate. Scarier. Worse, somehow, than just trading sex for money, or taking my clothes off for dollar bills.

"I know, Mom. It's nothing like that." I squeeze her hand three times. "I promise."

"Don't understand."

"It's kind of impossible to explain, and..." I sigh. "The hardest part of it is that if I do it, it'd mean I'd have to go away for a while. I'd still make sure I call you every day and come visit as much as possible."

Mom's eyes search me, deeply, carefully, thoroughly. "You...want this?" She wriggles slightly, seeking a more comfortable position, and I help her adjust. "Whatever it is...you want it, for *you*?"

I wince, shrug. "Yes, sort of. It's scary. I'm not sure it's a good idea. But part of me wants to see it through, and yes, it would be for you, but also for me."

"You'll tell me someday?" Mom asks.

I smile at her. "Yes, I'll tell you everything, someday."

"No sex you don't want." She squeezes my hand as hard as she can. "Promise."

"I promise, Mom."

"No taking off your clothes." She's working really hard to make this clear and concise. "Unless you *want* to. For you."

"I promise."

She blinks quickly, and I know she's fighting emotions. She doesn't like crying any more than I do, because she's a tough-ass chick, and when you're fighting for your survival day in and day out, working your ass to the bone to provide for your loved one, emotions are a liability. "Don't visit."

I frown. "What?"

"Call me."

"I mean, I'll do both. But of course I'm going to come see you as often as I can."

"Don't need you."

A knife to the chest. My turn to blink. "Mom. Yes, you—"

"No." She waves a hand, limp and weak, barely able to lift it above the bedspread, but her voice is strong. "You've done enough. Love you. Forever."

I can't hold it back. "Dammit, Mom." I wipe at my eyes. "I'm visiting you. I'll have to go away, I don't' know where or for how long, but I'll come see you as much as I can. You're my mom. My best friend. My only family. You can't get rid of me."

"Your life." She squeezes again, hard. "Not just about me. Won't be a burden."

Anger barrels through me, though this is an

argument as old as Mom's MS. "Goddammit, Mom. I've told you—you're not a burden."

"I *am*. Work all day, every day. Visit me in your free time." A pause for breath, and to sort through the words. "No friends. No boys. No dates."

I rest my head back against the couch. "I don't want to get into this again, Mom."

She lets go of my hand. With visible exertion she struggles to sit up. Turns to face me.

"Mom, what are you—"

Breathing hard, wobbly, she takes both of my hands in hers. Her dark brown eyes are set deep in her sickness and exhaustion-sunken cheeks; her weathered African-American skin is sagging and wrinkled even though she's barely twenty years older than me. She stares me down as only she can, shushing me into silence without a word. She doesn't have to yell or scold—it just takes *that* look, which not even MS can take from her.

"Makayla Poe." My full name—shit. "You have to live *your* life." She squeezes my hands three times, three times again. "Not for me, not anymore. Promise."

"I can't promise you that, Mom. I can't and I won't."

"Whatever it is you're about to do," a pause for breath, for thought, struggling for clarity of thought and speech, "you do it for *you*. Not me."

"Mom—"

"*Promise*, Makayla."

I blink back tears, and nod. "I promise."

I've never lied to her, and I'm not lying now. I know

I'm going to do it, and it is for her. But doing it for her is doing it for me—she slaved her life away until she physically couldn't get out of bed anymore, until she needed a wheelchair to get to the bathroom, until her hands were numb and lifeless, for me. Provided everything she could. For me. Saved pennies so she could move us out of Detroit to a safer community up here, so I could have a better education, so I could have a chance at a life that wouldn't include early pregnancy, drug addiction, incarceration, gangs, and who knows what else. She left her family, and we could never afford to go back down for visits, and then one by one her mom, sisters, brother, they all passed away one by one, until it was just her and me, alone up here, and it was all for me.

And then she started losing feeling in her hands, and woke up one morning blind in one eye, and the tables were turned. I never thought twice about having to quit school to go to work. There was rent to pay, groceries to buy, and then medicine and treatments for Mom, and then canes, and then walkers, and then a wheelchair, and then a nursing home. She took care of me, so now I'm taking care of her.

There's no question.

Everything is for her, because she's my *mom*.

but...I *am* curious about Paxton.

His family, his life—the lifestyle.

What it's like to not always be short a few hundred or a few thousand dollars.

A break from the struggle.

Play at being fake married, get a divorce, take the settlement, and put Mom in a better home. Pay up front for a year or two at a time. Get the best treatments, maybe even see if there's some kind of experimental treatments that could heal her. I know they don't exist, but as long as I'm dreaming, right?

Mom nods when I give her my promise, and then I have to help her get repositioned in bed, prop her up and adjust her so she's comfortable. The effort exhausted her totally, and within minutes, she's asleep.

I go home, and wrestle with my decision. I know I've already made it, but I'm still trying to convince myself I'm being stupid, that there has to be a better way. That I don't want this.

Who would want it? Luxury lifestyle aside, I'm letting myself be used. I'm putting myself in what is sure to be an impossible situation, with a man I don't know, who I'm not sure I like at all, or can even stand, honestly.

Yet, as dawn approaches and I haven't slept a wink, I know there's no way out of this. I've made my choice, and I'm just going to have to accept that I'm the biggest fool who ever was.

S UNDAY MORNING. NINE A.M., SIX DAYS AFTER THE TALK
with Paxton on his parents' deck. Usually, I have
to work on Sunday mornings, but I traded shifts
with a coworker at the breakfast place because she
needed the extra hours, so I'm left with a rare morning
off to myself.

I'm dressed in my bum-around-the-house pj's—
faded red cotton shorts that only sort of cover my backside, and a tank top with the logo of the pub I serve
drinks at in the evenings, which is too small around the
chest, leaving half my breasts bared on either side.

But it's just me in my little carriage house apartment, so who cares?

I'm sipping on a mug of hot black coffee, spoon-
ing some Greek yogurt into my mouth, and flipping
through a magazine, enjoying the feeling of not having
to be anywhere for several hours.

My apartment is a one-bedroom, one-bathroom
loft over a workshop garage, out behind the home of
the owner of the breakfast place. It's in a higher-end

neighborhood, within walking distance of the hotel, the cafe, the pub, and my gym, and I get a good deal on rent. But, it's tiny. Galley kitchenette, no dishwasher, electric stove and range, three steps across the entire living room, a bathroom so tiny I can sit on the toilet and touch all four walls and still not have room to shut the door if I'm on the toilet, and a bedroom so tiny my twin bed takes up the entire space, so most of my clothes are kept in clear bins I store under my bed frame, because the closet is too small for actual hangers and there's no room for a dresser.

But it's mine, and that's what counts.

I'm shocked into stupefied blankness by a hard, fast knock on my door—which is accessed by a staircase around the side of the garage.

"Makayla?" A deep, impatient male voice. "Makayla!"

I could ignore him.

I'm tempted to. I don't want to talk to him, see him—I don't want to be around him, because that will mean telling I'm dumb enough to agree to his cockamamie plan.

I'm in the act of standing up when Paxton waltzes through the door. I sit back down, snorting in irritation, and gesture at him. "By all means, come on in."

He nods. "Thanks." Missing the sarcasm entirely, it seems. He spies the coffee pot, and the drying mat with my other two mugs on it, and pours himself a mug of coffee, and sits down on my couch beside me.

"Yes, Paxton, please, help yourself to my coffee."

I glare at him. "This may be a foreign concept to you, I realize, but it's fairly customary, I think, to wait for permission before entering someone's home, and to ask before taking their coffee."

He blinks at me blankly for a moment, and then waves a hand. "Whatever. Sorry." He takes a sip of coffee, and then pivots on the couch to face me. "I need an answer. Mom is pestering me nonstop about this, and I really tried my best to give you a full week to think about it, but she's about to send out the invitations with Cecily's name on them." He scrapes a hand through perfectly coiffed brown hair. "So...I need an answer."

I pinch the bridge of my nose. "Tell me again how this will work. I need a few details."

He blinks. "That's a yes."

"I need some details before I say yes or no."

"But it's not no."

"Paxton!" I snap.

He suppresses a smirk. "A hundred and...well, now a hundred and fourteen days from today, we get married in St. Patrick's Cathedral in Manhattan. Everyone who's anyone will be there—senators and congressmen, A-list actors, famous musicians, ex-presidents and first ladies. The reception will be worse, or better, depending on your viewpoint. Elbow to elbow with the wealthiest and most famous humans on the planet. A private jet will whisk us away to, oh, I don't even know, Fiji maybe, or somewhere like that, for a month or so of nothing at all." He eyes me speculatively, gauging my response, which I keep restrained. "Then we move in together. You'll have to give up this place, which…I'm sure you'll be heartbroken, palatial as it is. I live in DC most of the year, or at least while Congress is in session. When it's not, I'm all over the place. Here, California, New York, Europe. You'll quit your job, of course, but if you're bored while I'm working we can find you things to keep you occupied, and before you get all up in arms, I don't mean shit like tea parties and fundraisers. Housekeeping at a hotel is fine if your only goal is making ends meet, but as my wife, even fake and temporary, you'll need an occupation that fits your station. You can go to school, and we can get you in pretty much wherever you want, you can take up photography, or horse riding, or…god, I don't know. It's up to you for the most part." He pauses again. "There will be events, of course, and these are a big part of the reason this whole thing is happening in the first case. They'll mean a designer measuring you, fitting you into a dress, and then a glam squad to do your hair and makeup. We'll arrive in a limo, be introduced when we enter, and it'll be a couple hours of mix and mingle. Depending on the event, I'll either have to make the rounds alone and do my networking that way, or you'll have to hang on my arm and look pretty and in-terested and maybe put in your two cents here and there if you want, but mostly just sort of support me by being there and make me look good. Chauvinistic perhaps, but that's the gig. Then the dinner, desserts, more drinks."

He tilts his head at me, thinking.

"You know," he says, "There's a lot more to this than I thought, now that I explain it all. Parties are hard, I guess. You have to be able to always have a drink in your hand, but never be drunk. That's a big one. If you get labeled as a lush, or get a reputation of being someone who gets drunk too quickly, or as a loud annoying drunk, or someone who disrupts parties, you never get rid of that rep. So handling your booze is super important."

Yikes.

"Being good at conversation is important. Have something to say, know when to listen, know when to just let me talk and when to rescue me from awkward situations. The mix and mingle of a party is an art. It's never just a party; it's always politics, always business. They'll remember what you say, and chances are some-one is either recording or will report what you say and how you act."

"So, no pressure," I quip, droll.

"You said you needed details." He shrugs. "I'm giving you details."

"How long will this last?"

He frowns. "I don't know exactly. We'll have to play it by ear."

I sigh. "I don't know how long I can play the game, to be totally honest. I'm not an actress, and I'm not very good at hiding my feelings."

"If you can play the part during public events, the personal, private stuff is less important. Family get-to-gethers are always awkward, and there is always some combination of people arguing or fighting about something, so the fact that you and I may not be actually in love with each other will not be noticed. I mean, shit, a good portion of the marriages in my family aren't *real* either, assuming you even believe in love and real marriage to begin with."

"And what about…" I sigh, not knowing how to put it.

"Finances?" Paxton suggests. "I'm going to go ahead and assume you're not looking for a payout, per se, because you just don't seem like that type."

"Good assumption," I say.

"You'd just be…my wife. The resources of my family would be at your disposal, no questions asked. Want a car? Buy a car. Want a house for your mom? Buy a house for your mom. Shopping trip to Beverly Hills with your girlfriends? We've got a fleet of jets on standby and expense accounts galore. You'll get a credit card with unlimited access, and as long as you don't raise any eyebrows, you're free to do pretty much whatever you want."

"What would raise eyebrows?" I ask.

Paxton shrugs, tilts his head. "Um. I mean, don't go out and buy a hundred-million-dollar mega yacht without talking to me."

I cackle helplessly. "I don't even know what that is or what I would do with it, Paxton."

He tilts his head. "What's your idea of a big purchase?"

I roll a shoulder. "Um…Taco Bell?"

He blinks at me, waiting for the laugh. "Come on, for real."

"Every once in a while, me and a few of the girls from the hotel will go out for a few drinks. Usually I drink well liquor but sometimes, like I said when we were drinking your fancy scotch, sometimes I'll spring for Johnnie Walker Red Label."

"What about, like, purses and shoes and shit?"

I snort, jerk my chin toward my bedroom. "Go look at my closet if you want."

He blinks at me, and then takes me up on my offer. Heads into my room, peeks in the closet, which I use mainly to store coats, which I have to tilt sideways and finagle the door closed over them. He glances at me, standing in the doorway watching him. "Where are your clothes?"

I point at the bed. "Look underneath."

He crouches, peering under my bedframe—yanks out the four clear plastic tubs, pops the top on one and flips through my stack of thrift store skirts and T-shirts, cutoff jeans handed down from a friend of a co-worker, a second tub containing my work khakis for waiting tables, logo work T-shirts from the cafe and pub, a third full of my hotel uniforms—black dresses, white aprons, black stockings—and a fourth tub of underwear, T-shirts, workout clothes, and pajamas.

He frowns up at me. "This is it?"

I shrug. "I've got a pair of work shoes, a pair of gym shoes, and a pair of heels for going out. What else am I supposed to have?"

"Purses? Jewelry?"

I cackle. "My purse I got from my mom, and I think she bought it in, like, 1995. I'm not allowed to wear jewelry at the hotel, and don't care to at the other places I work."

He stands up, replaces the tops of the containers, and slides them back into place. "How many jobs do you have?" He asks this as we go back to the living room, and the couch.

"Three," I answer. "The hotel, a breakfast cafe on Friday, Saturday, and Sunday mornings, and a pub on Friday, Saturday, and Sunday nights."

"When do you go out?"

I shrug. "If I do, usually Thursday nights. That's when Kim, Donna, Maria, Tamika, and me are all off."

"And I," he says absently.

I frown at him. "What?"

"It's not 'and me', it's 'and I'," he says. "Proper grammar is important to Mom."

I glare at him. "Really, right now?"

He eyes me. "That bothers you? Me correcting your grammar?"

I don't want to admit the truth—that I am bothered, but only because I don't want to admit that I don't even have a high school diploma. "Never mind."

He stares at me, and clearly understands that there's more to the subject, and that I have no interest in the conversation. "What do you do for fun?"

I shrug, sniffing a laugh of amusement. "Fun is for people with spare time."

He sighs. "Okay, well…you'll need to find a hobby."

"I haven't agreed to anything," I point out.

"Can we cut the shit, Makayla? Please?" He gives me a long, open look. "If you're not in, just tell me. I'll figure something else out. If you are, then I need to make plans for how to best blindside Mom with this for maximum effect."

I wipe my face. "You need a decision right now?"

He nods. "I do. Mom won't be put off."

I hold my coffee mug in both hands. Meet his earnest, intense golden eyes. "I'm in."

He hangs his head, exhaling a long sigh of relief. "Oh, thank fuck."

"I can't promise how long I'll be able to keep up the ruse, though, Paxton. Your mom doesn't seem like she's stupid, and I'm a terrible liar."

"You let me worry about Mom."

I laugh. "I've worked for her for four years, Paxton. I think I know a side of her you don't."

"I've been her son my whole life, so I think *I* know a side of her *you* don't," he answers.

"Fair enough," I say. "My point is, I'll do my best to play the part, but I'm afraid you've probably picked the girl least qualified to play the part of party girl arm candy. Just saying."

He quirks a corner of his mouth in a half smile. "And I think, truthfully, that may very well be part of why I picked you." He shrugs, waves a hand. "That, and because you're damned beautiful."

I blink. "I—You—what?"

He shrugs. "What? You think this would work if I picked some bag-of-hammers-looking chick? I told you, there's expectations."

"I thought I was meant to flaunt the expectations," I pointed.

He nods. "You are, because of your skin color for one thing, and because of your...um, station in life, if you will. You're beautiful, Makayla." He hesitates. "Honestly, I didn't even realize it at first. That stupid outfit Mom makes you guys wear hides what you really look like."

I can't help a snicker at that. "The whole goal is for us to be as invisible and unobtrusive as possible. We're not meant to be noticed."

"With you, it only sort of worked. Once I really saw you, it was obvious that you're far from average." He holds my gaze. "Very far. As far as you can get, really."

"Well...thanks?"

He nods. "So. This is it. I'm going to call Mom and get things in motion."

I gulp. "So, it's begun?"

"It has begun."

I'm not ready. Not in any way whatsoever.

9

SILENCE BETWEEN US.

"Now what?" I ask.

He exhales slowly. "I don't know. We have a hundred and fourteen days. But the wedding is already planned, so I hope you don't have any big visions of picking flowers and swans and shit."

Wedding.

Gulp. I've never considered a wedding. I don't know anything about weddings. Never been to one.

"Um. No," I whisper.

He detects something. "No? Really? I was expecting pushback on that."

I shrug. "I've worked two and three jobs at a time, eight to twelve hours a day, seven days a week since I was fifteen. I haven't exactly had the time to sit around mooning about my dream wedding."

He stares at me. "Oh. You really have no ideas or expectations?"

I stare back. "I thought you said it was planned out already, so what does it matter?"

"I mean, if you feel strongly about a specific flower arrangement, I could probably do something." He gestures at me. "And you'll have input on the dress. Not the designer, I imagine, as I'm certain Mom has already paid to have Vera Wang or someone design the dress last minute for a not-so-small fortune."

My head is spinning. I just agreed to *marry* this man. As in, I do, till death do us part, wear a white dress, take his name, walk down the aisle and, *get married*.

I stand up, dump my cold coffee down the sink, and stand there gripping the edge of the counter. "Holy shit."

He's beside me. "What?"

"It's just hitting me, what I've agreed to."

"It's not real, though, Makayla. I mean, yeah, you'll be really married to me, but I won't expect, like…"

I straighten, turn to stare at him. "About that."

He lifts his chin. "Maybe we should cross that bridge when we come to it."

I breathe a sigh of relief. "Yeah. Just, you know, don't try to—"

He rests a hand on my shoulder, intending to comfort me, I imagine. "Makayla. No. Don't even think that. I said we'll cross that bridge when we come to it, and I meant it. I do have a soul, you know."

His hand doesn't comfort me. The opposite, if anything. I brush it away and step out of reach, sit at my kitchen table. "I remember you saying something about an heir. Children being expected."

"If you're thinking I'm going to, like, force you to produce an heir like this is some kind of fifteenth-century monarchy, then I'm honestly insulted. I may be a self-important, entitled douchebag, but I'm not a shitty human, Makayla."

"How am I supposed to know that? I don't know the first thing about you."

"Nor I, you. You think I'm any more excited about this than you? I don't want to get married. I didn't, and I don't. I don't know what to do, how to approach this, how to handle you, this, us—the whole thing. I'm doing the best I can. So to put it bluntly, Makayla, no, I do not expect you to have sex with me on our wedding night."

"You don't *expect* it." I know my voice sounds bitter.

He growls. "Well, fuck, woman, what else am I supposed to say to you? We're going to get *married*. You're an attractive woman. If some part of me does hold out even a minuscule amount of hope that you may one day end up liking me enough for that to happen, even knowing the whole thing is fake and temporary, can you blame me? I'm doing the best I can with what I've got, okay?"

I huff a laugh. "I think we're getting a glimpse of what this is going to be like, huh?"

He glances at me, then, and laughs. "I guess so."

Silence.

"Again, I ask you, Paxton: now what?"

He shrugs. "I don't know. It's a little over three

months till the wedding. It would have worked for there to be a surprise wedding if it was Cecily, because she and I have been photographed together on and off for years, and speculation has run rampant about us getting back together, especially since she dumped that Linus Mackenzie tool, so a surprise wedding between her and me would make sense to the media." He pinches the bridge of his nose. "I have to think like Mom, and then outsmart her. Which is hard. So, um... with you, no offense, but you're nobody. Meaning, no one knows who you are."

I snort. "No offense taken, because it's just the honest truth."

"So, a surprise wedding with no precedent, no exposure, no rumors of me seeing anyone? That'll raise eyebrows. But I don't want it to be known that it's *you*, in particular. I want it to be a shock to Mom and my family and the media who it is I'm marrying, including what you look like, and who you are."

I frown. "I see the conundrum. Put out rumors without letting out the whole truth."

"Exactly." He paces back and forth, and I think I'm getting a glimpse of Paxton the Congressman. "I think the best plan would be to be seen together, but pay a specific photographer for specific shots that we leak ourselves, that show me with you, hints of you, but not details of what you look like or who you are, just enough to whet the tabloid frenzy's appetite. I won't tell Mom shit, and that'll drive her crazy. Just tell her

I've got it covered, and it won't be Cecily. If I promise to be there, with a suitable bride, she'll take me at my word."

"What about the invitations?" I ask.

Another shrug. "Not my problem. She'll send something out that says something along the lines of 'the deBraun family cordially invites you to attend the wedding of Paxton deBraun,' blah blah blah, and just leave off the bride's name. It's gauche, as Mother would put it, but unavoidable as I'm going to refuse to provide a name. I don't care about the appearances of it—that's Mother's problem, not mine."

"I see." A pause, and then I glance at him. "So all we really need to do is release a few photographs of us together?" I ask.

"No, no." He pivots away, but with only three steps across the living room his need to pace is tightly curtailed. "You'll have to move in. Get pictures of the moving truck, shots from behind with my arm around you as we go into my condo, some us on the town."

I swallow hard. "I…move in? Like, when?"

"Like, now." He faces me. "We, as a couple, will have to be at least somewhat believable for the wedding. Right now, you're stiff as a board around me. If I touch you, you shy away. I don't know how to act around you. You call me Paxton, and only my mom calls me that."

"Move in with you…right away." I'm faint. I was expecting a bit more time, I guess. "A moving truck would be silly, because I can't imagine your DC condo would require anything that I have here."

He waves a hand dismissively. "Obviously. It'd be full of prop furniture. A staged photo op. Have a real estate staging company fill a truck with a believable load of stuff from a normal woman's apartment, bring it in for the photographers, and then load it back up in secret through the private loading dock."

I laugh, despite myself. "What a ridiculous game."

He nods, serious. "It's all a game. That's what it is. But it's serious, and for keeps. And for now, I have to play it, or my whole future is shot."

He turns to me, a hand in his pocket—for the first time since he arrived, I take time to really look at him: dark wash jeans, just the right amount of tight, clean, straight. Orange polo, the front tucked in behind a black leather belt, the rest left loose, black high ankle leather boots, buckles and straps instead of laces or zippers. Casual, but still dressy and presentable and elegant. Hair perfectly just so—not gelled into submission or actually messy, just…effortlessly perfect, swept to one side, short on the sides and longer on top, a few strands draping over his smooth forehead.

"Do you want to keep this place?" he asks.

"What?"

He gestures. "The apartment, such as it is. Are you attached to it? I can pay the owner enough to make sure it stays open for you until you're ready to come back. Or, you can bring your personal effects and when we go our separate ways, I can see you set up in a new apartment with new furniture and stuff."

There's one logical, obvious answer. "There's very little that I really need, honestly. The apartment is just convenient. If I have to quit my job and move in with you, marry you, divorce you, and figure out a new life after that, then I imagine the life I have afterwards is going to be pretty drastically different than my life now."

He nods, his hand still stuffed in his hip pocket. "I'd say that's true."

"So." I shrug. "The apartment doesn't matter. It's just somewhere to live, really." I look around, and laugh ruefully. "And truthfully, I really don't like this place. Even for a dirt poor barely making it chick like me, it's tiny. But it's safe, and it's cheap, and it's mine."

"And your stuff?"

"I'll pack a suitcase with my makeup and comfy clothes and stuff, but from what you've told me, nothing I own will really be good enough for the life you're telling me I'm about to jump into."

"Also true. There's a lot of shopping in your future."

I grin at that. "Well darn. What a hardship."

He snickers. "Yeah, poor you. Have to buy a whole new designer wardrobe, purses, shoes, and makeup."

I look around again. "What's our timeframe?"

He glances at a wristwatch that blinds me with the amount of gold and platinum on it. "I have to be in DC for a meeting with some colleagues early tomorrow. I can help you pack, make some phone calls for you if need be."

My head whips up to lock eyes with him. "Wait… *tomorrow*? Like, pack and leave today?"

Paxton's eyes are actually somewhat sympathetic. "Um, yeah?"

"I have scheduled work shifts, Paxton. It's customary to give two weeks' notice before quitting a job."

"Say there's a family emergency. They'll figure it out, and it's not like you'll be back there anyway." He's so casual about it; but then, it's not his problem to worry about.

Or, I guess, it is now. Sort of.

"Fine." I feel like this is, somehow, jumping off a cliff—the first of a series of no-returns. Quitting without notice is anathema to me, being someone who takes my reputation as an employee very seriously. "I'll call my bosses."

"I'll handle the hotel," Paxton offers.

"If you handle me quitting the hotel, your mom will suspect something," I point out.

He growls. "Yeah, true." He rubs the back of his neck. "So what can I do?"

I shrug. "Sit there and be pretty?" I quip. "On second thought, you being here will just unnerve me. Just…give me a couple hours and I'll be ready."

He shakes his head. "No. I'm not giving you a chance to change your mind. And you gotta get used to me being around, Makayla."

I hate that he's right.

He just fills my apartment in a way I'm not used to. His presence, his scent, his bigness—my tiny apartment feels so much tinier with him in it.

Plus, dealing with Tanya at the hotel means bringing up Mom, since Tanya is aware of the basics of my situation, and I just don't even want to bring Mom into this.

I find my beat-up old Razr flip phone, the same one I've had since high school, and dial the café first. Bill, the owner and manager, answers. "Just Eggs, this is Bill."

I take a deep breath. "Hi, Bill, it's Makayla."

"Makayla, what's up? If you need a shift, I've got Lisa looking to have Monday morning covered."

I wince. "I, actually—um. I have a family thing, Bill."

"So you need time off?"

"Um. I—I'm sorry for the short notice, but I actually have to put in my notice."

"So, two weeks? Or now?"

"Now, I'm afraid. I'm so sorry. I've never quit without notice before, but it's not something I can avoid."

"Well, if it can't be helped, it can't be helped. Sorry to see you go, though. You're a great waitress and great to have around." Bill is also my landlord, I should point out. "You need a break on the rent? Or are you moving out, too?"

"I'm moving out. It's a sudden thing."

He sighs. "It was good having you there. But I get it. My mom died a few years ago, and I had to upend my entire life to deal with it."

This is the worst part of this situation, but I choke it down. "Yeah. Thanks for understanding. I'll make sure it's clean."

"Nah, don't worry. I know you're a neat sort. Hope things work out, Makayla. Good luck."

I sigh sadly. "Thanks, Bill. You're a dear for being so understanding."

"Hey, life happens, you know?"

Before I can think too hard, I call my manager at the pub—Brad. He's a brusque, all-business sort. "Makayla. Talk to me."

No beating around the bush with Brad. "I have a family emergency that's taking me out of state for the indefinite future. Normally I'd give two weeks' notice, but under the circumstances, I can't."

He huffs, annoyed. "Shit timing. I'm down three girls on the floor this weekend already, and you're quitting?"

"I'm sorry. Nothing I can do. I feel bad, but—"

"Fine, fine. Family first, I get it. Not great for me, but I'll figure it out." He pops gum. "Guess I need to make some calls about new help. Good luck."

"Thanks, Brad. Sorry again."

That call over, I have two down and the scariest to go. Those jobs just filled in the gaps. The hotel is my big paycheck, the job I can't afford to lose.

I glance at Paxton. "This is the big one. You're sure about this? Once I quit this one, there's no going back for me, so you better be rock solid fucking certain on this."

He nods, hands in his pockets. "I've got your back on this, Makayla. Even if it goes sideways somehow, I'll see you're on your feet when the dust settles. On my honor as a deBraun."

My thumb hovers over the entry in my phone for Tanya. "I am so stupid," I whisper to myself. "This is so stupid. Why the hell am I doing this?"

Paxton opens his mouth, but I hit the green phone icon, and wave a hand at him to forestall his protest or attempt at comfort or whatever it was going to be.

"Hi, Makayla," Tanya answers. "I hope you're not calling to switch shifts on me, because we're short today, and I've already had two girls call in sick, so I really, really need you."

I can't stifle the groan. "I—shit, Tanya. I'm sorry, I—"

She blows out a breath. "You have *got* to be kidding me. You're quitting."

"I have to. I'm sorry." Not entirely a lie, but it feels like it.

"Goddammit." We've worked together for too long for her to bother hiding her feelings behind some veneer of professionalism. "Tell me I've at least got two weeks before I need a replacement?"

My silence is telling.

"Your mom?" Tanya surmises; she knows the basics.

"Yeah," I whisper, unable to lie beyond that.

"Well, your check is here, along with an envelope to you which I assume is from Mrs. deBraun, and which I assume is a bonus for the penthouse job."

"I'll come get it later today." I hesitate. "I'm sorry, Tanya. I really am. I've never called in sick, never been late, and only rarely ask to switch shifts. You know I'd never quit last second without notice and without a damn good reason. I hate doing it, but I'm really out of options at this point."

She makes a sound that's half groan, half sigh. "I know, Makayla. I really hope things work out for you."

I swallow hard. "Me too, girl."

We say our goodbyes, and I hang up the call, toss my phone onto the table, and take a sip of my coffee—I grunt and spit it back, because it's gone cold; a glance at the pot shows that Paxton took the last full cup.

I groan. "Figures you'd take the last of it."

Paxton glances, and at least has the decency to look chagrined. "Sorry. I can make another pot."

I wave a hand. "Be easier to just go get a cup from North Perk." I gesture at the coffee maker. "That thing is older than both of us, and takes at least half an hour to make a pot."

He takes a moment to examine the surroundings—my kitchen, and the beat-up, thrift store table and chairs we're using, the chipped mugs, both thrift store finds, one with the faded logo of a St. Louis dry cleaning company, and the other an auto repair shop in Nome, Alaska; the ancient TV on a rickety stand, both also from thrift stores, and the TV is probably one of the earliest color TVs ever made; my couch, threadbare, with noisy springs and upholstery that's more stain than fabric.

"Sensing a pattern when it comes to the overall age of things around here," Paxton says.

I shrug. "Working girl barely making ends meet, Paxton. New stuff is for fancy people who can afford things like, oh, you know, paying *all* the bills in a month."

I stand up, toss my coffee in the sink, rinse out the mug, and set it upside down on the drying rack. "Well, I suppose it's time to start packing."

I stretch, leaning backward with my arms over my head, arching my spine until it cracks, and then twist side to side to crack it lower down—forgetting, momentarily, what I'm wearing and the company present. My boobs swing heavily side to side with my twisting, until one of them flies out. I cover it immediately with my hand and shove it back into place, but the damage is done—I glance at Paxton, who is staring at me with a blank, blinking expression, jaw tight, fingers clutching his coffee mug hard, as if suppressing his reaction requires maximum effort.

Blushing furiously, I tuck my hands under my armpits, covering my chest with my arms. "Sorry. I—yeah.

Um. I'm going to get dressed. You can stay, or…whatever. I don't even know."

I'm not a prude, nor particularly or overly modest, but for some reason, the wardrobe malfunction has me off-balance and embarrassed, even though I've gotten naked with men I've known a shorter time than Paxton. I don't really have any issues with my body, and I'm generally very confident about what I look like—and I know pretty damn well that most men are easily hypnotized by the natural monstrosity of my tatas alone, not to mention the rest of my curvaceousness. Paxton brings out something unique in me, though. I don't know what, or how to define it or label it or handle it, just that he makes me feel odd and self-aware and more self-conscious than normal. Not self-conscious, just…physically self-aware.

Maybe.

Ugh.

I turn away from him and lock myself in my room—and change into a tight, minimizing bra, a pale green crew neck T-shirt, and my least flattering light-wash jeans. Nothing like the outfit I was wearing when he hijacked me on the side of the road, or the pajamas I was wearing when he barnstormed my apartment. I run a brush through my hair and keep it out of my face with a hairband.

I really don't have much, so it's short work to pack: my clothes are already in bins, and I have another for shoes and belts and scarves and such, and then my toiletries, shower stuff, phone charger, and the few other sundry items all fit into my gym duffel bag. Everything I own is packed within twenty minutes—the furniture I'll leave for Bill, so he can rent the place fully furnished.

I exit the bedroom and find Paxton still at my table, nursing his coffee and scrolling through a social media platform on his phone. "So, you're dressed and ready to go." He swallows the last of his coffee and shoves his phone in the back pocket of his dark blue jeans. "I can help you pack."

"I own, like, eight things, Paxton. I'm already packed. Five bins, a duffel bag, and my purse." I shrug. "That's it."

He frowns. "I drove the Porsche here, which may fit a duffel at most." He digs a set of keys out of his hip pocket. "So we go to my parents' house and switch to the Rover, come back and get your stuff."

I let out a sharp breath. "Okay. Let's go." I frown. "Wait, so we're driving to DC?"

He laughs. "You kidding? No. We fly—private jet out of Pellston."

I boggle at him. "Private jet? Like, an actual jet you guys own?"

Paxton makes a face of amused hilarity. "Yes, Makayla, an actual private passenger jet we own." He stares up and to the left a moment, thinking. "Actually, I think Dad owns a few. Three or four big Gulfstreams he leases to various charter companies, and if somebody needs to use one, we just need to give them few hours' notice. But this jet is a heavily customized Gulfstream Three, for the personal use of our immediate family in the Northern Michigan area only. The others, extended family and authorized friends of family, can use the others, but this baby is for us only."

I cackle, a little overwhelmed. "Just because I'm so clueless, what's the difference between a normal private jet and a 'heavily customized' one?" I ask, using air quotes around his phrasing.

He chews on his lower lip in an attempt to not laugh at me. "Oh, only about a hundred million dollars."

I get a little woozy, and have to hold on to the counter. "A hundred…"

"A hundred million dollars," he finishes.

"Meaning, yours is a hundred million dollars *more* than the average?"

He nods. "At least. And I mean, you can get a little baby jet, like a Cirrus or whatever, for like two mil."

"Does that make yours one of the most expensive?"

"Like, most expensive ever? Maybe in the top, oh, ten or fifteen in the world, but nowhere near the top. That belongs to a sultan of somewhere or other I think. But his shit is gold plated on the inside and is worth like five hundred million or something stupid." He shrugs. "Which is cool, I guess, if you're into having things gold plated and diamond encrusted."

"And you're not?" I glance pointedly at his watch, which is both.

He follows my gaze. "Okay, well this watch is literally the one exception of everything I personally own, and it was a gift from my grandmother when I won my seat in Congress. It's not really my personal style, but Grandma gave it to me so I wear it."

I can't help a little smile. "That's sweet."

He frowns. "That feels a little condescending, Makayla." He crosses his arms over his chest. "Just because I'm rich and arrogant doesn't mean I don't love my family."

I blink. "I didn't mean to insinuate that, Paxton, and if I gave you that impression, then I apologize."

He waves a hand. "Whatever. Let's get this show on the road." But instead of heading for the door, he ambles into my room, and stares thoughtfully at my little pile of crates. "So, idea."

I lean in the doorway next to him, shoulder to shoulder. "Okay?"

"How about you take, like, a few changes of clothes, and that's it?" He gestures at the tubs. "Underwear, some jeans and shorts and T-shirts and workout stuff, a few things of your own in case you get, like, homesick or whatever, but leave the bulk of it? As soon as we get to DC, I'm hiring a stylist and personal shopper to outfit you with a decent wardrobe. So, really, you don't need any of this, because you'll be wearing all new stuff. I just figure you'd feel better having at least a little bit of your own stuff."

I sigh, a long, slow exhale. "I guess you're right.

All this is from the thrift store anyway." I set my purse down and open the duffel bag. "Just give me, like, five minutes."

He shrugs, and sits on the bed to wait, and watch. But, as soon as he sits, he frowns, and bounces on the mattress, which is so old it has actual springs in it. "How the hell do you sleep on this? I can feel the springs through the mattress."

I laugh. "It's what I've got, so it's what I use. Beggars can't be choosers. And I mean, I'm not a beggar, but when I got this apartment from my boss it was empty and I had no furniture and about a grand total to furnish it, including appliances."

He frowns. "I'm not an expert by any means, but I thought most landlords provided appliances?"

"He had just finished remodeling, and so he waived the deposit and gave me a discount on rent for the first year if I provided my own appliances. So, to the thrift store I went, for everything from T-shirts to my microwave to my kitchen utensils."

He grimaces harder. "You bought kitchen utensils from a thrift store."

I laugh at his disgust. "And underwear and bras."

He blinks. "Wow."

I shrug. "Hey, if you've never been poor, you don't know, and you don't get to judge. And besides, you always wash before you use."

I don't bother folding, I just cram a handful of underwear—thongs, boy shorts, period granny panties, my two best sports bras, my one bought-new full coverage bra and, for reasons I'm not entirely certain of, the one matching set I own, purchased on a whim because the set was clearance and my size. I've never worn the lingerie, and the tags are still attached—I'm not even sure what it looks like on me, or what I was thinking when I bought it, or why I'm including it.

I steal a glance at Paxton as I shove the racy, lacy red thong and demi push-up bra into the bag—thankfully, he's on his phone again and not looking.

Resolutely, I leave the lingerie in the bag, despite not having any clue what's going through that section of my brain.

Quickly, then, I put my favorite sleepwear, laze-around T-shirts and sweatpants, my most form-flattering jeans, my one nice going-out skirt and blouse, a few T-shirts, my work out tank tops and shorts, and—again, for reasons I don't care to examine too closely—my one slinky, revealing, tight, barely mid-thigh little black dress. Again, bought on sale because it fit me and was dirt cheap, and I had the idiotic idea I'd wear it someday. The tags are still on it, and I've never worn it besides trying it on in the fitting room.

Now, my toiletries, clothes, and my few personal effects are all contained in this one small duffel bag.

I zip it closed, and hold it, staring at it. "So, this is my entire life. Everything I own of value, not including the stuff I'm leaving."

Paxton nods. "Compact and efficient. I like it."

I snort. "I meant something kind of the opposite."

He pats me on the shoulder. "By the end of the week, Makayla, that will no longer be true."

I consider what he means. "Well, no. Not really. You will have bought me a bunch of stuff. That's not the same as it being mine."

He tilts his head, genuinely confused. "Yes—I'll have bought things for you, therefore they will be yours. If, or when, rather, we get a divorce, you'll keep it all. So, yours."

I shake my head and pat his shoulder like he did mine. "I realize you can't know this about me yet, Paxton, but that's not how I work. It's not who I am as a person. You buying me shit, giving me shit—that's *your* shit. I didn't buy it; I didn't earn the money that bought it. So it ain't mine." I hear my mother in my voice, the old her, the born-and-raised in inner-city Detroit, pre-MS, the vehemently and proudly independent, don't need nobody, won't ever ask for help version of her. I lift my chin, stare him in the eyes. "Don't think I won't be appreciative, mind you—but nothing you give me will be mine."

He frowns, stares back. "What the hell would you want me to do with a closet full of women's clothes and whatever?"

I shrug. "Your business. Donate them? Give them to the next girl?" I snicker. "Not like the next girl will be built like me, though."

His eyes flit over me, head to toe. "Point is,

Makayla, we're going to have to discuss this a bit more. When I give you something, it will be because I want to. And whatever it is, it will be *yours*. So when we separate, if you leave your stuff in my condo in DC, I'll have them delivered to wherever you are, and you can sell them or donate them as you see fit."

I sigh, smile. "I'd say we're at an impasse, then."

"Have you forgotten?" His grin is an arrogant smirk. "I always get my way."

I pat him on the cheek. "Well, buddy, you don't know me very well, do you?"

He doesn't laugh, and his eyes are deep and serious. "No, I don't." A pause. "Not yet, anyway."

Not yet. Not yet?

I put that odd little comment aside and shoulder my bags. "Well. Time to go, I guess."

He nods, pushes up off the bed and strides past me. I follow him, and then pause at the door. Dig my keyring out of my purse. Funny—there's only the one key for this apartment. I don't own a car, or a post office box, or anything else that would require a key. Not even a bike lock. I set the one key on the table beside the couch, and with one last glance around, leave the apartment that has been my home for the last several years.

I don't look back, once I'm out the front door.

10

PAXTON PRECEDES ME DOWN THE STAIRS, AND THEN AT the bottom, takes my duffel bag from me. Parked at a careless angle in front of the carriage house is the tiny little classic red Porsche of Paxton's. I expect him to open the trunk at the rear of the car, but instead he opens the front where the engine usually is. This is where he sets my bag. He closes the front trunk, and then rounds the hood to open the passenger door, and holds it for me.

I hesitate. Breathe out slowly, and then lower myself into the sumptuous black leather bucket seat. I clutch my purse on my lap and try to not tremble all over. This car has a much different feeling than the super Ferrari I was in a week ago—that was beyond luxury, hyper technologically advanced, like being in a futuristic spaceship; this, by contrast, is small, sporty, comfortable, open air all around rather than a small removable section of roof. When Paxton slides behind the wheel and starts the engine, the sound is a rumbly feline purr rather than the massive throaty predator snarl of the Ferrari.

He shoves the stick shift forward, nudges the gas, and the little car makes a tight circle, pauses at the end of the driveway, and then we're zipping out of the neighborhood and onto 31 back toward his parent's house.

I glance at Paxton: he's grinning, an ear-to-ear grin of sheer joy, the wind playfully ruffling his hair. I can't help a grin myself at the fun of being in this car—it's a visceral experience, a sense of connection to the world and the road.

He glances at me. "Well?"

I know exactly what he means. And I can't help laughing. "Okay, you were right. With *this* car, I get it."

He howls a triumphant laugh, and it's a joyful, easy, carefree sound; this version of Paxton...I like. A lot.

"You like it?" He says this as he yanks the shifter down, floors the gas, and the car surges forward down the highway.

I nod. "It's fun, and I don't feel like I'm going to make it dirty or damage it just by sitting in it."

He laughs. "I get what you mean. That Ferrari is actually intimidating to drive, even for me." We come to a curve in the road, and there's a subtle sense of leaning to the right. He eyes me, grinning again. "Wanna drive?"

I shake my head. "No, thanks."

He rolls his eyes at me. "Come on. It's fun!" A glance. "Or can you not drive a stick?"

I hesitate. "I, um. I don't drive."

He frowns at my answer. "Don't, or can't?"

I shrug. "Same thing."

"Explain."

"I grew up in Detroit, inner city. Mom didn't own a car, and never has. Same with me. We used public transportation in Detroit, and once we moved up here, we walked everywhere."

He shakes his head. "You never got your license?"

"Nope. I have never operated a motor vehicle." I laugh. "Closest I've come is sitting in the driver's seat of a fire truck during a field trip in third grade."

"Well that's...fucked up. Driving is one of life's great joys."

I sigh and laugh at the same time. "I'll have to take your word for it."

A pause, and then he shakes his head. "No. You're learning."

I roll my eyes at him. "Yeah, okay."

He eyes me as we pull into the deBraun driveway. "You are. Right now."

I narrow my eyes at him. "Right now? In your half-million-dollar matching-numbers classic Porsche five thousand or whatever you call it?"

"1956 Porsche 356 Speedster," he says, droll. "And yes, now, in this."

"Isn't driving a stick harder than an automatic?" I ask.

He shrugs. "Not really. A steeper learning curve, maybe, at first, but once you learn, you never really forget. And it makes driving an automatic easier."

I shake my head. "I'm fine. It's not like I'll ever own a car."

He tilts his head. "You could."

I roll my eyes at him again. "Oh, right, because I'm going to stroll into a dealership and buy myself a car using my fake husband's family's money."

Now it's his turn to narrow his eyes at me. "I won't be your fake husband—I'll be your *real* husband, it just won't be a love match."

I sit in silence—except for the purr of the engine. "You know what I mean."

"Yeah, I do. But it's important to remember that it may not be a real marriage in the sense you know it, where we fell in love and got engaged and planned a wedding and got married, but it will be a real marriage in every other way—you'll legally be my wife, and I'll be your husband. You'll take my last name, get an equitable division of property upon divorce, meaning you'll get a shitload from me out of the deal, because I'm going to conveniently forget to do a prenup."

I frown at that. "Won't your mom be all over that? Like, I would imagine she'll have that drafted and ready to sign before I ever set foot in the church."

He waves a hand. "I'll handle it. Even if she does somehow force the issue, you have my solemn promise upon my honor and my life that I will make sure you're set for life when we divorce."

I sigh. "Part of me just wants to push all the details away and pretend this isn't happening, just go with the flow and not think about anything." I look at him, and the truth bubbles up out of me unbidden. "Truth is, I'm actually really scared."

He doesn't dismiss this as I expect him to. "I'm not going to say I'm exactly *scared*," he says slowly, "but I will admit to being a little...apprehensive."

"What the hell do *you* have to be apprehensive about, Paxton? You're the man. You're the rich one, with the connected family, the education and the career and everything. I'm the woman, the one legally tying myself to a man I don't know from Adam, for a vague promise of being 'taken care of' at some future date, at which point I will have a divorce on my record and another man's name." I rub my face, shuddering a sigh. "I'm the one risking everything. I quit my jobs, and if something goes wrong I'll have no money, no jobs, no furniture, no apartment...and I'll be stuck in Washington DC with no way home, and no home to go to."

"You don't have any family you could crash with?" he asks. "Not that you'll need to, I'm just wondering."

I shake my head. "Father has never been in the picture, grandparents have all long since passed. Only child, no aunts, no cousins. Just my mom, and living with her is...well, it's not an option."

He eyes me in silence for a long, long time. "I guess I didn't realize that."

"Like I said, Paxton, we don't know anything about each other."

He chuckles bitterly. "You have an advantage though—you can find out a lot about me with a quick Google search." He puts on the parking brake, pushes open his door, and gets out. "Come on, now. Get behind the wheel. Time to learn how to drive."

I blink at the sudden change of topics. "Uh, no?"

He grins. "You'll enjoy it. Just try."

I sigh. I have often wondered how much easier my life would be if I had a license and a car. I would never have imagined my first driving lesson would be in a car like *this*, but hey, here I am.

I unbuckle, circle around the hood and slide behind the wheel. Buckle up. Grip the wheel in both hands and familiarize myself with the wheel, the gear shifter, and the three pedals.

Paxton settles in next to me, his eyes on me. "Okay, so. The steering wheel is pretty obvious, I hope."

I give him a look. "Yes, Paxton, I am familiar with how a steering wheel works. I do know that much."

He shrugs. "Hey, you've never operated a car, so I'm just covering all the basics." He taps the shifter. "This changes the gears. The numbers indicate where the gears are—first, second, third, and fourth," He traces the tree diagram as he says each gear. "So, you start in first, up here, and then follow the pattern. It becomes second nature after a while." He gestures at the floor. "Three pedals—gas on the right, brake in the middle, clutch on the left.

"Already lost," I quip. "Not really. But how do they all work together?"

"Well, the clutch pedal, on the left, pulls the gear out, and then you move the shifter and release the clutch pedal, and the engine moves into the next gear. You take your foot off the gas while you have the clutch pedal down, and push the gas down again after it's in gear. Try pushing in the clutch."

I push it in. "Okay."

"Now put the shifter into first—all the way to the left, and forward."

I do so.

"Okay, now—" he cuts himself off. "Wait, the parking brake is on. Put it back in neutral and take the brake off." Once this is done, he gestures at the shifter. "Okay, try again." Once the shifter is in first, he juts his chin up. "Cool. Now, very slowly, very gently, let out the clutch, and at the same time, push in the gas. You'll feel the car start to move, feel the engine taking hold as the gear engages."

By minute increments, and with a death grip on the steering wheel, I let off the clutch pedal and depress the gas—and, as he said, at a certain point I feel the difference in the steering wheel, and hear it in the engine. The motor hums louder and higher pitched, and then something catches, and the car begins to roll forward—and then I let off the clutch entirely and the car bolts forward, startling me into releasing both clutch and gas. The engine stalls, and the car rolls to a stop.

"That was good!" Paxton says.

I frown. "No, it wasn't. I stalled it."

He waves a hand. "Eh. Everyone stalls their first time. I told you, there's a learning curve. This time, when you feel the motor catch, try to find the balance where you're not letting off all the way all at once until the car is moving. But don't jam the gas pedal down or we'll jolt. Smooth and easy and slow."

So, I try again, and this time, I get a bit farther before it stalls out. Within ten minutes of somewhat frustrated effort, I have the knack of it, and we're trundling slowly down the driveway, which curves and dips and rises; I keep it in first and under twenty miles per hour, learning the feel of the wheel and the gas and the brake, accelerating and slowing down, turning this way and that…

I glance at him with a smile. "This *is* fun."

He chortles, leaning back in his seat, a long thick arm draped over the back of my seat. "Babe, you're going literally eleven miles per hour. Wait until we've got you a license and you can do ninety on the highway. *That*'s where the fun is at."

"Speed?"

He lifts a shoulder. "I mean, yes. I really love going fast. There's nothing in the world like getting eight or nine hundred horses howling on a track. But no, I just mean…" He waves a hand at the open sky overhead. "Driving with the top back, the wind in your hair, the flat four singing behind you…sun shining, not a care in the world, nowhere to go but wherever the highway takes you." He sighs, a great lungful of air sucked in, held, his head tipped back to bathe in the golden sunshine, and then a happy, whooshing exhale. "Like I said—it's one of life's greatest joys."

I bring us to a stop in front of the garage. "Two things I know nothing about—not having a care in the world, and life's greatest joys."

Paxton starts laughing, and then lifts his head to look at me, and realizes I'm not joking. "Makayla, Jesus. That's awful."

I snort, shrug. "I mean, I'm not being all poor me. I got nothing to complain about. My momma loves me, I've always had some kind of a roof over my head and food to eat and clothes to wear. My life has just been focused on the grind, you know? Surviving day to day."

He prods the clicker attached to the underside of the sun visor, and a garage door opens. "Well, Makayla Poe, that's about to change."

PAXTON DOES THE FINICKY WORK OF PULLING HIS
Porsche into its spot in the cavernous garage,
and then retrieves my duffel from the front
trunk.

"Is it still called a trunk, if it's in the front?" I ask, as
he closes the lid and hangs the keys in a lockbox on the
wall. "Or is it the hood?"

He smiles at me. "They call it a frunk."

I laugh. "Frunk. What a funny word." I eye the expansive garage. "So now…inside?"

He shakes his head. "Nope. Now I have Johnny
drive us to the airport."

"Don't you have to pack?"

He waves a hand, careless. "Nah. I keep everything
I need both places." He tilts his head. "Well, wherever
I go regularly. I've got at least minimal wardrobes and
toiletries and all that shit here, in DC, LA, Manhattan,
Aspen, and London."

I snort, a helpless giggle of hilarity. "You have
houses in all those places?"

He shrugs, with a *well yeah* expression on his face. "I live in DC while Congress is in session, and I have business interests in LA, New York, and London, and when I want to get away from everything, I go to Aspen."

I glance his way. "Business interests?"

Another shrug. "Sure. I have plans for a long political career, but I'm also interested in diversifying my assets, just in case."

"What kind of business?"

He blinks my way. "Ummm, this and that. Luxury real estate in LA, telecom-slash-media in New York, import-export in London. Just dabbling in various things my family has ties to, you know? Easy investments with minimal oversight from me, until and unless I want to start leaning into those endeavors."

I laugh. "What a weird, wild world you live in, Paxton." I gesture at him. "Well, lead the way, I suppose."

He waves toward a side door I hadn't noticed the last time I was here. "This way."

Through the rows and rows of gleaming cars, each one worth more than I've ever made in my entire life—probably more than what Mom and I have made in our lives combined—and then we pass through the door in the far side of the garage, which leads to…another garage.

I pause in the doorway as I see yet more rows of vehicles. "Seriously?" I say with a cackle. "How many cars do ya'll have?"

He taps his chin. "Hmmm. No clue, never added them all up." He gestures to the larger garage we just left. "Those are the collection." Another wave of his hand to this other, much smaller garage. "These are the daily drivers, the noncollector cars. Just your average, run-of-the-mill, everyday cars."

I stroll through and examine the cars here: I see two Range Rovers—one brand, sparkling new, the other older and more beat up, but not a collector item, apparently—a long, sleek, new Mercedes Benz sedan, a boxy, white Mercedes SUV, a quick-looking little blue two-door BMW, a handful of motorcycles ranging from choppers to antiques to crotch rocket sport bikes, and an older and well-used Mercedes convertible sedan.

I laugh. "Not a single thing here is run-of-the-mill, Paxton. I think you're wildly out of touch with reality."

"Well, yeah, probably," he says with a chuckle. "My first car at sixteen was a one of ten ever made Jag."

"Jag?" I ask.

He frowns. "Jaguar?"

I snort. "Oh. Right. Sorry, I just know literally zero about cars."

Paxton laughs. "Clearly." He points at the new Mercedes sedan. "We're taking that. I just have to find Johnny."

A voice from behind us. "Here, sir."

Paxton jumps, whirls. "Dude, you are a ghost. Were you in the SAS or something?"

John doesn't react at all. "No, sir. Something rather more challenging: the British Butler Institute."

I snicker, thinking he's joking. "The British Butler Institute. Good one."

John only stares at me. "I was serious, ma'am."

My eyes widen. "It's a real thing?"

"Yes, ma'am."

"Oh, sorry. I didn't mean to laugh at you." I wrinkle my nose. "What do you learn in butler school?"

"How to be a butler, ma'am." A beat of silence as I work out how to respond. "That was a joke, ma'am." He smiles, a smooth curve of his lips. "Posture and bearing, elocution, etiquette, things like that." He turns to address Paxton. "What can I do for you, sir?"

"We're heading to DC, so we need a ride to Pellston, and I need you to have them warm up the jet for me."

John nods. "Yes, sir. Of course." A pause. "Will you require a meal, or a particular beverage selection for the trip, sir?"

Paxton waves a hand in dismissal. "Nah. It's a short hop." He eyes me, and then turns back to John. "Um, one thing. She was never here, okay? I'm working something out with Mom, and I'd like my association with Miss Poe kept...private. Yeah?"

A subtle nod. "Certainly, sir. Mrs. deBraun is on holiday in Marseilles at the moment, so that shouldn't be a problem."

"Good to know," Paxton says. "She can be hard to reach when she's on vacation."

"She made a point of being unavailable. A mental recharge, she called it."

"Recharge, or retard?" Paxton mutters.

"I'm sure I wouldn't know sir," John says, but his tone is openly disapproving.

I whack Paxton's arm. "Not cool, Paxton."

He grumbles. "Whatever. I was joking."

"Yeah, well, some things aren't funny," I say.

He waves a hand in that dismissive way he has. "Whatever. Let's go."

John nods. "A moment, sir, and I'll bring the car around front." He takes my duffel bag. "There's coffee on, if you'd like some, sir, ma'am."

"Ooh, coffee!" I say, excited, and then glance at Paxton with a glare. "SOMEONE helped himself to mine."

"Shall I set out cream and sugar for you ma'am?" John asks.

I shake my head. "No, thank you. I like it strong and black, like me."

He smirks. "Certainly, ma'am." With a short bow of his upper body, he turns and heads into the house, and Paxton and I follow him.

By the time we're in the kitchen, John is nowhere to be seen, but two insulated travel mugs bearing the logo of Beach by deBraun wait on the counter, full of steaming black coffee, the lids beside each one. Paxton screws the lid on one, hands it to me, and does the same for the other. I sip, and the coffee is as much better than mine as the house is—that is to say, the coffee I buy makes Folger's look expensive, and this coffee is some kind of gourmet, designer stuff.

"Wow," I say, after the first sip. "Best coffee I've ever had."

Paxton nods. "Mom takes coffee *very* seriously. She bought several coffee farms in Indonesia, South America, and Africa, hired a master roaster, and started a distribution company, all for the sole purpose of getting the best, freshest beans possible. Each twelve-ounce bag costs at minimum fifty dollars. Some of the bags can go for upward of a hundred."

I snicker. "For *coffee*?"

Paxton gestures at the mug I'm sipping from. "You did say it was the best coffee you've ever had."

I shrug, nod. "Very true. It does taste…expensive."

I marvel, as I sip. This family goes far out of their way, sometimes to ridiculous extremes, to get the absolute best of literally everything. It's almost funny.

Apropos of nothing, Paxton heads for the front door. "I'm guessing John will have the car around, now." A glance at me. "You ready?"

I shake my head negative. "Not at all." I laugh, and follow him. "But here we go anyway, right?"

Last time I was here, I saw the garage, the kitchen, and the deck—this time, I get more of a tour as Paxton leads me to the front door. Miles of marble, clean white walls, pops of color here and there in the form of knick-knacks and statues and wall hangings and paintings; I see one painting on the wall near the front door that looks, to my uneducated eye, like a Picasso. I stop to look at it more closely, and Paxton stands beside me.

"That's an original," he says.

"Of course it is," I mutter. "I mean, who doesn't have an original Picasso."

"If I told you how much Dad paid for it at the auction, you'd probably faint."

I nod. "Yeah, I don't think I need to know. I couldn't fathom the amount anyway."

"An original by a master like this is actually considered an investment, though," Paxton says. "It retains its value. It's insured to an absolutely eye-watering amount, even for us." He gestures at the glass case surrounding the painting. "The case is fireproof, waterproof, and crushproof. The house could burn down around it, and this painting would be intact."

I shake my head, sighing. "Incredible." I just look at the painting a while longer, because who gets to see an original Picasso in person, outside a museum?

Paxton is looking at me, rather than the painting, I notice. "You like art, huh?"

I shrug. "I mean, sure. Who doesn't? And plus, it's just a cool opportunity, you know? A real, original Picasso, without paying to go into a museum and fighting the crowds? It's just cool."

Paxton grins. "I've got some pretty cool original pieces at my place in DC you may like to see, in that case."

"Like what?" I ask.

His grin is mischievous. "Let it be a surprise?"

The foyer of the home is a palace in and of itself, with a giant chandelier made of dangling crystals and Edison bulbs, an acre of marble, with Greco-Roman statues flanking each side of a pair of curving staircases which frame the foyer space. We walk out through French doors which are easily six feet wide and twenty feet tall, made of heavy dark oak to contrast with the white marble floor and white ceiling.

Outside, another grand, sweeping staircase like you'd see at a courthouse or something, descends to a wide circular driveway of cobblestones ringing a stunning fountain, the centerpiece of which is another Greco-Roman statue of a mostly nude woman tastefully covered in the folds of a dangling robe, one foot touching the waters of the pool, a jar under one arm from which water pours. Knowing this family, the statue is probably an actual antique statue from Ancient Greece or Rome, as with the statues in the foyer.

I glance at Paxton. "The fountain and the statues inside, are they...?"

He laughs. "Real? As in from like two thousand years ago? No. They're hand-carved replicas of actual pieces from a museum in Athens, but they're not actual real statues carved by the ancients. Shit like that has to be in a temperature-controlled museum environment. Keeping them here out in the open would be highly irresponsible."

"Oh," I say, feeling relieved for some reason.

"I can't tell if you're disappointed by that, or relieved."

I laugh. "Me either."

Paxton laughs with me. "You know, I think Uncle Nicholas does actually own a piece of legitimate Roman statuary, but it's on long-term loan to...the Berlin Museum, I believe."

I snort. "Figures."

Waiting at the top of the circle is the long, low, sleek, black Mercedes sedan, which isn't a limousine, as in stretched, but when I get in its clear this vehicle is, yet again, something extraordinary. The seats are...beyond words. Stitched, quilted white leather, supple and soft to the touch, so comfortable I feel like I'm sitting on a cloud. There are only two seats in the back, so it's not designed to carry a lot of people, but rather one or two people in extreme luxury. Large digital screens were installed on the rear of each front seat, providing each passenger with his or her own individual viewing experience, and each seat also includes recliner-style extendable footrests, and enough footwell space to fully extend them. Upon further inspection, I realized that the rear compartment is adjustable, so if there are only two passengers, it could be arranged as it is now, and if space for four passengers was needed, two additional rear-facing seats could be folded down.

Paxton is watching me examine my surroundings, and I see the expectant look on his face.

"Okay," I sighed. "I'll indulge you. What is this thing I'm in? I'll admit it's impressive."

Paxton face palms himself. "Impressive."

I shrugged. "Yeah, it's nice. Comfy."

A laugh, disbelieving, as with everything else he imagined I would be in awe over. "It's a Mercedes-Maybach Pullman."

I shook my head. "Okay?"

A sigh. "Unbelievable. Basically, the version of a limousine used by royalty, as in literal kings and queens and Sultans. It's bulletproof, for one thing."

I cackle. "Just in case terrorists want to assassinate you, way out here in Northern Michigan, huh?"

A shrug. "Right? Dad bought it. He keeps it here most of the time, but if he has to travel abroad, he takes the 747 and brings this with him."

"The 747?" I ask.

"Customized to carry several vehicles, plus three executive suites, a movie theater, and a full kitchen," he clarifies.

"Of course," I say with a snort. "How else should he travel?"

Paxton laughs. "You think I'm out of touch with reality? You should meet Dad. His idea of slumming it is…" He pauses, tilts his head. "Well, to be honest, he doesn't even know what that is. I doubt he's been inside any means of transportation within the last twenty-five years which he doesn't personally own, and which costs less than half a million dollars."

I blink. "I…wow."

"Right now, he's in Marseilles with Mom, I'm guessing. He flew into Pellston in the 747 with this car, collected Mom, and they flew to France, where they were taken by helicopter to their Mediterranean mega yacht, leaving the Pullman here because they won't need a car in France, as they won't leave the boat."

"As opposed to their Caribbean mega yacht, I presume?"

"Precisely. Far more convenient to simply have one in both places than try to move it back and forth and have to plan far enough ahead to send it over when you want it."

"But of course," I drawl.

Paxton just laughs. "You make fun, but it's just how they do things. They have the money, so why not?"

I shrug, nod. "Makes sense, I just…" A laugh. "It's all beyond my ability to fathom, I guess."

A silence, but not an uncomfortable one. I watch the scenery pass, and I can't help but marvel a little at the complete silence within this car—the soundproofing is perfect, without even a hint of road noise. I feel separate from the world, a completely opposite sensation to being in Paxton's little Porsche.

I glance at him. "I like your car better."

He smirks. "My 356?"

"The one you picked me up in this morning, yes."

His grin widens. "Totally different experiences, right?"

I nod. "Exactly what I was just thinking. I like the air and the sense of being in the world, whereas in this I just feel like I'm floating in a moving castle, separated from everything."

"Well, that is the purpose of this car."

"To make you feel separate from the unwashed masses?"

He frowns, but nods. "Yeah, I guess. I mean, that's an unkind way of putting it, and not every wealthy person is like that, but the essence of your point is accurate enough."

We chat more on the rest of the drive, but there are long silences, and I'm somewhat baffled by how comfortable I am already with Paxton.

Although, now and then, there are moments that are distinctly *not* comfortable. Moments where I'm looking out the window and feel his eyes on me, moments where his gaze is piercing and scrutinizing and yet unreadable, and I wonder if he's going to say something, but he doesn't. We're separated by the console between us, yet I feel him filling the car with his larger-than-life presence, where even silent and still he is somehow just *more*.

Thirty minutes in the car, and we're pulling onto a section of tarmac somewhat distant from the rest of the airport. The jet that's waiting, engines idling, is not small. Sleek, white, with six or so oval windows, and a truck-borne staircase leading up to the door. John pulls the limousine up within a few feet of the base of the stairs, puts the vehicle in park, and moves with a speed that is somehow unhurried around to open the door first for me, and then Paxton, who unfolds himself from the seat with a smooth elegance. A tug straightens his polo; a pass of his hand sweeps his hair aside.

Effortlessly perfect.

Annoying.

I feel…frumpy. Underdressed. Awkward, like a newborn giraffe. I wish, stupidly, that I'd dressed up a little more. Worn nicer jeans, a better top. Compared to Paxton's elegant perfection, I'm a sleazy plebeian with no taste.

I push my self-consciousness away—I am who I am, and I'm not trying to impress him or anyone. He picked me, and I'm not going to pretend to be someone I'm not just to please him. Like me or don't, take me or leave me, I don't care—that's been my attitude my whole life, taught to me by Mom, who is the most self-confident, self-possessed woman I've ever known. Even Camilla deBraun can't compare to my mom when it comes to sense of pride in self—Mom survived just about the worst that life can throw at a person, and retained her sense of self and pride in who she is; it's this attitude I have inherited, which I've also developed for myself through my own experiences. I can stand on my own two feet; I can make my way through life without anyone's help. I have nobody to impress. Never cared about what I do or don't own, or what I look like.

Not going to start now, that's for damn sure.

I lift my chin, stiffen my spine, and wait for Paxton to precede me up the stairs—I'm about to head up when I see John carrying my duffel bag; I take it from him, despite his protestations that it's his job to carry it for me. He doesn't work for me, and I'm not about to start letting people wait on me hand and foot just because I'm hanging around Paxton deBraun.

I toss my duffel bag on a seat, and sit in the seat beside it—in the row in front of Paxton. I feel his confusion, but I ignore it. I'm so confused, so conflicted.

I don't know how much time passes before the airplane begins moving, and the tarmac outside is whizzing past, and I have to grip the armrests and clench my jaw. I breathe hard.

"Hey, it's okay." Paxton, beside me. Touching my shoulder. "Never flown before?"

The pressure on my ears, on my chest, pressing me into the seat—it's terrifying. I shake my head.

His hand is gentle, gripping my shoulder in a friendly, comforting way. His voice is a low buzz in my ear. "Breathe, Makayla."

I suck in a ragged breath, and realize I was holding it only after my lungs fill with oxygen. I reach out blindly and grab his hand, and somehow his hand tangles with mine, fingers twined with fingers, and I clench it as hard as I can.

After a while, the pressure relaxes, but my terror doesn't—I'm at the window seat, and outside I can see the world spread out like a quilt far, far, far below.

My terror isn't as much about being this high up in a tiny little metal tube—it *is* that, but not *just* that.

It's him.

Holding his hand…and it's *comforting*.

I'm leaving behind everything I know.

Moving in with a man I've now met twice, three times? Marrying him?

What the hell am I doing?

To his credit, Paxton doesn't try to talk to me—and smart of him, too. I'd probably bite his head off. I'm feeling vulnerable and scared, and those feelings make me cranky. Plus, I still have a death grip on his big, strong hand, a fact I want to ignore.

Eventually, once a few minutes have passed, I'm able to calm myself down, take a deep breath or ten, and release Paxton's hand.

He shakes it, and I see white fingerprints dimpled in the skin. "Damn, girl. You've got a grip."

I wince. "Sorry."

He just grins, winks, and thumps his chest with both fists. "Ook, me big strong man," he says in a gruff voice. "Me tough."

I can't help but laugh. "You know, for all your many faults, you're not a caveman."

"Many faults, huh?" He pretends to preen. "Like what, pray tell?"

I snort. "Um. Where do I start? Obscenely, absurdly

arrogant. Entitled. At least a little vain. Wildly out of touch with reality. Spoiled."

At each fault I list, he clutches his chest, as if my words are arrows. Making a dramatic, wounded face, he leans toward me. "And, may I ask, do I have any positive qualities whatsoever?"

"Not that I can tell," I say, my voice dry. I bite my lip over the grin that threatens to spread. "Fine. Maybe one or two."

"Like?" he prompts.

"You're not too bad to look at. You're obviously very smart, very well educated, you're one of the youngest members of Congress in US history." I roll a shoulder. "You're pretty funny. Easy to talk to, in spite of being so damn arrogant."

I realize I'm much more at ease now, and that this entire conversation has been a subtle and effective ploy on Paxton's part to calm me down.

I sigh, rub my face with both hands. Give him a kind, thankful smile. "Thank you, Paxton."

He doesn't ask for what. "Hey, flying can be scary."

He looks around at the interior of the jet—which is much like the car we took here, an example of luxury taken to its furthest extreme short of being gold plated and diamond encrusted. Cushy, hand-stitched, plump white leather captain's chairs, complete with extendable footrests, cup holders in one armrest, and a bank of buttons on the other...for massage functions, it looks like. A monstrous flat-screen TV fills the majority of the bulkhead between the passenger cabin and the cockpit, which turns on seemingly of its own accord, tinkling piano jazz. I glance at Paxton, and realize he has an iPad that he used to control the TV.

He grins. "So, this is your first time flying, huh? Gonna spoil you for flying commercial."

I roll my eyes. "Like you would know what flying commercial is like."

He arches an eyebrow. "I flew commercial once." He fakes a dramatic shudder of disgust. "It was awful. Filthy plebeian peasants everywhere, and that was in first class."

I laugh. "Poor baby, had to fly in icky first class instead of his parents' ultra-luxury private jet."

He laughs. "Fly commercial sometime, and tell me you wouldn't fly private if it's available. And, honestly, it's not about the amenities, really. Seats are seats, and the ride quality is pretty much the same. It's the privacy, and the convenience. No lines, no security, no baggage check, no waiting around in the gate area, no crowding in with two hundred other people. None of the noise and the crying babies and annoying, chatty people in the row with you." He gestures. "This? It's quiet, it's private...it's just better."

"Yeah, but I mean, obviously everyone would rather fly private. It's not like people are sitting there like, yeah, I could have my own jet but I just prefer being squashed in the back of economy class."

"Well obviously, but it's also not like I can change

the fortunes of the entire country." He gestures at the jet again. "And this isn't even *mine*, it's my parents'. I just had the ridiculous luck of being born into a wealthy family."

The conversation wanders after that, to favorite movies aside from *Princess Bride*, music, funny or embarrassing drinking stories, and suddenly, I feel a shift in the movement of the jet.

I must stiffen, because Paxton smiles at me reassuringly. "Relax. We're making our approach."

"Shouldn't the captain make an announcement or something?" I ask.

"That's commercial. Our guys just fly the jet. If there's something important, he'll come back and tell me himself."

"Like what?"

A shrug. "Like if there's a diversion or something, or if we were to hit a rough patch of air with no way of avoiding it."

"What the hell is a rough patch of air?" I ask.

He chuckles. "Air currents, I guess. I don't know. Turbulence. That's what they call it, a rough patch of air."

I swallow hard. "Doesn't sound fun."

He makes an *eh* face. "Like hitting a section of road with a lot of potholes, basically."

"You must fly a lot," I say. "You're so blah about all this."

He nods. "All the time. I live in DC, but I hit up New

York and LA a couple times a month, and London, not regularly, but several times a year."

"What's London like?"

He grins. "Amazing. If I were going to live anywhere just because I like it, it'd be there. DC is where I have to live because I'm in Congress, but I don't love it. When my time on the Hill is over, I leave pretty fast. New York? No thanks, not on your life. Too big, too fast-paced, too many cranky people. LA is...I don't know. It's LA. Not my scene. But London? Yeah, baby. Fun, fast, interesting people, good food, culture...it's *old*. A sense of history, like you're walking these streets and you know Darwin and Shakespeare and Dickens, Winston Churchill...they all lived here, walked the same streets. You can live in the same building they lived in. You can see plays in the actual Globe Theatre."

I sigh. "Sounds amazing."

"Never been, I take it."

I laugh at that, and hard. "I've been precisely two places—Detroit, and Petoskey."

"What about, like, Mackinac Island?"

"Hard to go on vacation even to Mackinac Island when you gotta work seven days a week to make ends meet. Even if I could afford a day off, I couldn't afford the ferry ticket, and couldn't afford to do anything while there. Shit, I couldn't *get* there simply because I ain't ever owned a car." I hiss, annoyed. "I've never owned a car."

He tilts his head. "Why'd you correct yourself?"

I hesitate. "I lived in Detroit with Mom until high school, then we moved up here—up there, rather. I talked like my mom. Like someone from Detroit. Nothing wrong with that, in and of itself." I hesitate again. "But, when we moved up here, I stuck out. It's mostly rich white kids in the schools up here, so that alone set me apart. But talking different, too? I made a point of changing the way I talked, so I sounded less like Mom and more like the rest of the kids. The old accent comes back sometimes, and I correct myself out of habit." I shrug. "Besides, Camilla won't let us speak with obvious accents."

He blinks. "Wait, really?"

I nod. "Oh yeah, absolutely. The front desk clerks are actually required to receive 'elocution training' from a Hollywood acting coach, so as to speak with region-less neutrality." I snort, using air quotes around the phrase. "Even we lowly housekeeping staff are given a handful of lessons so we don't sound like we're from wherever we're from. Obviously, you have to speak at least halfway decent English to even be hired. No fresh off the boat hires allowed."

Paxton shakes his head. "That's stupid. No one cares how the housekeepers talk."

I eye him with an arched brow. "Because who would bother even talking to them, right?"

"Exactly—" he cuts off, looking at me. "Don't take insult where I don't mean it, Makayla."

"Actually, I agree with what you're saying. She

wants us to be essentially invisible. Like the hotel cleans itself, or there's like magic cleaning gnomes or something. Yet we have to speak proper English and be articulate and without accent. Sort of clashing ideas, you know?"

"Mom has always been very particular about things," Paxton says by way of explanation."

I feel a variance in the pressure, a sense of weight-lessness. "What's happening?" I ask, hating how squeaky, breathless, and panicked I sound—and feel.

His hand finds mine. And, to my great chagrin and deep confusion, I immediately twine my fingers in his and squeeze hard.

"We're landing," Paxton explains, as calm as can be. "It'll be nice and easy. Our pilots are the best. Ex-military, most of them, and our regular pilot out of Pellston was a copilot on Air Force One for a few years. So, you're in the best possible hands."

I glance out the window, which is a mistake—the ground is rushing up at the airplane with dizzying speed, the runway getting bigger and closer and bigger and closer. I gasp in helpless fear, turn my head away from the window and bury my face in Paxton's shoulder.

He laughs, curling an arm around me protectively. "Okay, so flying's not your thing." He's laughing at me, the bastard. But it's somehow not unkind. "It's okay, Makayla. It's fine." I feel him bend a little, glancing out the window. "Okay, here we go. Squeeze my hand as hard as you need to. We're going to touch down in... five...four...three...two...one—"

BUMP—SQUEAL.

I'm pretty sure I crush his hand, I squeeze so hard at the jolt and the bark of the tires, and then I think the worst is over, but it's not—there's a roaring sound, like a hurricane howling outside.

"That's the brakes, babe. It's normal. We're slowing down." Paxton's arm curls me into him, and he smells like expensive cologne: spicy but smooth, almost sweet, a rich scent that's not overpowering.

I do NOT want to feel so comforted by him. It's not right. That's not what this is. Not who I am. I don't need comfort. I don't need anyone, and I don't want anyone.

I'm doing this for the money. For Mom.

But fear is stronger than my desire to pretend I don't feel what I'm feeling, so I breathe in his scent, and let myself enjoy, just for a moment, the comfort of his strong arm around me.

This is a comfort I've never felt. I've never been hugged by a man.

Fucked, yes. Hugged? No.

I swallow hard, choking down the dizzying burst of emotions that bizarre realization brings up in me—and then the roaring stops and the feeling of being crushed forward by momentum slackens.

"See? Done. Safe on the ground." He doesn't let go, but he does loosen his grip on me so I can pull away on my own time.

I do, after a moment. I sit up straight, brush my springy curls back over my shoulders, and clear my throat. "I, um. Sorry."

He tilts his head, puzzled. "Sorry? For what?"

I gesture at him. "For being such a baby about it."

He smiles, shakes his head. "Don't be."

I expect some idiotic remark about not minding having his arm around me, and judging by the mischievous sparkle of his deep brown eyes, I know he's thinking it.

It's a legitimate moment between us.

"What?" he asks, half laughing.

I shake my head. "Nothing."

"No, you're thinking something. Expecting me to say something stupid, it feels like."

I bite back a grin. "I was, actually."

He arches an eyebrow. "Something along the lines of, 'hey, if it'll get you back in my arms, let's fly all the time,' I imagine?"

I snicker. "Along those lines, yes. Although that's a clunky and awkward line if I've ever heard one, and I feel like you're smart enough to be smoother than that."

He shrugs. "While that may be true, I think what I'm smart enough to know better than to say dumb shit like that to a woman fresh out of a panic attack."

"Well, at least there's that going for you." I frown. "I wouldn't call it a panic attack. More just...raw fear at a scary and new experience."

The jet halts with a gentle lurch, and then an attendant opens the door from the outside, and a staircase is put in place, and the attendant, a blonde, middle-aged woman wearing a blue power suit, ushers us off the plane, thanking Paxton by name—Mr. deBraun—with a polite nod and thank you to me. Paxton thanks her back, preceding me down the stairs, where another sleek black Mercedes awaits. This one, while still absurdly luxurious, isn't one of those Pullman things, but seems to be somewhat similar.

The ride from the airport is long and quiet—I'm at war with myself over my behavior on the plane, and specifically how nice it was to have his arm around me, how amazing he smells, and how I don't want to like it.

The war is that another part of me, deep inside, a small quiet voice, is whispering that I *am* marrying the man, after all, so why shouldn't I, at a minimum, not mind him, if not outright like him? He's been pretty nice to me, so far. He's sexy as sin. Rich as hell. Seems to have at least some kind of decency as a person, judging by his reaction to certain things his mother has done and said.

After a good thirty minutes of silence, Paxton pivots a little on the seat, leaning backward against the door and window. "You're awful quiet."

I stare out the opposite window, and shrug—we're on a freeway like any other, with an early afternoon sun shining, bathing everything in yellow-golden light. "Just…thinking."

"Care to share?"

I chew on the inside of my cheek. "Not really."

"Come on. One thing."

"I'm the farthest away from home I've ever been. The farthest away from my mom I've ever been." Crap, I shouldn't have brought her up.

He absorbs what I've said, and thinks a moment before answering. "You're pretty close to her, huh?"

I swallow hard; keep my face turned to the window so he doesn't see the tear that trickles down my cheek. "Yeah. Super close."

Silence.

"Um, well. You know, uh—I wouldn't always be able to go with you, but my car and driver and the jet are always available to you. Let me know if you want to go home for a day or two, and I'll have the jet warmed up and waiting, and if I'm using Liam and the car, I'll get a service to take you to the airport. Whenever you want, Makayla."

I make a show of fixing my hair, but it's an excuse to wipe at my face, steady my breathing, and then smile at him—but it's a small, tight one. "Thank you, Paxton. I appreciate the gesture."

He frowns. "It's not a gesture. It's reality. You could say we're engaged, right? In my world, that means you have full access to the family resources. Especially since the whole reason we're doing this is to make sure *I* still have access to those resources."

I exhale shakily. "Engaged. We're engaged." It's not

just my breath that's shaky—it's all of me. "What the hell am I thinking?"

Panic sets in—my lungs seize, my heart hammers erratically, and my thoughts whirl crazily.

"Makayla?" Concern paints his voice.

"*This* is a panic attack," I whisper.

"Hey, hey, just breathe. Breathe, Makayla." He physically turns my body so I'm facing him, and I know I'm crying now, but I have no control over it—I can't breathe, can't get my lungs to work, and the inability to breathe is terrifying, worse than taking off or landing.

"C-c-can't—" I gasp, my voice raspy, harsh.

He lifts me bodily off the seat and deposits me in his lap, wraps both arms around me, cradling my head against his chest—I hear his breathing, and feel the steady thumping of his heart. He sucks in a deep breath. Holds it.

"Breathe with me," he murmurs.

I try. Fail. Lungs won't cooperate.

He lets the breath out slowly. "Count with me, okay? Ready? One...two...three...four...five..." And then he inhales again, a slow filling of his lungs, holds it, and counts again.

Slowly, patiently, he repeats the process, counting to five, breathing in, counting to five, breathing out. It's something to focus on, and gradually I feel myself mimicking him. A tentative, shuddering breath. Manage to make it as far as three, and then my breath explodes out, and I have to fight to bring it back in. And then I'm sobbing, hating myself for this weakness, this panic, for needing the comfort Paxton is providing.

He doesn't waver.

Just breathes, and counts.

I find myself matching him, eventually. Get a full inhalation, hold it for five, exhale, and count again.

His arms are strong and hard, yet his embrace is gentle. His hands are on my shoulder and my waist; his breath is on my scalp, his chin in my hair. He's all around me, and I'm breathing because he's breathing.

How long does it take to gather myself? I have no concept of the time. It feels like forever, and yet it is only a moment. When I can open my eyes and breathe and behave like a rational human again, I straighten away from his embrace.

His golden-brown eyes are warm and concerned. "Okay, now?"

I nod, can't summon a smile. "Yeah." I want to look away in embarrassment and shame, but I don't. Not sure why, because those two emotions are top dog in the pile-up inside me, but I just can't. "No, but yeah."

"No, but yes?" He uses the tip of a middle finger to brush a curly tendril of hair away from my eyes, and it's too intimate a gesture and I can't handle how that makes me feel, so I slip off his lap and move back to my seat, and buckle up.

"I'm over the panic attack, and I'm not going to cry anymore, but I wouldn't say I'm okay." I look out the window, and realize we've stopped. We're in downtown

Washington DC, parked along the curb. A smirk from Paxton at my seat belt has me laughing despite myself. "I didn't realize we were here."

He smiles, but it's distracted. "So, we're here."

I nod, a sarcastic expression on my face. "So I've noticed."

He gestures out the window. "You have no way of knowing how this is going to work, I'm realizing."

"How what's going to work?" I ask, and then look in the direction he indicated—there's a small cluster of men and women with cameras being held back by several large men in black suits and mirrored sunglasses. "Are those guys Secret Service?"

He chuckles. "Nope. I don't rate protection, being a lowly first-term House rep. They're private security."

"How did they know we're here? How did the photographers know?"

"Well, Liam, my driver, is also head of my personal security detail, and it's his job to get bodies where I need them, so he alerted the crew here in DC while we were on the drive over." A gesture at the photographers. "As for them? This is a pretty high-profile address, and a lot of DC power players live in this building, which means there are always photographers lurking around waiting for a car to show up so they can get shots of whoever it is arriving."

I watch the activity outside: security keeps the photographers at a distance, but they push and leverage and angle to get a shot of the car.

Turning back to Paxton, I push my hair back and stiffen my spine. "So. What are we doing?"

"Liam will open the curb-side door, and I will slide out first. I'll offer you my hand and help you out, but I'll keep both Liam and myself between you and the photographers." His gaze is serious. "This is the first the media will know of you, and it'll be just shots from a distance, over my shoulder. No details, not enough to identify you, but enough to get the speculation started."

"So this is a big deal," I say.

He nods, serious. "It is." A hesitation. "I've um—I've been photographed with plenty of women before, this can't be news to you. But I've never been photographed bringing a woman *here*, because I never have. This fact will not escape notice."

"Why not?"

"Why won't it escape notice? Or why haven't I brought anyone here?"

I shrug. "Either. Both."

"It's just the kind of thing the twenty-four hour news cycle loves to pounce on, especially the celebrity-obsessed cycle. The media, for some reason, is just fascinated with me and my romantic involvements. Although, entanglements may be a better word." A careless wave. "So, you can just be guaranteed that they'll make a big deal out of the photos that are about to happen. And that's gonna get back to Mom, which is all part of my plan to fuck with her stupid Machiavellian machinations in my life."

"Mockya-what-what?"

He chuckles. "Machiavellian machinations. Ivy League bullshit for she's a meddler, and I'm about to foil her plans." He leans forward. "Whenever you're ready, Liam."

A voice like a razor rasping over a whetstone. "Certainly, sir."

I shudder at that voice. "He sounds scary."

Paxton laughs. "The Boogieman has nightmares about Liam."

"That's a good thing?"

"Yes, it is," Paxton says, still laughing. "He's been with our family for twenty years. Loyal to the last breath, and scary as hell, but the nicest guy you'll ever meet."

I see a black-suited body move to stand in front of the rear curbside passenger door, waiting. A beat, two. Paxton taps on the window with a knuckle, and it's clearly a prearranged signal, because upon the tap, Liam swings the door open and steps to put himself between the gathering crowd of photographers—the noise, as he opens the door, washes into the interior of the once-quiet car like a wave, palpable. Paxton gracefully exits the car, straightens his shirt, tucks the front in behind his belt, brushes his hand through his hair to neaten it a little, then turns to smile and wave at the photographers.

And then he leans down, smiles brightly at me, eyes dancing, teeth white, arm stretching his sleeve as he reaches in for me. His hand folds around mine, and I let him help me out of the car—my legs are shaky, knees wobbling. Not ready, not ready, not ready—

Flashes blink and wink and strobe, and I realize I'm dressed two steps up from looking like a hobo. This is my debut, apparently, and I'm wearing my worst jeans and a baggy T-shirt—all because I didn't like how much I liked the way Paxton was looking at me at my apartment.

"Wish you'd mentioned that I'd be photographed today," I murmur as I stand up. "I'd have dressed a little nicer."

"You'd have been more nervous than you already are about everything, and you didn't need that pressure. Besides, when we're ready for them to get good pictures of you, we'll arrange it and you'll be looking your best and you'll be ready for it." As promised, both he and Liam are standing between me and the photographers. "Ready?"

He doesn't wait for my answer, which would have been "no." He gently but firmly pulls me into a walk, Liam ahead of us, head on a swivel.

Liam: Medium height, seemingly of average build, graying black hair cut short and neat, clean-shaven, wearing a black suit and sunglasses. But despite his average size, he moves likes a predator, and exudes confidence and threat.

Liam opens a door, Paxton ushers me through first and follows me inside. The noise from outside is immediately silenced, a hush from within the condo building's foyer falling over us. I get a sense of brightness and airy elegance, and then we're on a wood-paneled elevator, Liam on one side of me, Paxton on the other.

I look up into Liam's eyes. "Hi," I say, inanely.

He smirks, a ghost of a curve touching his lips. "Good afternoon, Miss Poe."

I roll my eyes and shake my head. "Call me Makayla, please."

"As you wish, ma'am."

I snort. "It's like that, is it?"

Liam glances at Paxton, who just shrugs, lifting his palms facing up. "Doesn't have to be, I guess."

I smile at him, now. "Better." I eye him. "Did you go to British Butler School, too?"

Liam arches an eyebrow. "Nope. I went to Iraq, by way of the United States Marine Corps Reconnaissance Training Company."

"Oh."

Paxton leans toward me, speaking in a stage whisper. "That means he made bad guys go bye-bye real good."

I glare at him. "Wow, Paxton, thanks so much for that translation. Whatever would I do without you?"

"Just trying to be helpful."

The ride is brief, and then the doors open to a short, wide, white-carpeted hallway with a single door at the end. Liam uses a keycard to open the door, preceding us both inside—Paxton waits until Liam returns with a signal which apparently means all is clear.

Liam waits with his back to the open door, and Paxton leads me in to what I assume is a penthouse condo.

White marble floor with gold veins glittering through it, white tray ceilings golden with hidden lights, art lining the walls, each piece lit from above. An elegant, arching, polished wood bench here, more art than furniture. A glimpse through open French glass doors into a masculine study: huge dark wood desk, stuffed-to-bursting bookshelves lining three walls, a deep leather chair in a corner with a polished bronze floor lamp, a paperback novel upside down on the cushion, waiting to be picked back up. The foyer/hallway opens to a formal sitting room opposite the study, the sitting room occupied by a grand piano, music books in several layers on the music rack, a shelf behind the piano stuffed with more sheet music and books, the fall lifted to leave the black and white keys exposed; unexpected, that piano, and even more unexpected is the evidence that it is used and is not merely decoration.

Beyond the study and sitting room is an open-plan kitchen and living room, a hallway off the living room leading to the bedrooms. Floor-to-ceiling windows and sliding doors form one side of the space, overlooking the river, and outside is an expansive flower garden terrace and outdoor living area.

I stand in the transitional space between the kitchen

and living room, turning in a slow circle, examine the condo; it's masculine but not aggressively so, warm and inviting, lived-in but luxurious, expensive but not gaudy.

My first instinct is to put on gloves and start cleaning, even though it's already clean—it's just not spotless to Camilla's Beach by deBraun standards.

My second instinct is to stop breathing and wonder what the hell I'm doing in a place like this.

Paxton stands beside me, drapes an arm casually over my shoulders. "Welcome home."

13

I DON'T KNOW WHERE MY DUFFEL BAG IS—SO MANY PEOPLE
have carried it for me at this point that I've lost track
of where it is.

Is Washington DC in the same time zone as Michigan?

Where will I sleep? Does he expect me to sleep with
him?

Do I want to?

He's a man, and one with a media-verified high-oc-
tane libido, so if he's not expecting me to sleep with him
he's at least hoping to and probably looking for ways to
make it happen.

The second question is trickier. Do I want to sleep
with him?

Maybe.

No.

Yes.

I don't know.

Welcome home?

Home.

Home?

I turn and step out of Paxton's arm, heading for the terrace. But the door won't open, and I get a little panicky trying to open it.

I stop, fighting for breath, and bite my lip. "I need to get some air," I rasp.

Paxton steps beside me and unlatches something. "It was locked," he says gently, sliding the door open. "Here."

"Thank you," I bite out.

The terrace is breathtaking. Flowers of all kind in full bloom, dwarf Japanese maples, carefully trimmed spruce shrubs, a profusion of greenery and flowers and trees I don't know the names for, all artfully interwoven with stone flags and trickling streams and gurgling mini-waterfalls, hidden lights...it's gloriously peaceful and calming, and I find a hand-carved wooden bench tucked into an alcove beneath the outspread arms of a cherry tree. Slumping down into it, I breathe in carefully; holding my breath, I straighten my spine, rest my hands on my knees, palms up, close my eyes, and slowly release my breath in a precisely measured four-count; I exhale to the same measured four-count, rest with my lungs empty for another four-count, and inhale once more. After a few repetitions, my pulse has slowed and my breathing is more normal. I can't say the anxiety and turmoil in my brain have slowed, but it's not dominating my physiological mechanisms anymore.

"Do you have anxiety attacks a lot?" I hear him ask, and feel him beside me.

I glance at him—he's resting a buttock and thigh on the edge of the sculpted brick wall, which runs in a gentle, sinuous curve around behind the bench. I scoot over on the bench to make room for him, and he offers me a smile as he takes the spot.

I shrug. "Sometimes."

"Frequently enough to have a breathing response," he says.

"I don't know if it's an actual medical anxiety attack or panic attack, I just know sometimes stress and worry get the better of me, and it's hard to breathe and my heart goes a little haywire." I don't look at him. "I don't get them, like, every day or anything, but when I do get them, they hit hard and fast."

"Where'd you learn the breathing technique?"

"My supervisor at the hotel, Tanya." I sort through what to say. "I was going through some personal stuff and had an attack or whatever you want to call it while I was at work. Tanya has had them for ages, and actually saw a therapist about them—Tanya's therapist taught her, and she taught me, and I've used it since."

He hesitates. "So, why the anxiety attack now?"

I frown at him. "Um, because I quit all three of my jobs, got rid of my apartment, left my mother, and moved across the country to a big city I've never been to, where I don't know a single soul, and all with a man I barely know who I'm about to marry in less than four months." I laugh, and know he can hear the note of hysteria in it. I suck in a breath, hold it, and then I feel a barrage of words tumble out of my mouth like an avalanche. "We're not in love, we don't know the first thing about each other, I'm terrible at relationships, you and I are from completely different worlds and I'm a fish out of water in the worst way and I have no idea how to navigate in your world and this life I'm suddenly living, and I can't figure you out for the fucking life of me and worst of all I can't decide if I even *like* you yet a part of me wants to sleep with you and I can't decide if that would be the worst mistake I've ever made or the best thing ever because it's been a really long time and I'm going crazy and why the *hell* did I just say that to you?"

I shoot to my feet and half run half stumble away from Paxton and the bench to the other side of the terrace, resting my arms on the polished steel railing of the glass partition separating the terrace from the world below. I hang my head and tremble uncontrollably.

I feel him approaching—for some idiotic reason, my entire body is hyper-attuned to his physical presence. Even facing away, with my eyes closed, I feel him behind me. He's moving slowly, probably trying to figure out how to handle me.

He leans against the railing beside me, his arm touching mine. "Makayla, listen to me." I feel his eyes on me, but I can't bring myself to look into those absurdly compelling golden eyes. "Look at me, please."

I force my eyes to his. "What, Paxton?"

He turns slightly, not quite facing me. "I thought

I made this clear already, but I'll try again. There is no pressure whatsoever to make this a real relationship if you don't want to—whether physically or otherwise. I get that I've ripped you out of your life. Now, I'll be honest here, and I know you're going to say I'm being arrogant if not condescending, but...I feel like the life I'm about to give you, both in the temporary time we're married and afterwards, is a pretty big step up from the life you were living before me. But still, you've left everything familiar, and that's scary." His eyes search me. "You seem like someone who will appreciate honesty, so here's some blunt truth for you: Yes, I'm attracted to you. Yes, I'm a heterosexual male with a pretty wild libido, and you're a beautiful woman about to share my home with me, so yes, certain...possibilities have entered my mind. Part of me is hoping something will happen between us. We're two single adults cohabiting a home, and will soon be legally married, so it's not like it's a ridiculous notion for me to entertain."

He touches a finger to my chin, keeping my gaze on his. "But—and you need to hear me and understand me very clearly—I make no claims, set no expectations, and will never demand anything." His eyes heat, spark. "I can't say I won't test the waters with you, though, and I can't say that if I sense you're open to an advance that I won't press it, because I sure as fuck will. But if—*if*—something happens between us, Makayla, it will be because *you* want it to. Because you allow it, if not seek it out yourself."

"I don't know how to respond to that," I murmur.

"You don't have to. I don't need a response." He straightens, pushing away from the railing. "I have some preliminary work to do before my meetings tomorrow morning."

"I need some alone time anyway." I meet his eyes. "Something you probably need to know about me, now that we're living together—I'm not exactly an introvert, per se, but I'm the kind of person who needs time alone to recharge and to process my emotions. So, if I tell you I need time alone, it's really not about you or not wanting to be around you, it's—"

He grins. "You don't have to explain that one to me, Makayla. I'm the same way."

I tilt my head. "Really?"

He nods. "Absolutely." He laughs, but it's tinged with bitterness. "Which made boarding school and military school absolute hell, because there's no such thing as alone time."

"You really got sent to military school?" I ask.

He laughs again, this time less bitterly. "Yes, I really did. I'll tell you about it sometime." He waves at the house. "I'd offer you a tour, but it's pretty self-explanatory. You saw my study; my bedroom is obvious, as are the guest bedrooms. Take your pick, and make yourself at home."

"What if I pick the master bedroom?" I ask, smirking, not sure why I feel the idiotic need to play with fire like this, especially so soon after an anxiety attack.

He grins, a wide, bright, amused flash of teeth. "Then you'll be sharing with me." He breezes back inside. "Find me if you need anything," he says, tossing the words over his shoulder.

And just like that, I'm alone, on a massive terrace overlooking the jeweled heart of Washington DC.

My new home.

I shake my head, unable to fully comprehend what that means. It doesn't feel like home. It feels like I'm visiting someone.

I can't go home.

I don't have a home to go to.

Shit, shit, shit—the panic starts to rise again, and I grip the railing and force it away, focus on the traffic below and the view of the Potomac. Once I have it under control again, I decide to go inside and explore a little. It's about half the size of the penthouse suite at the hotel, but that makes it cozier and homier. I don't know if cozy is the right word, though. It's every bit as luxurious as the hotel, every bit as expensive as his parents' home, but somehow seems more personal. I go back to the foyer and look at the art on the walls; he'd told me he had some original pieces here, and I'm wondering what they are.

The art decorating the foyer hallway walls are black and white landscapes, of trees and mountains and ocean surf exploding over rocks. In the living room above the mantel over the fireplace is a glass case much like the one at deBraun's home in Michigan; within the case is an oil painting of a young woman pouring milk into a bowl.

"Recognize it?" I hear Paxton ask behind me.

I snort, glancing at him. "Hardly."

He stands beside me, staring up at the painting with me. "That was an incredibly difficult piece to procure, and if it was widely known in art circles that I own it, there would probably be quite an outcry." He grins, pleased. "It's Han van Meegeren's forgery of Vermeer's *The Milkmaid*."

I hear the expectant pause, and just roll my eyes at him. "I hope you're not waiting for me to faint in awed shock."

He groans, annoyed. "You know who Vermeer is, don't you?"

I shrug. "Sure. A classic painter. He did that one painting with the girl wearing the blue scarf?"

"*Girl with a Pearl Earring*, yes. Among others." He gestures at the painting. "That is a forgery of another famous Vermeer painting."

I frown. "Why would you be proud to own a forgery?"

Another of those sighs that seem to indicate long-suffering patience with the hopelessly uncultured. "Because Van Meegeren's forgeries are famous and valuable in their own right. It's quite a story, really. Short version is, Van Meegeren was a painter and wanted to be famous, so he started copying the style of the masters, Vermeer, Frans Hals, van Baburen, and other mostly Dutch painters. He started gaining attention for how closely his paintings resembled the work of the Old Masters, and this earned him a lot of criticism. He felt misjudged and that his genius was being underestimated, so he set about forging the works of the masters, rather than merely copying their style. It took him years to figure out the process, and he eventually got an art expert to accept a forgery of a Vermeer as authentic." He pauses, thinking. "Honestly, this could be a movie. Anyway. One thing led to another, and Hermann Göring, the famous Nazi and art collector, was sold one of van Meegeren's paintings as an original Vermeer, which eventually led to van Meegeren's arrest and subsequent trial by the Allies after the war, when Göring's hidden collection was discovered. He was actually compelled during the trial to produce, in front of witnesses and reporters, a copy of Vermeer's *Jesus Among the Doctors*, simply to prove that the painting owned by Göring was his work."

I stare, blinking. "Wow. So...this painting is one of those forgeries."

He nods. "Yes. He produced quite a few, and this is considered one of the best." A sigh. "Eventually, I'll let one of the museums somewhere put it on display, but for now, I just want to enjoy it myself."

"Why not an actual Vermeer?"

He snorts. "Because there are only thirty-five authenticated original Vermeer paintings in the world, and they're all in museums, with one being in private hands, and the other having been stolen from a museum in Boston in 1990."

I bite my lip to hold back a grin. "Well. Thanks for the art history lesson."

He sighs. "Wasted on you, was it?"

I shrug. "No. I know something now that I didn't before. And it's a cool painting with a cool story."

"That's why I wanted it. Yeah, an original Vermeer is worth hundreds of millions of dollars, but the story behind that one is way more interesting." A self-conscious laugh. "Plus, they look pretty much the same."

"How do you go about telling an original from one of those fakes?" I ask, figuring I'm probably getting myself another lecture.

A shrug, interestingly. "It's a technical process I know nothing about. Chemical testing, like carbon dating, sort of? I'm not an art history major, I just like cool shit." He indicates the painting. "I couldn't tell you much about Vermeer or his paintings, I just know the story behind van Meegeren because I own the painting." Another laugh. "I don't want you to get the idea that I'm some beret-wearing art history dork."

I bite my lower lip. "Oh no. Can't have that. It would ruin your rep as the coolest guy in school."

He eyes me. "You're mocking me, aren't you?"

I widen my eyes, shake my head. "Why no, Mr. deBraun, I would *never* do that."

He walks away, laughing. "Sure you wouldn't. I see how it is. See if I tell you any more cool stories about the cool shit I own." He indicates another painting on the wall in the hallway leading to the bedrooms. "Figure that one out on your own."

With that, he vanishes into his bedroom and closes the door behind himself.

I, of course, go to the indicated work of art and examine it. It's small, a charcoal portrait sketch. In the lower left-hand corner is a barely legible signature which looks, to my decidedly inexpert eye, like M.M. Caravaggio. Another famous name I've heard here and there, but know zero about.

I sigh, and decide there's no way I'm asking him about it now. I'll get another art history lesson for sure.

Right?

Why should I care?

Apart from the fact that I definitely saw nothing compelling about the spark in his eye and the confidence in his voice as he speaks, nothing interesting about the way he continually surprises me. I mean, I had him pegged as an air-headed spoiled rich white boy. Smart enough, sure, because you don't get through an Ivy League education by being stupid, and he is capable, sure, because he *is* an elected member of Congress. But still, Paxton deBraun is a spoiled rich white boy, and little else.

So what if he collects interesting art with a unique story? So what if evidence points to him playing the piano? Why should I care? All I'm here for is the chance to get Mom taken care of.

That's all this is. It's a long game. Not a con, just…

I push that line of thinking aside and decide to pick my room; interesting, though, that he's assuming I'll want to sleep alone, in my own room.

I did at least half assume that he'd expect me to sleep with him, to share a bed with him.

His reassurances to the contrary are…comforting, to at least some degree.

The two guest rooms are identical, for the most part—different art on the walls, different beds and furniture, but mostly alike. Lots of light colors, white walls and ceiling, with pops of color here and there— the overall aesthetic of the guest rooms is neither masculine nor feminine, just neutrally appealing.

I pick one simply because I like the artwork better: another black and white landscape photograph of a beach, and an oil on canvas painting of a mermaid sitting on a pile of coins and treasure, combing long reddish hair, rocks framing the crashing sea in the background. Another piece of art by a famous painter, probably, but I'm ignorant of who or what—I just think it's pretty, and it reminds of the ocean, something I've never seen but have always wanted to visit. There's an en suite bathroom of course; marble floor, a marble-lined shower stall with a glass door, a claw-foot soaking tub, a pedestal vanity with a waterfall faucet and a lovely, delicate, gold-gilt oval mirror.

When I go back into my room after examining the bathroom, I find my duffel bag on the bed, which is freaky as fuck. I heard nothing, and as far as I know, Liam isn't here.

I find Paxton in his office, and knock on the door-frame; he's sitting at his desk, working on a laptop, wearing glasses with a dark frame on top, which some-how makes him look distinguished and intelligent rather than nerdy.

He looks up, nudging the glasses higher on his nose. "Yes?"

"I think your shit is haunted, Paxton."

He frowns while chuckling. "Why do you say that?"

"I picked a room, went to look around the bath-room, and while I was in there, my bag mysteriously appeared on the bed."

Paxton rolls his eyes, rubbing his forehead with a knuckle. "That's Liam's idea of a practical joke." He tilts his head up, shouting. "LIAM!"

A few moments later, I jump when I feel Liam brush past me. "You bellowed, Mr. deBraun?"

"No more of the spooky shit, okay?" Paxton turns his attention back to the computer screen; we're both clearly dismissed.

Preceding me out into the foyer, Liam snickers, turning to grin at me with a wink. "Gotcha."

"If by get me, you mean freak the shit out of me, then yes." I arch an eyebrow at him. "Do you have spy cameras or something?"

He shrugs, endeavoring to look innocent. "Certainly not. This is Mr. deBraun's private home."

"You do!"

He holds up both hands palms out. "There are no cameras, Makayla. I swear—on my honor as a Marine Recon."

"Then how?"

"A magician never reveals his secrets." He smirks. "Suffice it to say my nickname in my squad was Spooky." He laughs. "Or, more frequently, 'goddammit, Liam, you spooky fucking bastard!'"

I restrain a grin. "Well just be careful. You may be a spooky hard-ass Marine, but I was raised in Detroit. Spook me at your own risk."

Liam just winks. "Look at this way—I only prank those I like."

"What do you do to people you don't like?" I ask.

Liam's face goes scary. "They disappear." I blink, hoping he's joking but not sure...until he cackles, face breaking into a grin. "I'm kidding, Jesus. You think I just go around killing people I don't like?"

I shrug broadly. "How the hell am I supposed to know?"

"I was a Marine Recon, not an assassin." A pause. "I know a couple, though. Nice fellas, just don't get on their bad side." He winks at me again.

"Such a joker, you are," I say with wry amusement.

He heads for the door. "For real though, it was a joke. I'm not spying on you; there are no hidden cameras. Sort of a welcome to the club initiation."

"You coulda just said 'welcome to the club.'"

A shrug and a wave. "Nah. Where's the fun in that?"

And then I'm alone yet again; passing by his study, I see Paxton still working, the screen reflected in his glasses, a loud, fast, constant clacking of the keys punctuated by an occasional pause.

I pace around the penthouse for a while, examining artwork, poking through the kitchen, sitting on the couch and leafing through magazines...

I begin to realize that my biggest problem with this whole situation won't be Paxton, but...boredom.

14

I ENDED UP BORROWING A BOOK FROM PAXTON'S OFFICE—I had expected his library to be full of dry, stuffy, Ivy League-education crusty bullshit, but instead, I'd found a dizzying variety of subjects and genres: histories and biographies, psychology and self-help, classic literature ranging from *The Odyssey* to *Catcher in the Rye*, political treatises from Ancient Greece and Rome, as well as autobiographies from modern politicians like Madeleine Albright and Bill Clinton and Barack Obama, and genre fiction of all kinds, ranging from sci-fi and fantasy to historical fiction and even a few romances. I was, honestly, amazed.

While I perused his bookshelves, Paxton remained at his desk typing, thinking, and typing, a focused expression on his handsome face. Eventually, when I pulled out a biography on Rockefeller and stood flicking through the pages, he sat back in his chair, poking at his teeth with the arm of his glasses.

"That's a wonderful biography," he said. "One of the best around on Rockefeller."

I gestured at the shelves. "How many of these have you read?"

He frowned slightly. "Well…all of them."

I blinked—there were thousands of books here. "All of them?"

He nodded. "That's why they're here: I love books, real books. I buy them, read them, put them on the shelf. Sometimes I read them more than once, but not often—only if it's really good. But yes, I've read every book on this shelf at least once." He indicated the small table next to the deep, reclining armchair under the lamp; stacked in piles on the table were at least a dozen books, hardcovers and paperbacks, fiction and nonfiction. "That's my T-B-R pile."

"To be read?" I guessed.

A nod. "Yep. I like to pick at things. I'll read a few chapters of a novel, a few chapters of a biography, back and forth. There's always a lot of hurry up and wait in Congress, too, and while a lot of my colleagues like to waste it pretending to look busy sending a flurry of emails, I prefer to keep a book or three in my briefcase."

"So when do you do your emails, in that case?"

He indicated his laptop. "I keep working hours, and I divide it into chunks. My working hours today include emails, some topical research on the agenda of things I'm discussing with my colleagues tomorrow morning, and a few other odds and ends. But once I'm done here, I'm done. I don't send any more emails, and I don't read them, either. Keeps me sane, or I'd be a hamster on a wheel…like so many of my colleagues on the Hill."

I'd nodded, impressed. "Makes sense." I lifted the book in my hands. "May I borrow this?"

He'd nodded, but laughed. "Yes, Makayla."

I'd frowned. "Why the laugh?"

"Because you live here. This is your home, now. Everything here is yours. Want a bottle of wine from the cellar? Take a bottle. No need to ask. Want to take a car? Take it." He blinked, frowning. "Well, that perhaps should wait till we get you licensed, but you get the idea. It's not borrowing, it's using something you have the right to use as a member of this household."

I'd sighed, tried a smile. "That's going to take some getting used to, but thank you."

Thus, I find myself sitting out on the terrace in another little nook—this one featuring surprisingly comfortable wicker furniture, a glass of iced tea sweating nearby.

Three hours after borrowing the book, I'm still barely two chapters in, but enjoying it.

I'm startled, then, when Paxton appears, taking a seat in the other wicker chair. He smiles at me. "Enjoying it?"

I nod. "Yeah, it's good."

He eyes my progress, a baffled look crossing his face. "Taking your time, huh?"

I flush, shrug. "Um, no, not really. I'm just a really slow reader."

"Oh. Sorry, I didn't mean—"

I wave him off. "It's okay. I bet you could've finished this by now. I'm just…not much of a reader, honestly. I think this is the longest I've sat and read in my entire life."

He frowns. "Really?"

"Yeah." A shrug. "I've worked full time since I turned fourteen. School wasn't as much of a priority as helping Mom keep a roof over our heads and food on the table. I skipped a lot of school, and I was honestly lucky to even graduate. There's just never really been time in my life for sitting around reading. I've worked two and three jobs, ten to twelve and sometimes sixteen-hour days since I graduated high school, just out of necessity." I laugh. "Honestly, I feel guilty, just sitting here. I feel like I'm missing work, like I'm flaking out on my responsibilities. It's hard to focus."

He nods. "I know this may shock you, but I actually do understand that, to a degree. I've never had to work just to keep clothed, housed, and fed, but idle time is a foreign concept to me. My family values one thing: achievement. Success. It's why I got kicked out of the prep school. Why they sent me to military school. Why even now, what I've accomplished isn't enough. Get elected as one of the youngest members of Congress in American history? Not enough—run for Senate. I'm driven to succeed, compelled to it, because anything less is considered failure."

"Not the same, but at the same time, I know I can't imagine that kind of pressure any more than you can understand what it's like to not always know where your next meal is coming from, or if you'll be able to pay utilities *and* eat this month."

He frowns at me. "You've really had to choose?"

I laugh. "All the time. Usually, it means you put off a utility bill another month and hope they don't shut it off, *and* spend less on food so you can try to catch up." I tilt my head at him. "So, even though you have a seat in the House, that's not good enough for your family?"

He nods. "Well, mostly for Mom. Dad would've been happiest if I'd been willing to apprentice under him and take over the reins of his company. Unfortunately for him, I've never been interested, which I suppose is a large part of the reason for his overall disinterest in me as his son."

I blink at that. "Disinterest?"

A nod, but no hint of sadness in his voice, although I do detect a tinge of wistfulness or bitterness in the way he glances away from me. "Best word I can find for it. Once I made it clear when I was, oh, thirteen or fourteen, that I had no interest in going to work with him and starting in the mailroom and all that, he just sort of...stopped being interested in me. Stopped caring. I was provided for, I had everything I could ever want—if I asked for a half-million-dollar car for my birthday, I'd get it. Want an apartment in Princeton? I got it. Love and affection and acceptance from my father? Not so much." A dismissive grin. "Don't worry, I've been to therapy over it. No lingering Daddy issues here."

I sigh sadly. "Well, at least one of us can say that."

"You can't?"

A shake of my head. "Hell no. Mine abandoned us when I was born, and it's done a number on me in a lot of ways, some of which I probably haven't ever identified. Therapy ain't free, and I've never had the time for it even if I could afford it."

We sit in silence for a minute, each of us lost in our own thoughts. Eventually, Paxton sits up straight and smiles. "Well. Enough of the heavy shit. You hungry?"

As if on cue, my stomach growls. "Clearly that's a yes," I say.

"In or out?"

"Huh?"

"Eat here, or go out?"

I shrug. "Um...I don't know. I'm fine either way."

He frowns. "I'm not choosing."

I sigh. "I honestly have no frame of reference, Paxton. I eat at the cafe in the morning, and dinner at the hotel in the evening. Occasionally I'll pick up something on the way home, but not usually. So if you have some fancy chef waiting to make a fifteen-course meal, go for it. If you have standing reservations at the most upscale restaurant in DC, fine."

This gets me a laugh. "It's *dinner*, Makayla. You're taking this far too seriously."

I can't help but laugh, because he's right. "Okay, whatever. Let's eat out, then. But you pick the location."

"The question becomes a matter of fancy versus casual."

I gesture at my outfit—the loose, ill-fitting jeans and wrinkled, baggy boys' crewneck T-shirt. "I'd think this makes it pretty obvious."

He smirks. "We could go shopping first."

My stomach growls again. "No, I'm too hungry to wait. I haven't eaten anything but some yogurt today."

He frowns, gesturing impatiently at the kitchen. "You should've eaten something, in that case. The kitchen is fully stocked with just about anything you could possibly think of."

I sigh. "Paxton, look, I'm just not there yet. This doesn't feel like home—it feels like I'm your guest, and I'm not comfortable just poking around your kitchen and helping myself to your food. Plus, you probably only have shit like caviar and some kind of fancy salad."

Paxton cackles. "Do I seem like someone who eats that kind of bullshit?" He stands up. "Come on. I know you have nicer clothes than that in what you brought with you—the only reason you wore that is because you were embarrassed that I caught you in your sexy little pj's." His eyes reflect his enjoyment of the memory. "So, go change into nicer jeans and a sexier top, and we'll go get some food." He pauses. "Real food. No fancy salad, unless that's your thing."

I stand up and follow him, grumbling under my

breath: "Sexy little pj's my ass. You just liked the free show."

It was supposed to be under my breath, but he obviously heard me. "I admit I didn't mind that portion of the program," he says, holding the door and meeting my eyes.

I have no response for that, so I just go to my new bedroom and change—nicest jeans, nicest top. Meaning, the dark-wash jeans have a liberal amount of stretch to them so they fit more like leggings, which does wonders for my thighs and booty, which are both pretty damned wondrous, between genetics and exercise. The top is a tight, filmy ivory camisole over my one good bra, with a lightweight, pale coral three-quarter sleeve sweater over it. Paired with my one set of decent heels, and a quick updo of my hair and some light makeup, I feel...not fancy, but acceptable for a dinner out on the town in the company of a man as wealthy, sexy, and influential as Paxton deBraun.

Paxton is sitting at the island, perched on a barstool, sipping sparkling water from a green glass bottle, reading a paperback. When he hears me emerge, he turns on the stool, sees me, and slowly sets down the book, eyes widening slightly.

"Damn, Makayla. Maybe we don't need to go shopping after all."

I snort. "This is my one nice outfit."

He shakes his head. "Well...damn. You look amazing." He doesn't seem to be blowing smoke up my ass either, because his eyes rake over me several times, lingering at my hips and chest more than once before latching onto my eyes. "You ready?"

I nod. "As I'll ever be."

He eyes me again. "Don't you need a purse?"

I shrug, holding up my little wristlet that contains my ID, debit card, and a small amount of folded-up emergency cash. "Nah. No keys, no phone, and I'm not a touch up my makeup kind of girl. This is all I really need."

He grins. "Minimal. I like it." He digs in his pocket, withdraws his cell phone, and tosses it on the counter. "Let's go pick a ride."

I follow him to the elevator. "You're leaving your phone?"

He nods, lifting his left wrist on which is a large black rectangular smartwatch. "Any of my people need me, I'll get notifications here. If they don't have my personal number, they don't need to get ahold of me."

We take the elevator down to an underground garage; the collection here is a tiny fraction of what's at the house in Michigan: a modern Porsche convertible, a Range Rover SUV, and a classic motorcycle with a sidecar, along with a couple hulks covered by white drop cloths.

I eye him. "Well?

He stares at me. "Well what?"

"I'm waiting for the inevitable lecture on the cars."

He chuckles. "These are just practical everyday

vehicles. Porsche for sunny weather, Rover for nasty stuff." He gestures at the motorcycle and sidecar. "That's the only piece of any real interest. It's a World War Two era military motorcycle and sidecar, which saw actual action in the European theater, and was later restored by a company in Florida. It's a recent acquisition, and I've never actually taken anyone out in the sidecar before."

I can't help a grin from spreading across my face. "This seems as good a time as any, right?"

He stares at me in disbelief for a long moment, waiting. When nothing further is forthcoming, he laughs. "Wait, really?"

The boyish excitement in his voice is…well, it's honestly fucking adorable. And it makes me grin so hard my cheeks hurt.

"Yeah, really. It sounds like fun. I've never been on a motorcycle, and I've always wanted to try it." I narrow my eyes at him. "You do have a motorcycle license, right?"

An arrogant roll of his eyes. "Obviously. A license, as well as evasive and defensive driving training by a professional motorcycle racer." He indicates the sidecar. "I guess I assumed you'd want to arrive in style, in a car, rather than something like that. A sidecar isn't exactly the quietest or smoothest ride, and it'll wreak hell on your hair."

I laugh. "I'm pretty much the opposite of high maintenance, Paxton. And this is dinner, not a gala, right? So…I'm up for a little adventure."

His grin broadens, as if he can't quite believe his luck. As if the women he's used to dating wouldn't be caught dead in a motorcycle sidecar. His excitement is palpable, and contagious.

There are two helmets, one hanging from the handlebar of the motorcycle, the other on the seat of the sidecar. Both are vintage-looking, and knowing Paxton, actually vintage. I realize I'll have to tie my bun lower down to get the helmet on properly, so I let it loose from the high top bun and retie my hair down at my nape, and then strap on the helmet.

Paxton watches all this, a grin on his face.

I can't help but laugh again. "This is really exciting for you, isn't it?"

He nods. "Very. I never expected to have anyone around who'd be willing to ride in the sidecar. I could probably compel Liam to climb in for a quick ride, but that wouldn't be the same."

"Well, you're welcome…for being open to adventures," I say, climbing into the sidecar.

He laughs. "And it will be an adventure." He grins as he swings a leg over the saddle and straps his helmet on. "Full disclosure, here—riding in a sidecar is a whole different ballgame, and while I've had practice with it, I'm by no means an expert."

I eye him. "So should I be worried?"

"Nah. Just letting you know. It could be a little… rough, at first. It just handles totally different, due to the unequal distribution of weight and wheels and all."

He starts the motorcycle, and it comes to life with a rattling snarl, and then idles with a smooth, even chug. A glance at me, a grin, and then we're off. Slow, at first, heading up the ramp to the exit, where a sensor of some kind detects us, opens a garage door, and then we're out in the reddish-gold light of evening. A quick, leaning right turn into traffic, and then I'm pushed back into the seat as Paxton accelerates. The feeling of open-air and speed and connection to the world around me and the road beneath me is ten times what it was in the little Porsche—exhilarating, wildly exciting. I whoop loudly as he opens the throttle and we zip forward.

We can't go very fast, because traffic is pretty thick, it being evening rush hour in DC, but it's still fun, and Paxton clearly knows side roads and alleys to get around the worst of traffic—many of which are only really accessible to us because of the fact that we're so small. It's a sadly short ride—as we soon pull down a narrow street and into a small parking lot. I wasn't sure where I was expecting him to take me, but this doesn't fit any of my expectations. It's a little pub off the main road, called The Sovereign. All dark wood and leather-topped stools with brass buttons, red-cushioned high-top chairs, cozy booths ensconced in thick, dark wood panels, filled with young, well-dressed people conversing in low tones under the exposed wood beams and old-world rustic light fixtures.

He gets us a quiet corner booth, orders a beer for himself and eyes me expectantly. I just shrug. "I have no clue. I don't really drink beer all that often." I gesture at Paxton. "Order for me. You clearly have more refined taste than I do."

He eyes me speculatively, considering, and then orders me...something. I don't know what. Something with a fancy name. When it comes, it turns out to be a tasty and refreshing light lager, and we sip in silence as we peruse the menu—elegant takes on classic hearty fare. He gets a burger, and I, on a whim, decide to go way outside my comfort zone and try duck leg confit.

At my selection, Paxton grins. "Good choice. It's excellent."

"Trying something new," I say.

It's a surprisingly low-key and highly enjoyable experience. We drink good beer, eat good food, and our conversation is easily endless—mostly due to Paxton's enviable skill as a conversationalist. He can talk with equal ease about nearly everything—we cover sports, music, movies, Hollywood star drama, and he relates a few entertaining stories from the Hill. Nothing heavy, nothing deep. Just me and him, a meal, and light conversation.

It's too easy.

I like it way too much.

I notice too many things—the effortless elegance in the way he eats, the gracefulness of his movements, the way his jaw flexes as he chews, the sparkle in his eyes as he tells something funny about a gaffe made by one of his colleagues. The way his arms stretch his sleeves, the cords in his forearms. The way he occasionally brushes his thick dark hair back from his head in a carelessly sexy gesture that leaves my heart palpitating weirdly.

He has three beers by the time he's finished eating, and takes his time finishing the third after the end of his meal, and I notice he's careful to liberally punctuate his sips of beer with swigs of ice water. Considering we're returning home in a motorcycle with a sidecar, which he's admitted he's not an expert in operating, is very reassuring.

As for me...the duck leg confit is so fucking good I have to restrain myself from making too many moans of delight. Being unused to beer, I probably drink the first couple a little too fast. The third goes down even more smoothly, and I'm not drinking water with it.

But fuck it, right? If I can't cut loose a little now, then when?

Paxton's third beer seems to last forever, while I'm on my...fifth? Conversation seems to loop and circle and drift, and his attention never wavers. It's a weird feeling, for me, being the utter center of someone's attention. He glances at his watch a couple times, but immediately dismisses it without a second glance or taking his attention from me.

After I don't know how long, he finally tosses back the last swallow of beer and slides the empty glass aside. "You want another?"

I shake my head, and realize I'm a little wobbly. "Um, no. Probably shouldn't."

No grin, this time, just an intense, opaque smolder, golden-brown eyes regarding me without blinking, without giving away anything but raw intensity. "You sure?"

When I stand up, I do indeed wobble a little, and glance sheepishly at Paxton. "Yeah, I'm good."

A small smile. "Ready to head home, then?"

"Yeah, just let me pee first."

It doesn't even hit me until I'm in the stall how easy "head home" slid through my mind. Maybe it's the beer, but the panic isn't as strong, this time.

Paxton is waiting by the front door—and he's just waiting. No impatience, no checking his watch, just content to stand and watch the patrons in the pub, and wait for me.

He doesn't notice me right away, and it gives me a chance to get a look at him without him knowing I'm staring.

And damn, the man is beautiful. Rugged, but elegant. Just enough stubble, but still clean cut. Powerfully built without being bulky. Lean, but not skinny. Well-dressed, but not flashy. And fuck me, that hair. So thick, so richly brown, artfully messy.

I swallow hard. Down girl.

Rein it in.

But…why? Why should I? I'm going to marry the man in a little more than three months. Why shouldn't I get something out of it? He's an expert at casual, and I'm certainly not about to fall in love. It would just be a little bit of fun. Something to make a fake-but-real marriage a little better for the both of us.

I know it wouldn't be a thing, and he certainly does too. A marriage of convenience doesn't have to be a joyless, sexless business arrangement, right?

So why am I hesitating? He's sexy. He wants me. God knows why—I'm a far cry from the glamorous goddesses he usually dates.

I'm quiet as we get back on the road—the rush hour traffic has thinned, so the ride is much faster, which means it's even more fun, but shorter.

I spend most of the ride trying not to look at Paxton, and trying not to continue the endlessly circular arguments for and against sleeping with him.

The problem is, the more I try not to think about it, the more I end up thinking about. And the more I think about it, the fewer compelling arguments I can come up with for why I shouldn't sleep with him.

He's still just as arrogant as ever, and just as entitled, and just as much of an insufferable know-it-all, but there's also a lot more to him.

I mean, yeah, he's damned beautiful, but is that enough of a reason? God, it's not just his looks, though. It's the way he looks at me. The intensity in his eyes. The spark and the heat, the curiosity. Like I'm a gift-wrapped enigma he wants to open up and figure out.

Do I want to be unwrapped and figured out? Do I want to know what those hands can do? They're big, strong, clean, clever.

What can his mouth do?

I got a glimpse of what hides under his clothing… and I wonder about that, too.

We arrive back in the underground garage, and the elevator ride back up is quiet. It's not exactly late, but it's been a crazy day and I'm in a weird place emotionally, as well as in a new place physically, and I'm tired.

Suddenly drained.

The alcohol is fading, and I'm still a little unsteady, but that could be exhaustion.

I realize we're standing in his foyer, just outside his study, neither of us speaking, just looking at each other. His eyes search me. More of that speculative, curious heat. A hint of amusement. Desire.

"What?" I ask.

He shrugs. "This is weird for me."

"What is?"

"Going on a date with a beautiful woman, bringing her *here*, and then…not knowing what to do next."

An unexpected admission, from him. Oddly vulnerable for someone so obviously used to being in control, in command, taking what he wants and never thinking of the consequences.

"What to do next?" I breathe.

"With you." He pauses. "With…us."

"Us."

"I'm trying to figure you out. What you want, what you don't want."

I sniff a laugh. "Yeah, well, makes two of us."

He scrubs his stubble. "I guess that explains it."

"I'm not playing games or intentionally trying to be confusing."

"I know."

"This is just...new. And confusing."

"I know."

I lick my lips. Alcohol-loosened lips let slip truths: "I'm trying to figure you out, too."

"What is there to figure out?" he asks.

"You."

He smirks. "I'm not hard to figure out."

"Yes you are."

"No, I'm not." He sidles closer. "I've got nothing to hide, Makayla. My shit is all out in the open. Wanna know something? Ask. You may not always like the answer, but you'll always get the truth."

"So what is it you want from me?"

Closer. Until I have to tilt my head back to look up into his golden-brown lion's eyes. Until my chest brushes his. "Everything."

I gulp, swallow a lump of air and nerves past a dry throat. "What's that mean?"

He shakes his head. "That's not a tell you thing, that's a show you thing."

"I saw you. Some of you. In the hotel. Before you were awake. I saw...it. Not all of it, but enough." I don't have a single damn clue why the hell I'm saying this.

He doesn't quite smirk, but it's clear he's holding it back, and only just barely. "Autonomic physiological response." He does grin, this time, and it's wolfish, mischievous. "Then, it was. Right now, not so much."

I can't help looking down at his zipper—something is happening, that's for damn sure. "I haven't done anything. We haven't, I mean. I'm not even sure this counts as flirting."

He nods seriously. "Exactly." He presses closer, and now my breasts are flattened against the hard anvil of his chest, and his hips bump mine. "That's the trouble with you, Makayla. You don't have to *do* anything to get me hard as a fucking rock. You existing at all, you being within twenty fucking feet of me does it to me."

I feel my body responding, and I step back from him. Thighs press together. Heat gathers low. Pulse thunders. Nipples harden—and this last one is obvious. And you can be damn sure Paxton sees it.

"I think I have a similar effect on you," he murmurs, eyes fixed on my all-too-apparent headlights.

Even through the bra and the camisole, my nipples are prominent, and hard. It's a fact of life for me, and part of the reason I wear sports bras so much—I get tired of the attention, and I can't help my physiological response to temperature and whatever else makes my nipples hard. Which, to be honest, is a mystery to me. A strong wind blows, and my nipples stick out. See a hot guy on the street, think a dirty thought? Headlights. It's so annoying. And right now, I'm turned on like crazy, and that's making my nipples stand as tall and hard as cell towers.

He reaches out, and I flinch, but he only gathers a long curling wisp of flyway hair and twists it around his index finger. "Are you sober, Makayla?"

I stare up at him. At his lips. Wondering what he tastes like. "I…yes. Mostly."

"Mostly?"

I shrug. "I was a little buzzed at dinner."

"How buzzed?"

I frown. "I don't know. A little wobbly. I felt good. It's wearing off pretty fast." I notice the hitch in his eyes, a stutter in the heat. "Why?"

He gathers the curl around his finger until it tugs against my scalp, a knuckle brushing my temple. His eyes flick to my lips. Hips nudge mine, chest crushing against mine, and I wonder if he can feel my pulse. "I really want to kiss you."

I stop breathing. The way he's looking at my lips, it would be a hell of a lot more than just a kiss. "Paxton…"

He's closer.

Closer.

His big deep golden eyes are piercing, fiery, raging with need, boiling with conflict. "Makayla…tell me again. How sober are you?"

"I'm not drunk," I whisper, and it's the truth. How rational I am right now is up for debate, but I can't honestly blame the alcohol.

"I really want to believe you," he whispers.

"Why?"

"Because if you were drunk, I couldn't do this…"

And his lips meet mine. Soft. Warm. Damp, strong. Seeking. Questing, tasting, testing.

I don't breathe, don't move. I can only process, only register the fact that Paxton deBraun is kissing me. That it feels really, really *good*.

That I like it.

That I want more.

A furious, boiling intensity of heat and need explode through me at the moment his lips touch mine. And it's just that—

Just a kiss, at first. His lips touching mine, but no more.

And then he pauses for breath, and the sudden rush of cool air between our hot mouths is shocking. And that rush of oxygen is a blast of sanity, in which I pull back and stare up into his eyes, and see the same drowned awe.

A tiny, innocent, ten-second kiss.

But I'm…

I'm not okay.

And neither is he.

I step away, and he lets me.

If I wasn't sober before, I am now.

Except now, I'm drunk on the kiss, and high on the need to know what more would feel like.

Instead, I push past him and nearly run to my room. Close the door. Lock it.

Lean back against it, heart hammering.

I touch my lips with two fingers, which tremble.

Damn it—I am in *so* much trouble.

If *that's* just a kiss, a short and innocent one at that?

Oh god, oh god.

So much trouble.

15

"**O**KAY, ONE MORE LOOK," JULIE SAYS, handing me a set of hangers laden with clothing. "This one's going to be the most fabulous yet, just you wait."

I've tried on at least thirty different looks at four different stores, each look—or, as I more prosaically call them, outfits—chosen by Julie, the personal shopper and stylist hired by Paxton to give me a style. Julie is Asian—Korean, maybe? I'm not sure—small, petite, beautiful in a sleek, prim, sophisticated way, with an obnoxious tendency to overuse buzzwords like *lovely*, and *fabulous*, and *gorgeous*. She sounds, in an odd way, like an extravagantly gay man stuck in the body of a four-foot-nine Asian woman.

I suppress a sigh, taking the stack of hangers over my forearm and heading into the changing room. This look is a layered one: slim, tight-fitting leggings in a light gray / dark gray camo print, in a thick, almost denim-like textured fabric, with a gauzy, feathery, brilliantly white sleeveless top, over top is an open, knee-length, plum sweater with heavy, chunky wood buttons and an overly wide lapel. Finishing the look is a pair of white TOMS, a medium-sized Gucci handbag, and jewelry and bangles—simple silver bracelets on both wrists, with a black leather cuff on one and a twisted braid of black leather with a copper pendant on the other, and a black leather choker necklace.

When everything is on, I step out of the changing room and face Julie, waiting as she taps her pursed lips with a long, manicured fingernail. She reaches out without saying a word and removes the necklace.

"There, much better. I like the choker, but it's too much. It overloads the look. You're best with just the bangles on your wrists. Besides, you have such a lovely neck, it's almost a shame to distract from it." She smiles, nodding as she steps back. "Good, good, very lovely. This is a perfect look for a casual sort of day. You could wear this to go shopping and a nice lunch, and even a lovely casual dinner. It's comfortable and sophisticated, but not too dressy." She pushes on my shoulder to get me to spin, going so far as to lift the tail of the sweater to check out how the leggings fit around my butt. "The leggings fit you perfectly. You'll probably want some kind of sweater or something layered that's long enough to cover this fabulous bottom of yours, because it's just so gorgeous it'd steal the show, and we want to present ourselves to the world with class, don't we? We can flaunt our bodies, but overemphasizing our assets detracts from the overall sophistication of a look, you know."

I physically stop myself from rolling my eyes, but I do love the outfit. As I've loved nearly all of them, once we narrowed down a general theme. We've discovered that I value comfort over fashion, that I don't mind showing a bit of skin, and that I like understated pieces rather than anything gaudy or showy or flashy.

Julie flicks her fingers at the changing room. "Okay, back into your unfortunate clothing. We'll discard them once we're back at the penthouse."

She hates my clothes—the jeans are cheap and ill-fitting, she says, and my top is far too plain and doesn't do my shape any favors. Well, no shit—the jeans were three dollars and the top was one dollar, from a big-box resale store.

I stopped calculating how much is being spent after we passed the first thousand, which included two outfits from the first store. A rough guess would be easily twenty grand just in actual clothing, meaning tops and bottoms. Julie has also picked out brand-name handbags, jewelry, watches, and shoes. The back of the Range Rover is piled high with bags, and I honestly am overwhelmed beyond any capacity to cope with the amount of money being spent on me. I nearly fainted when Julie nonchalantly slipped a pair of shoes on my feet which had a price tag of two thousand dollars, and did get light-headed when she slid a purse onto my shoulder which cost five thousand. Just for starters, Julie said. Simple stuff, first. The basics.

She swipes Paxton's black credit card like it's her mission in life to pauperize him via this shopping trip, and genuinely doesn't seem to grasp my discomfort with the price tags.

When I gawp helplessly at a nine-thousand-dollar price tag on a flimsy silk sundress—which, admittedly, looks absolutely breathtaking on me, but still, *nine thousand dollars* for a little bit of silk and thread—she just laughs and tells me to stop looking at the price tag.

The camo legging outfit was only the halfway point apparently—after that we moved on to three more stores and at least a dozen looks at each. Julie has me try on a bunch of outfits and then pares them down to about half, sets aside the keep pile, and starts over again, pulling more outfits and trying them on me and cutting some. Each store takes at least an hour; we've been shopping since nine in the morning and it's past three in the afternoon, now. We haven't even stopped for lunch, although we did zip through a Starbucks drive-thru for iced coffees and pastries.

Finally, at the eighth store and an absolutely mind-boggling amount of clothing tried and purchased, I slump into the rear passenger seat and eye Julie with a glare.

"No more," I say in a dramatic gasp. "I give. Mercy."

Julie laughs, a light bell-like tinkle. "Had enough, have you? Fine. We'll call it a day. At least you have a basic wardrobe to work with now. You still need a few formal looks for business dinners, and I have to get you into some evening gowns for galas, but Mr. deBraun said we have a bit of time before gala season starts."

"There's a gala season?" I ask.

Julie smiles widely, giddy. "Oh, yes! Best time of the year. So many fabulous looks, so many gorgeous parties to go to, it's just the best." She sighs happily, as if envisioning a parade of clothes floating in front of her face.

I glance back into the trunk at the dozens of bags, at what has to be over a hundred thousand dollars—which she considers just the basics—and my head spins. And I still have to get fitted for evening gowns, which I assume will each cost the equivalent of an entire mortgage for an average family, *before* shoes and jewelry, not to mention hair and makeup.

Julie says she doesn't handle that end, and that Mr. deBraun has a whole day planned for me at a spa. Which sounds equal parts incredible and terrifying.

We get back to Paxton's building, and Liam pulls into the private garage. Julie heads for the elevator, while I round to the back of the car, open the trunk, and start loading up with bags.

Liam and Julie both stop dead in their tracks, staring at me blankly.

"What in the world are you doing, Makayla?" Julie asks, genuinely baffled.

I, equally baffled, speak slowly and clearly, in case she's actually as stupid as the question is. "I'm unloading the car, Julie."

Liam narrows his eyes at me, a look that, if given to a man, would mean a fistfight and broken bones. "That's my job, ma'am."

I sigh. "Oh. Right. Only poor people unload their own purchases."

Liam pats my shoulder. "Now you're getting it." He grins at me. "It's just that Mr. deBraun pays me an exorbitant amount of money, and I take my job very, very seriously. This is one of those duties."

I set the bags on the ground and meet his eyes. "You're a Marine Recon. You risked your life fighting a war to serve this country. And now you're unloading bags for rich people?"

"I do a *lot* more than that," he says, his voice low and rough. "I protect. I serve." He gestures at the car. "Driving you around and unloading a few bags is just a fraction of the job, and it's one I'm honored to have."

I realize that everywhere we went, he was never far away. His eyes, hidden behind mirrored aviators were watchful, in the way a raptor perched in a tree watching a rodent scurry below is watchful. He was still, and quiet, and calm, but exuded deadly threat and ultimate confidence.

He smiles at me, his voice lighter, now. "What I'm saying is, please let me take care of the bags. Luisa has a light snack prepared for you upstairs."

Luisa—Paxton's...everything else that Liam isn't. Liam is the driver, the bodyguard, the personal assistant, and Luisa is the housekeeper and daily cook.

Which, I'm told, is not the same as the personal chef. Luisa takes care of breakfast and lunch and your average dinner, but if Paxton wants a special, fancy dinner he calls Jean-Paul, the chef. Who, of course, lives in the building and is on call twenty-four hours a day.

What an odd life.

I head upstairs with Julie, who makes a beeline for my room and my closet, eagerly waiting for Liam to bring up the first load of bags so she can start removing tags and sorting. Resigned to not having anything to do with any part of the process except wearing the clothes, I head for the kitchen in search of the "light snack" mentioned by Liam.

What I find is a charcuterie board with an assortment of freshly sliced meats and cheeses, assorted nuts, fresh local honey, fruit, olives, crackers, mustard, and jams. There's enough food on the wooden cutting board to last me at least half a week, longer if I were to stretch it out, and this is a "light snack."

I shake my head in marvel as I sit at the island, picking at the board and sipping Pellegrino.

I hear the door opening and closing as Liam comes and goes with bags, and I hear Julie rattling hangers and sliding them on the bars of the walk-in closet in my room—which is so large I could fit my entire apartment back in Petoskey in it with room to spare. I picture the closet, and then the clothing we purchased today, and realize everything we got will still only fill *maybe* a third of the closet. Nowhere near even half.

And I begin to grasp an inkling of the scope of what Julie meant when she referred to the haul of clothing as "just the basics" and "a decent start."

So much.

So, so, so much.

I hear the door open again, but this time it's accompanied by Paxton's voice—irritated, impatient.

"...I know, Mom. I *know*. But what I'm telling you is, I don't care. Send out whatever you want, or don't send anything at all. This wedding is your shindig, so do what you want. As long as what you send out doesn't have that bitch's name on it, I do not give a single sparkly shit..." A pause as he listens to what Camilla is saying, and I hear his footsteps on the marble approaching the kitchen. "Yes, I know you saw it...yeah, well, wouldn't you like to know....no, I'm not telling you. Familiar, huh? Well, I mean, I've seen the photos, and it could be anyone. No, I'm really not telling you who she is. You'll find out at the wedding. Yes, Mother, I'm absolutely for real."

He appears in the kitchen, dressed in dark blue jeans that fit just right—tight, but not skinny—over heavy black boots, with a white button-down under a black blazer. A casual but dressy look, somewhere between a suit and tie and his jeans-and-polo look from yesterday. He's got a leather briefcase in one hand, the leather a rich, deep, polished, aged brown, and his cell phone in the other hand pressed to his ear. He locks the phone between his shoulder and ear, sets the briefcase down, shifts the phone to his left hand, and uses his right to fold a piece of Dubliner cheese inside a roll of prosciutto, shoves it into his mouth and holds the phone away while he chews. He perches on the stool next to me, gives me a quick, friendly wink and grin, and then steals a long swig of my sparkling water. He holds the phone away, rolling his eyes at the volume of his mother's voice, and then puts it on speaker, sets it on the counter, and puts his finger to his lips.

"—Someone appropriate for your station in life, not to mention suitable for your aspirations in life, Paxton. You cannot simply surprise me on the wedding day with some cross-eyed, silicone-breasted bimbo from some dive bar in Anacostia."

"Mom, Jesus. For real? The hell is wrong with you?"

"Well, I certainly have no understanding of how you've gone about selecting your companions."

"God, you're horrible," Paxton mutters under his breath. "You said, and I think I'm quoting you pretty accurately here: you said I could bring Cecily, a Kardashian, or a hooker, you didn't care, as long as she played the game your way." His voice ices over. "Well, Mother, I'm playing your game. But I won't play it your way, and neither will she. We'll play it *our* way, and I'm only playing it until I don't need you anymore."

A sigh, bitter and furious. "You are so…*petulant*, Paxton."

"Learned from the best, Mother."

"I hope you don't mean me," she says, her voice hard and brittle.

"I sure as hell do."

"I'm nothing so pedestrian as petulant."

"What you are, they don't have words for. Cold, calculating, manipulative, and selfish only begin to cut it."

"I believe you forgot cunning and vindictive," she says.

A laugh. "True."

"Let's not bandy words, Paxton. Who is she?"

"I told you, Mom, I'm not telling. You'll find out along with the rest of the world."

"At least tell me you're taking the requisite precautions?"

"What would those be?" he asks, wrapping salami around a soft white cheddar and dipping it in mustard.

"An iron-clad prenup. I had Marek send you one."

A devious grin crosses his face as he chews, winking at me again. "A prenup? Nah. I like to live on the edge. Risk a little."

"You *can't* be serious, Paxton." Raw, stunned disbelief. "That would be absurdly irresponsible, even for you. I won't allow it."

"You don't have a choice."

"I certainly do, I'm paying for the wedding."

"A wedding you arranged! A wedding I didn't want! Your stipulation was that I had to get married—I have to be at the altar, and I have to say I do. You said I could bring whomever I wanted, as long as I got married and cleaned up my image. Well, that's what I'm doing. I'm bringing a woman to the wedding, and she's about as far from a hooker as you can get, and that's all I'm saying. Who I marry is up to me. The details of my marriage will be up to me. If I want a prenup, I'll get one. If I don't want one, there won't be one. You want to cut me out of the will over it, go for it. I don't need your money. I'm not doing the marriage to stay in the will, and you know it."

"Then why are you doing it, Paxton?"

"Because, despite what you may want to believe, my political aspirations go far beyond just climbing the ladder to more influence, more power, and all that. I do the job because I like it. I like serving my constituents. And to get where I want to be, I need the family's connections, and I know damn well that you'll cut me out of those if I don't do this—and you are also right about my image. So I'm playing your game, but only up to a point." A pause, and he resumes, but this time his voice is low and slow, carefully considering his words. "Despite your best efforts to convince me of the opposite, you're still my mother and I do love you. You're just this side of pure evil, but you're the mother I have, and I'm not quite willing to walk away from you just yet, and unfortunately for me, that means I have to play along with your stupid plans."

Silence. "I'm not certain whether to be touched or offended, Paxton."

A self-conscious laugh. "Me either, honestly."

Another silence, this one rather lengthy—Paxton

spends it noisily munching nuts. "It's rude to chew into the phone, Paxton," Camilla says with an annoyed sigh.

"Yeah well, I don't care." He chomps louder. "Goodbye, Mother."

"You really won't tell me?" she says, sounding... well...petulant. "Nothing? A first name? Where you met her? Her net worth?"

A laugh, around a mouthful of olives and crackers. "No, Mom," he says, once he's swallowed. "I'm not telling you dick."

"So vulgar." She sighs. "Well, have it your way then. But you'll be at the wedding? You're taking this seriously?"

"Yes, we will be there." A pause, his golden-brown eyes on mine, serious, deep. "And yes, I am actually taking this seriously."

A hesitation. "Is she there with you?"

"Yes."

Camilla's voice goes predatory and threatening. "Listen to me, whoever you are—if you take advantage of my son, you will regret it. I promise you that. You do not want to cross me."

I'm tempted to speak up, to give voice to my derision, my frustration, my anger, but I don't. Not just because Paxton is shaking his head and glaring at me, but because I really do want to see the look on her face when I walk down that aisle.

Ohhh shit, shouldn't have thought that. I should

not have thought that. I am in no way ready to walk down the aisle—to get *married*. I get dizzy, and carefully set my bottle of water down so I don't drop the glass on the marble.

Paxton hangs up the call without saying goodbye to his mother, and eyes me. "You okay?"

I shake my head. "No, not at all."

"Don't let her scare you."

I arch an eyebrow at me. "Oh? Are you going to tell me her bark is worse than her bite?"

Paxton pauses, laughs, and then shakes his head. "Actually, you probably should be a little scared of her. But my point is, don't let her threats get to you. I won't let her get near you once this is over. I'll handle her."

I focus on breathing steadily. "Actually, that's not my problem right now."

"Then what is?"

I hum the wedding march: "Bummmmm bum-bum-bum...Bum BUM bum-bum." I shake my head, dizzy again. "I am not ready for that. Not even a little bit." I wave a hand. "I thought, I really do want to see the look on your mom's face when *I* walk down the aisle to you, and it made me dizzy."

Paxton stares at me blankly, slowly lowering the rolled-up meat and cheese he'd been eating. "Now why the hell did you have to go and say that?" he mutters. "Now *I'm* dizzy."

"It's easy enough talking about getting married, but thinking about it being a reality?" I shake my head, rubbing my temples with my middle and forefingers. "That's totally different."

He blinks at me. "Yeah, no shit." He breathes in deeply, holds it, lets it out slowly, and I feel him regaining control over himself. "Well, it's the path we're on. I chose it, and so did you."

"Doesn't mean I like it," I say. "It's still scary as hell, and I don't know how I'll cope with it. I'm only making it through right now by not thinking about it."

A sigh. "Yeah, I know what you mean."

I shake my head at him. "You're not giving up as much as I am, Paxton."

"You also stand to gain a hell of a lot."

I don't have an answer for that.

"Speaking of which," Paxton says. "How'd shopping go?"

I shrug. "It was a lot."

"Am I poor now?" he quips, cackling.

"Yes, I think you very well may be."

"Well, let's see what the damage is." He opens an app on his phone, taps and scrolls, perusing the list of recent transactions, totaling them up, muttering to himself. "Ten, plus twelve is twenty-two, plus another fifteen is thirty-seven, plus thirty-five is…seventy-two, plus ten and another ten is twenty, which makes ninety-two, plus eleven and another thirteen…that's…one-oh-three and then…one-sixteen." He nods. "Not bad."

I stare. "That's how much Julie spent? A hundred and sixteen thousand dollars?"

He nods. "About what I was expecting."

He seems so casual about it, and I just can't understand how he can be casual about spending a hundred and twenty thousand dollars in a single day. That's more than I've ever made in my life, total.

He seems to see my discomfort. "That seems like a lot to you, huh?"

I boggle at him. "Yes, Paxton, a hundred and sixteen thousand dollars does seem like a lot to me."

He snickers. Stands up, waves his hand for me to follow him. I do, and he leads the way into his bedroom, and his closet, which is twice the size of the one in my room; his closet is full, but it's obviously been organized and spaced to make it look full, and he obviously has plenty of room for more...easily double what he has right now, more if he compressed them a bit. One entire wall is dedicated to suits—grays, blues, blacks, a couple tan suits, pinstripes, houndstooth...

He walks over to the suits, slides three aside, and glances at me. "A hundred and twenty grand." Another three. "Another hundred and fifty." He gestures at the rest. "And so on. I go to London each year and have three or four new suits made, and I drop at least a hundred, sometimes double, just on suits. Shoes, coats, ties, watches, cuff links...I drop easily a quarter mil, sometimes half a million."

I blink, and can't swallow or breathe. "I...but... *why?*"

A shrug. "The suit makes the man, so they say, and

nothing makes a man like a bespoke Brioni suit." A laugh, somewhat self-conscious. "And plus, I can, so I do. It's fun."

I glance at the rack of suits. "So that's like, half a million dollars just in suits on that rack?"

"Oh, easily." He waves a hand. "I donate a few every year to make room."

"You donate a fifty-thousand-dollar suit? To who?"

"Whom, you mean," he corrects automatically.

I snarl. "What the fuck ever."

He laughs. "Sorry, sorry. That was rude of me." A pause. "Anyway, I donate them directly to a charity org I founded. It works to get homeless people jobs—provides showers and haircuts, suits, rides to and from interviews, a meal before and afterward, and if they get the job, enough professional clothing to get through a full week without having to recycle outfits." He heads out of the closet as he drops this on me. "I don't specify the worth of the suits, obviously, because that would be tacky."

"So there are homeless men out there wearing a fifty-thousand-dollar custom Brioni suit and they don't realize it?"

"No," he says, "there are *former* homeless men out there wearing a fifty-thousand-dollar custom Brioni suit without realizing it." A cocky grin. "The difference is vital."

I frown. "Let me guess, the charity organization and the donations look good on the campaign trail."

He laughs easily, but it doesn't quite reach his eyes. "It does, yes."

I hesitate, hating the squirmy, leaden sense of having deeply offended him. "That was shitty of me, wasn't it?"

He shrugs, still giving me that grin that doesn't reach his eyes. "No, you've got me pegged."

"Paxton—"

A sigh, a wave of his hand. "It's fine."

"No, it's not. That wasn't fair of me. There's more to you than that, I'm realizing, and I'm sorry."

He blinks, the hardness in his eyes softening a little. "That charity is not publicly tied to me. It's called Dress For Success, and it's run by a nonprofit I started back in college, under a DBA that can only be traced back to me if you know how to look."

"DBA?"

"Doing business as," he says. "A way to do business under a name other than your own."

"And you started it in college?"

He nods. "It was part of a project for a business class. I went through all the steps, but for the project you weren't supposed to actually go through with it and make it legal, you were just supposed to know *how* to do it. But I figured, I've already done all this work, why stop there, right? So I created the 501c3, registered it, built the charity structure, borrowed financing from Mom and Dad to fund it and hire staff. It took a few months of extra work, but I got it off the ground and set it up to run without any input from me, and hopefully without anyone knowing it's my work."

I tilt my head at him, taking a seat on the stool beside him. "Why don't you want people to know?"

"Because that's not the point of it."

"What is, then?"

"To help." He meets my eyes. "As you've pointed out numerous times, I'm spoiled rotten. Entitled. Born with a golden spoon in my mouth. I know it. I've always known it. I guess I felt like...I needed to do something to offset it. Like, in order to be able to consider myself even a remotely decent person, I had to do something to give to other people. If I profited from it, even in terms of reputation or publicity, it would counteract the whole point of it."

I can't help but laugh a little—it's a soft, quiet huff, not meant to mock. "I'm not sure that's how being a good person works, Paxton."

Another of those maddening, insouciant shrugs. "It's all I've got. Being a good person doesn't come naturally to me, after all. I'm two parts asshole, one part selfish prick." He smacks his legs. "So. Let's see your haul."

And just like that, sharing time is over, and there's no chance to even think about his revelation, because he literally and legitimately has me show off several of the outfits for him. I've never paraded around in front of someone so much in my life, and it's odd. For Julie, it was purely business—she was being paid to assess how I looked.

Paxton?

I'm not sure what his motivations are. First, he has me try on a few casual outfits, and then some of the dressier ones. Finally, wearing a pair of soft gray linen pants and a yellow top with a plunging neckline and shoulder cutouts with a low wedge heel, he nods, smiling at me.

"That's the one."

I blink. "The one, what?"

"The perfect outfit."

"Perfect for what?"

He ignores my question, moving over to stand in front of me. He reaches up, his thick arms framing my face, and slides my springy mass of curls out of the loose half-bun I had it in. My hair flops and bounces down around my shoulders, and he nods again.

"There, better." He ambles over to the jewelry box on the bureau, sorts through it, and finds a simple but pretty pendant, a tear-drop crystal set in fine platinum. He examines it, wrinkles his nose, flicking the big center crystal. "Is this Swarovski?"

I shrug. "I dunno. I think? I know it's real platinum, because the clerk behind the counter made a big deal out of it."

He tosses it back into the box, careless and dismissive. "We can do better. Julie should know better than to fuck around with fake garbage."

I frown. "That is worth more than everything I owned, combined. It's pretty and not at all garbage."

He eyes me. "We can do better. We'll stop and see Abner on the way, get you something real."

I sigh. "Paxton. On the way *where*?"

"Your first official function as my fiancé."

My heart hammers, and I try in vain to swallow. "And what would that be?"

He grins, and it's that mischievous smirk that always gets me in trouble. "A business dinner."

"Business, or politics?"

A shrug, his eyes twinkling. "In this case, both. The couple we're meeting are heavy-hitter angel investors, and they're interested in investing in a company I'm launching this spring. He is also a colleague—he's the personal secretary to the Majority Whip. We're having an informal discussion about some topics I'm trying to get pushed through, and I'm hoping he can get his boss's support."

"Why not go through the actual person?" I ask.

"Because I'm a lowly first-term House rep—I don't get a meeting with the Whip, I'm just not important enough. But I know Matthew from Princeton, and I've done him some favors. He owes me, and I'm calling one in. Get my bill in front of your boss, and I'll make sure your measure gets pushed through the House without any major restructuring."

"I see. You did him favors back in college, and you call it in all these years later?"

A shake of his head. "Not in college, no. More recently."

"What did you do for him?"

He tilts his head. "It's not really my place to say."

I blink, my eyes widening. "Oooh, mysterious. Something nefarious, I bet."

He chuckles. "Ehhh, who are you gonna tell? Just don't let on that I told you, okay?" He sighs, thinking. "Matt has a gambling problem. He counts cards, and he's good at it—too good, and therein lies the problem. He likes to win, and he does, a lot. Too much. He got into some trouble in Atlantic City, the kind of trouble that can start piling up and get real dangerous real fast. I made some calls, greased some palms, and got him out of hot water."

"Wow," I say. "Not what I was expecting."

He grins. "And yes, I helped him out because I knew he'd owe me a favor." A wink. "But I also did it because he's my friend and I really didn't want to see him being fished out of the river on the evening news."

My eyes widen. "That kind of trouble?"

He makes a face. "Yeah, that kind of trouble."

"Maybe he should stay out of casinos, then."

Paxton laughs, a loud guffaw. "His wife would agree." A thoughtful frown. "Although, he doesn't go to casinos, he's too high a roller for that. He goes to the kind of games that happen in a secret back room where you have to get invited and know a verbal code and a handshake and put a deposit down just to get dealt in."

I laugh. "I always figured that was only in movies."

"I mean, I'm exaggerating for effect a little—there're

no codes or handshakes, but it is secret, and it is invite only, and he really does have to buy in for amounts that would make even me hesitate."

I nearly choke at that. "You didn't bat an eye when I spent a hundred grand today." I frown. "Or, rather, when Julie did."

"Exactly. He plays in very rarified circles. Millions of dollars—tens of millions, even—get won and lost at these games. Thus the trouble he was in, and why the favor I did him means I get the bill in front of his boss when I'd otherwise never get the time of day."

I shake my head, laughing. "What a strange world you live in."

Paxton shrugs, nodding. "You're not kidding." He waves at me. "Okay, well, you look incredible. Let's go politick, shall we?"

"I'm not wearing makeup, and my hair is a disaster."

He eyes me, bobbing his head side to side. "I mean, I personally think you don't need that shit, but this being a pretty important meeting, I guess I'd better call Amanda."

"Who's Amanda?"

"A one-woman glam squad. I've worked with her for years, getting people ready for events."

"People," I say, drily.

He arches an eyebrow. "I make neither apologies nor excuses, Makayla, and I hope you don't expect them." He doesn't wait for a response from me, but dials a number. "Amanda. I need you here. Right away. No, just something quick and minimal. She doesn't need a lot—you'll see. Okay, thanks. See you in fifteen."

I marvel. "She just drops whatever she's doing?"

"Well, yeah. I pay her a premium on top of her usual rates and, in return, if I call her in, she doesn't ask how high when I say jump, she just starts jumping."

He pours us each a glass of red wine from a decanter and brings them to us, and we continue munching on the charcuterie.

"So, what do I do at this dinner?" I ask.

He shrugs. "Be yourself. Smile, laugh, tell jokes, listen."

"Why are you bringing me?"

"It's a dinner with my friend and his wife—it would be awkward and uncomfortable for me and them if I showed up alone. Makes talking shop impossible—then his wife either has to listen to our conversation, or we can't talk shop for fear of boring her stupid. Having a date is vital—makes the whole dynamic work."

I cringe. "So I have to be girly and social with a woman I've never met?" I laugh bitterly. "You definitely hired the wrong chick for this, Paxton."

He narrows his eyes at me over the rim of his wineglass. "I didn't *hire* you, Makayla. This isn't a business arrangement. I'm not paying you. You're not doing a job."

I sigh. "Feels like it."

"Well, then, you need to fix that misapprehension

real fucking fast. That attitude will stink on you worse than shit-stained underwear."

I make a disgusted face. "Paxton! That's so gross!"

He shrugs. "This is Washington, babe. We're all liars, cheats, thieves, manipulators—and worse: lawyers. If there's one thing we're all pros at, it's sniffing out weakness. If you go into these meetings and events and dinners feeling like you're just a hired girl, everyone will feel it, and they'll chew you apart." A hesitation. "And me with you."

"So then why am I here?" I ask. "Why me?"

"How much truth you want?" he asks.

"Make it real, Paxton. Never lie to me, and never sugarcoat it."

He nods. "I respect that, and I ask the same from you in return." He tosses an olive in his mouth, washes it down with wine. "So here's the truth. You asked me this already, and I answered truthfully. But you want to go deeper, obviously. You challenge me. You don't fall for my shit. You're not intimated by me, or by my mom."

"Wrong," I cut in, laughing a little. "Your mom scares the poop out of me."

He laughs with me. "And well she should. In a world of barracudas, she's a Great White shark." He waves a hand. "But the point is, you don't let that slow you down or make you feel like less. You're in a whole new world, and you've got your head high, and you're not just laying down and rolling over." A hesitation.

"Truth is, most women in your position would have slept with me already. You haven't. You've got the grit to stick to your guns. You've got pride. You're smart."

I hold up a finger. "Smart, yes. Educated, no."

He waves a hand, dismissing my distinction. "Not important—not as long as you project confidence." He sips again. "You go into this dinner, and I want you to be the woman who snorted at my mother in the penthouse. The woman who tells me I'm an arrogant entitled prick." A grin. "Just don't actually call me that in front of Matt and Isla."

"If you act like one, I'll call you one." I sip my wine for the first time, and as I expect, it's as rich and expensive tasting as I would expect from wine in a cut crystal decanter. "Can't have just part of the attitude, Paxton."

He nods. "Well, I suppose that's the risk I'm taking, huh?"

And then Amanda is here—tall, black, willowy, lean, talkative, with a wild burst of natural hair, she's an explosive flurry of activity and energy. She sits me in the chair in front of the vanity in my closet, fingers rifling and twisting expertly through my hair, fingering the ends, tugging on the curls, examining my scalp, scrunching handfuls this way and that, chattering nonstop—a flow of words that washes over me like a river around a boulder. It's clear I'm not expected to respond, and I don't.

"Wow, you just have the most amazing hair! You obviously haven't had a trim in a long time, though—I mean, look at these split ends, girl. No time for that to-day, but get it done. I'd even go several inches off." She lifts my hair and tucks it under itself to mimic the look of shorter hair. "Like this, maybe. Not super short, un-less you're fierce enough to really pull that off, but at least a little bit to keep the ends healthy. Gotta mois-turize more too, your shit is dry, honey. You're doing great with your face, though. Nice healthy pores goin' on...I'm guessing you don't wear a lot of makeup, or not frequently. Wish I had that confidence, I'm telling you—I can't go anywhere without my face on..."

And so on like that as she kneads some kind of goop into my hair and plays with it seemingly at ran-dom, and then adds something else and keeps playing, and then suddenly my hair looks...incredible. Loose, bouncy, glossy, with perfect shape, falling around my face and neck to frame my features and draping against my shoulder blades just so.

I gape, amazed. "What the hell did you do? I've spent hours trying to get it to look like this, and you did it in minutes."

She just grins. "Magic, honey." She winks, tweak-ing a curl here and there. "I'll show you next time, as-suming Paxton gives me more of a heads-up." She says this with a glare in the mirror at Paxton, who is leaning against the doorframe, half watching and half scrolling on his phone.

Paxton just grins. "Too easy. You needed a challenge."

Amanda blows a raspberry. "This is a touch-up. Your girl here is motherfuckin' gorgeous, and all-natural. Now, asking me to get her ready for the Met Gala on this time frame, now *that* would be a challenge."

She's in front of me, now, blocking my view of myself in the mirror as she works her wizardry with brushes and pencils and sponges, each movement as precise and intentional as a painter's. Another few minutes, and Amanda steps away with a dramatic flourish.

I gasp. "Wow. I mean, just…holy shit!" I stare at myself in the mirror.

When I apply makeup to myself, I usually end up looking like me, just with makeup on, and obviously so. This is…art. It's seamless, and subtle. Emphasizing some features and downplaying others—making my already prominent cheekbones look sharper and more dramatic, my somewhat hard, square jaw look softer, my eyes look wider, deeper, more pronounced. My skin glows, almost as if lit from within.

I meet her gaze, and it's obvious she knows she's a miracle worker. "Seriously. You have to show me how to do this."

She laughs. "Oh hell no. If I did that, I'd be out of a job. It ain't magic if you can do it yourself, honey."

A few minutes later, Amanda is gone, with a hefty roll of cash tucked into her purse—I don't know how much, and I don't ask. Paxton spritzes a little more cologne on himself, tucks his dress shirt in, adds a black leather belt and a yellow tie to match my outfit, and then holds out his hand for me. To my own surprise, I take it and hold his hand on the way down to the garage. He opens the passenger door of the Porsche—this one is new, gleaming white with red leather interior. The engine purrs like a giant lion, and then snarls as we zip out of the garage and onto the street.

The top is up, because of my hair, but it's still an exhilarating ride, even with the slog through rush hour traffic. We reach the restaurant, an upscale, hush-hush, reservations a year in advance sort of place. A valet takes the car; Paxton steps out, takes my hand, and walks with me to the front doors, spiriting me inside before anyone has a chance to see us.

He pauses before he goes in, however, glancing at me. "You ready for this?"

I laugh, a little breathlessly. "Not even a little."

"You'll be fine. Just be yourself."

His smile is dazzling, breathtaking, and somehow reassuring. His hand in mine is reassuring, and familiar. His huge, towering, sheltering presence beside me is… right.

It shouldn't be this way.

I swallow hard, suck in a deep breath, hold it, let it out, and nod firmly. "Let's go."

16

THE DINNER DATE GOES SURPRISINGLY SMOOTHLY. I discover I'm somewhat better at idle small talk than I thought I was—it turns out all you really need to do is smile and nod while the other person talks, make some sort of inane response, ask a leading question now and then, and so on in circles. Talk about clothing, exercising, movies—fortunately, my one pastime in my very limited free time has always been going to the movies. I save my change, stuff a bag of SkinnyPop in my purse, and go see movies. It's my big splurge. So, I can talk movies all day long.

I know nothing of politics and care even less, but I discover over the course of the next few weeks as I accompany Paxton on more dinner dates and lunches and cocktail mixers, that most of the women I'm expected to mingle with know about as much, and care about as much, as I do. They're perfectly content to talk about makeup and purses and which car their husband recently bought them, and their most recent jewelry acquisition. I do a lot of listening, because talking about things someone else bought me just seems stupid and shallow and vain and materialistic—and my penchant for listening more than I talk quickly gains me a reputation in Paxton's circle of friends and acquaintances as being a good listener.

So, even better, I don't even have to talk. Just listen, act like I care about what they're saying, and I'm good. Don't have to pretend like I know as much as them, or that I'm as cultured or educated. I keep my mouth shut and let them make their own assumptions.

Most of the events Paxton brings me to are fairly small, casual things. Dinners with a couple or two, meet some folks for drinks at a local bar and let the men talk politics and make backroom deals over high-priced whiskey while the women compare ten-thousand-dollar purses—lots of standing around in expensive heels, nursing the same glass of red wine for an hour, nodding until my neck is sore.

Drive home.

Hold hands with Paxton.

Think about the kiss.

Pretend I'm not attracted to him.

Pretend I don't like him.

Pretend I'm not wondering what it would be like to sleep with him.

I want to—a lot. But I refuse. I can't. If I sleep with him, I'll start thinking this is real. I can't sleep with him precisely because I'm starting to actually LIKE him. I stand at his side sipping wine and listening, and

I discover that he's very, very, very smart. He's passionate about his job—his headline issues are gun control, climate change, homelessness, social equality, and education reform. Which, honestly, is unexpected. I suppose, as in so many other ways, I went into getting to know him with certain assumptions in my mind. That he was just a shallow, vain, arrogant, entitled brat.

He's so much more. He's not in politics for the power or the fame or the influence, and certainly not for the money. It's clear he's in it to make changes. Because he cares.

I don't WANT to like him. I want to keep pretending he's just a spoiled rich white boy with a big ego. But he's not.

Every night we go home, we linger in the kitchen until late, talking. We sit at the island and share a snack and a nightcap, and...Paxton unloads.

I'm not sure when it started. At first, it was just a chance to kick off my shoes and get a little snack before bed, and somehow it's turned into my favorite part of the day. Even if we don't have an event or a dinner, he works late, and that's his time to unwind. Pour some whiskey, have some ice cream or nachos, and vent.

He just wants me to listen, I've realized. I don't have to follow what he's talking about.

Like tonight.

The wedding is in a month; I'm scheduled for my dress fitting tomorrow, and Paxton's bill—meant to establish baseline funding for research on homelessness and how to solve it—is getting voted on. He's been working on this bill for months now; every dinner date, every cocktail mixer has been focused on pumping up support and getting votes. He's mega stressed.

I'm freaking out myself, because I'm getting fitted for my wedding dress tomorrow—alone. There's a selection to choose from, and Julie will be there to help me decide, and then it gets fitted and altered, and it's just me because I have no friends, no family here in DC.

I haven't seen Mom in almost two months, and I'm dying inside. I call her every day, or nearly, but it's just not the same as seeing her, sitting with her, holding her hand.

What if she's deteriorating? What if something happens and I'm not there? Paxton bought me a cell phone, and I've given the hospice my number with instructions to call me if anything comes up. But it's not the same.

I have to see her. I have to be there with her. She has bad days and good days, and she needs me on both.

And I'm not there.

I'm here, in DC, playing dutiful fiancé to a wealthy, influential, rising political star.

There have been reports of me, some blurry photographs taken from a distance by desperate paparazzi, but Paxton has been careful to make sure the media has no clue who I am. There are rumors, of course. The buzz blogs are going nuts with speculation as to whom America's most eligible and desirable bachelor is making the DC rounds with. There are reports, descriptions, lies, truths...the rumor mill is churning. Paxton is avoiding his mother's phone calls, which are nonstop, now.

Paxton is talking, but for once, I'm unable to focus. He notices.

"Makayla?" His voice cuts through my mental scrum.

I blink at him. "Huh?"

He laughs ruefully. "You're somewhere else tonight."

I sigh. "I'm sorry. I'm not being a very good listener tonight."

He tilts his head. "You know, I've been venting to you every night for weeks now, and I'm realizing I do all the talking."

I chuckle. "You've never had anyone to vent to, have you?"

He shakes his head, swirling ice and whiskey. "No, not really." A glance at me. "You?"

I shrug. "My mom, usually." A pause. "But that's a tricky situation."

"Why is it tricky?"

Nope, not ready to go there with him. It's too close, too vulnerable. I shake my head. "It's a long story."

He glances at his watch. "I've got time." A warm, dizzying smile. "Talk to me, Makayla."

What to say? "I just...I miss her. I haven't seen her in two months, and that's the longest I've ever been away from her. She has some health issues, too, and I just…I worry about her."

"Health issues?" He seizes on that, of course.

I stifle a groan. "I just need to go see her."

He waves a hand, the dismissive wave that says *consider it handled*. "Go see her, then."

"I'm picking the dress tomorrow and getting fitted." I rub my forehead. "And then there's the dinner with Dom and Catalina Wednesday, and cocktails Thursday…"

I know his schedule, now.

He frowns. "Go see her."

"But this is why I'm here."

He shakes his head. "I can manage without you for a few nights." A strange, unsettling smile. "I did manage for a while, you know."

I laugh. "I know. It's just…this is why I'm here. It's why we're together."

He nods, shrugs. And then his eyes find mine and there's an odd light in them, an unsettling openness. "I managed without someone for years…my whole life. I was fine. I didn't want a wife." His gaze doesn't waver. "Weird how quickly I've gotten used to you being there. How much I've come to rely on you being here with me."

I swallow hard. "I don't do anything."

"You do more than you know." He looks down at his glass, swirls. "Just you being there helps me mentally, somehow. Like, I know you're there. If a conversation is becoming something I need an escape from, you're there. You give the women something to talk about besides my love life, and honestly you make me look better with the men."

I frown at that. "How so?"

He smiles, one that says *You really don't realize?* "Because you're so fucking stunning."

I shiver, shrug a shoulder, shake my head. "I'm out of place. I don't fit."

"Which is exactly why they're all smitten with you."

"No one is smitten, Paxton."

He arches an eyebrow. "At cocktails last night, the guy I was talking to most of the night, Mick Branson? He couldn't stop talking about you. How his wife was girl-crushing on you, and how he couldn't figure out what a ten like you is doing with a five like me."

I snort, my trademark blast of sarcastic laugh. "Yeah, okay. *I'm* the ten, *you're* the five. Good one, Paxton."

He frowns. "You think it's the opposite?"

I shrug again. "I mean, no. I don't think I'm a five. I know I'm pretty. It's mostly my build, but I know I'm okay. I'm comfortable and confident in who I am and what I look like, so don't think it's self-deprecation. But you're way out of my league, Paxton. You're the elite. Women want you, and men want to be you. You have everything. It's fucking annoying, actually. I wanted to assume it's because you're rich and beautiful, that you're shallow and vapid. But you're not. You smart and you genuinely care." I'm fully aware of how bitter I sound.

He frowns at me, head tilted, eyes searching. "That really bugs you, huh?" he says, half-laughing.

"Yes!" I shout. "It does! You can't have literally *everything* going for you! It's not fair."

He doesn't laugh with me. "I don't have everything."

I eye him speculatively. "Oh? And what are you missing?"

He takes a sip of whiskey, and doesn't answer for a while. Eventually, still staring into his glass, he answers. "More than you know, Makayla."

Something in the silence stops me from asking what he means.

After what feels like several minutes of silence, he finishes his whiskey, pushes his empty ice cream bowl away and slides off the stool. He makes it as far as the hallway before he stops and turns back to me.

His expression is opaque, unreadable. "I'll drive myself tomorrow. Liam will take you to the fitting, and I'll have the jet on standby for you, with John on the other end waiting to take you to see your mom."

"Paxton, it's fine. I can get a ticket on my own."

He laughs. "Well, yeah, I'm sure you *could*, but why would you?"

I sigh. " It just feels weird."

"What does?"

"Using your things. Spending your money on clothes and purses, taking your family's private cars and jets, using your drivers." I shrug, helpless to explain it. "I don't know how to cope with it. It's all too much."

He walks back over to me. Stands over me, serious and brooding. "You've done more for me in the last few weeks than you'll ever know, Makayla. I know for a fact that I've got votes from people simply because of how their perception of me has changed just by having you there." He tugs on a spiral of curly hair. "So take the jet, okay? It's the least I can do."

He turns on his heel and vanishes into his room without a backward glance, his shoulders rounded, hunched.

He's been moody, lately.

Anxiety over the wedding? I know I'm feeling it, and I don't have a career and a reputation on the line, nor millions and billions of dollars and invaluable personal, business, and political connections.

I go to my room, strip, and climb into bed, but it's a long time before I fall asleep.

I think of the heavy, almost sad hunch of Paxton's shoulders.

The brooding darkness in his eyes.

I want to take it away, but I can't. I don't know how. He's not mine—it's not my place or my nature.

I'm quiet on the ride to the airport—Liam tries to engage me in conversation several times, but I'm not feeling it, and he eventually gives up.

The dress fitting was quick and painless. There was a rack of incredible white bridal gowns, each by a high-end designer. I tried on a dozen, and Julie and I settled on the one that looked best—simple, a sleeveless sweetheart neckline; it's a mermaid style, and the plunging neckline is truly daring, and would be well-nigh immodest if it weren't for the gauzy lace. As is, I don't think my breasts have ever been pushed up so high, nor quite so eye-poppingly prominent. I protested this at first, but Julie overrode me. Let what God gave me shine out, she said. It's just enough of too much to be absolutely perfect. It also fits nearly perfectly, just needing some adjustment in the hips and bust, because I'm so ridiculously curved in both areas.

After some measurements, the dress is taken away to be altered by a team of professionals hired specifically by Camilla for this—no in-house alterations here, thank you very much.

I hope the sarcastic eye roll is evident, because it's just so over the top.

Once the fitting is done, Liam whisks me off to the airport—a pleasant surprise is waiting for me: a bottle of chilled white wine, courtesy of Paxton, and a packed bag, as the fitting had been early this morning and I hadn't had time to pack.

He even made sure to include two of the best

purses in my new collection, as well some of the jewelry which had, at some point, appeared in a glass box in my room—two-carat diamond solitaire earrings in platinum with a matching three-carat pendant necklace, four-carat diamond tennis bracelets, a sapphire pendant necklace, several more pairs of earrings ranging from simple small diamonds to elaborate tear-drop pieces. When I asked Paxton how much it had all cost, he'd just winked at me and told me not to worry about it.

Obviously, it's all real, and the potential value of it all makes me nauseous.

Thirty thousand feet up, sipping wine and watching a rom-com on the TV screen…and my phone rings.

"Hello?" I answer.

"Miss Makayla Poe?" a smooth female voice asks.

"Yes."

"This is Jennifer from Harborview Nursing Home. How are you this morning?"

Panic, immediate and throttling. "Is it Mom? Did something happen?"

"No, god, I'm sorry, I should have led with that— no, Miss Poe, your mother is doing very well. No, I'm actually calling because we've been going through accounts, and it seems you're somewhat behind. You've always been very prompt, and as a token of appreciation we're waiving the late fees, but we do need you to get current as soon as possible."

I swallow hard—before I left with Paxton, I'd given

them every dollar I had except for the $250 emergency cash in my wallet. I'd hoped the amount would have covered me for longer than this, but apparently I had miscalculated.

"Okay, um." I'm already on a sliding scale based on my obviously dire financial situation, and I know they're doing me a huge favor by even giving me this notice, but the amount in question is still way outside my ability to pay, now that I've fallen behind. "Okay. I'll handle it. Thank you for the notice."

"You're welcome and thank you again."

I end the call and carefully set the device aside—it's the first cell phone I've ever had, the newest sleekest handset, and I'm paranoid about dropping it. I barely know how to use it.

Sigh.

Now what do I do? I have no money. I'm not working. I have nothing of my own to sell. I could ask Paxton to take care of it, but knowing him, he'd go buy the whole nursing home. I can't go to Paxton. I can't be any more reliant on him than I already am. I take care of Mom, because she took care of me. It's my problem. I just don't know how to fix it.

God, I'm so stupid. I should never have done this. Why did I think it was a good idea? Quit my jobs, leave my mom, marry a stranger...all in some vague hope of someday somehow being able to make things easier. What did I think I was going to do in the meantime? Pay for her hospice care in excess purses?

Wait, though.

I finger the fine leather and intricate stitching on the Gucci handbag on my lap. This is the kind of bag I never even dreamed of owning, and here it is.

Worth at least two thousand dollars.

I open the small hard case Paxton packed the jewelry in: a necklace and earrings worth easily five grand, if not more.

That may not get me current, but it would help, and at least buy me time.

It's shitty, though.

They're gifts.

But what else am I supposed to do?

A little Googling later, and I've created an account on a luxury goods resale app. Post pictures of the purse and the jewelry...

By the time the plane lands, I've got buyers for all three items, at nearly full value. Beginner's luck, probably. I hadn't expected it to work so fast.

I ask John to stop at a UPS store so I can put a few things in the mail—he looks at me with curiosity, but says nothing. When I go into the UPS store with a purse and come out without one, he raises his eyebrows, but says nothing.

With the items marked as shipped, my buyers send payment. The money goes through, hits my account, and by the time I'm at Mom's nursing home, I can write a check to take care of the next couple of months.

Now I just have to hope that Paxton doesn't notice.

"WHY DID YOU…" SHE HAS TO STOP FOR breath. "Why did you come back?"

I glare at her. "Mom. You thought I would just vanish? Never come back?"

She glares back. "Told you. Live your life, Mack."

"I am. I just miss you."

She softens. "Miss you too, baby."

"It's harder than I thought it would be," I admit.

Mom frowns. Silent, thinking. "If you're gone, how are you paying for the home?"

I sigh. I'd been hoping she wouldn't ask. "I'm making it work."

"How?"

"Mom, come on."

"No." She shakes her head with as much resoluteness as she can summon. "Tell me."

"Don't, please."

"Tell…me."

"I'd have to tell you everything."

"So tell."

My throat catches. I can tell her now, because I have an agreement with Paxton, and I won't back out. Mom won't ask me to, because I gave him my word, and I don't go back on my word. Mom set that in stone for me from day one. You make a promise, you keep it.

"Remember Paxton?" I ask, my voice heavy and flat.

She nods. "You hated him."

"I didn't hate him, I just…" I swallow hard. "I've agreed to marry him."

Mom blinks once. And then, slowly, with visible effort, she sits up, shaking and sweating from the exertion necessary for something so simple. "You *what?*"

I nod. "In a month." I close my eyes, because I can't admit the rest with her eyes boring into me. "I've been living with him in DC."

"Why?"

"It's complicated." I weigh my options. "His mother is forcing him to get married. I think I mentioned the situation, but it's for political reasons, mainly. The plan is, we'll get married, stay married for a while, and then get divorced. He has a bad reputation, playboy and all that. Well deserved, but really, it's not who he is. It's just an image he has, and getting married, having me around cleans that up. Then, when we split up, I'm taken care of. And I mean taken care of in a way you cannot even fathom."

"You sleep with him yet?" Mom's eyes are sharp; MS has robbed her of her physical mobility, but her mind is as sharp as it ever has been. More so, maybe, because it's all she has now.

"No."

"You want to." She doesn't phrase it as a question.

"He's good-looking. And a lot nicer than I thought. He comes across as arrogant—well, he *is* arrogant. But there's more to him."

Mom's smile is wicked. "You *like* him."

"It's an arrangement. It has an expiration date. I can't like him." It's odd, the twinge deep down inside when I say that.

"Mack." She raises her eyebrows at me. "It's okay."

"No, it's not."

"How'd you pay?" She shifts tracks faster than anyone I know. "We were behind, now we're not."

"How do you know?"

She smirks. "I have my ways."

"Not important. I took care of it. I'll always take care of it. No matter what I have to do."

She straightens again, eyes blazing. "Rules, Mack." She's getting tired, making it harder for her to speak.

"I am following the rules. The rules are keeping me from sleeping with him. This isn't sexual, Mom. It's an arrangement. I play wife for him, help him with his image, and then we will develop irreconcilable differences. We both move on."

"And you get money."

I shrug. "I don't know. Something like that. A house, probably. A trust to make sure things are set."

She sighs. "Doing this for me." She seems sad, now. "You lied."

I swallow, blink back tears. "Mom, come on. I was drowning. Three jobs, sixty, eighty hours a week and all my money went here." I blink harder. "I was lonely, and he seems to like me. It can't be anything, but it's still nice to be liked."

She nods, weakly. "He know about me?"

"He knows that my mom has health issues."

A bitter bark of a laugh. "He know his money is going to take care of an angry, sick old black lady?"

"It's not his business."

"You marryin' the man, Mack. It is." A pause, as she gathers strength again. "How did you pay?"

I sigh. She won't stop till I tell her. "Sold some things he bought me."

"Like what?"

I look away. "A Gucci bag. Some diamond jewelry."

Mom's eyes widen. "Damn, girl." She grins. "What else you get?"

I hide a smile. "Mom, it's not mine. I shouldn't have done it, but I was desperate. I can't ask him for help."

"Won't, you mean." She rolls her eyes. "He got you shit, it's yours. You sellin' it is your business." Humor is gone, then. "He won't like it, Mack. Don't need to know him to know that."

"I know," I whisper. "I know."

"Tell him."

"No. He'll pity me. He'll do something nuts, like buy the whole nursing home."

"So? Then no more problems."

"It's not his problem. It's mine—ours."

She shakes her head. "Stubborn girl."

I grin at her. "Learned from the best."

Her eyes flutter. "Ain't stubborn. Just know when I'm right…and I'm always right."

"I know, Mom."

She flicks them open, fighting sleep. "Give it a real shot, Mack."

I shake my head. "No. I can't."

"Why?"

"It won't work."

"How d'you know?"

I blink back tears. "I just do. He doesn't want it to. He never wanted a wife. He just picked me because I'm a fuck you to his racist mom, and a way to toy with the expectations of the DC political scene and the media buzz around him."

She grins. "Listen to you."

I shake my head. "I'm keeping my heart and my body out of it."

She grabs my hand. Squeezes hard. Eyes bug wide, burning fierce. "*Try*, Makayla Poe. Try. Please, for me. Try."

I shake my head. "I can't. I can't."

She squeezes even harder. "Mack." Her voice is pleading. "Look at me."

I look—it's hard, it hurts like fuck to look. She's so thin, so weak. Fighting as hard as possible, because she's a tough old Detroit-raised bitch who don't back down from nobody and nothing. But she's tired. She hurts.

"I see you, Momma."

She shakes her head, because that's not what she meant. "No. Listen." A long pause. "I know you...you don't want to hear it. But I'm...gone soon. Not much time left. I can feel it." I open my mouth to protest to scold her but she squeezes my hand so hard it hurts and I shut up. "I *feel* it, baby Mack. I feel it."

"Momma, come on."

She shakes her head. Her eyes laser into mine, and I can't look away. Don't dare. "Won't go till you're not alone."

"If you go, I'm alone."

She shakes her head. "Gotta let me go, baby. I'm *tired*." She squeezes again, three times, hard. "But you—you have lived your whole adult life for me. No more, baby."

"Momma—"

She cuts in. "He a good man?"

I consider. "Yes, I think he is. Completely out of touch with reality when it comes to money, but he's a good person despite that."

"He respect you?"

"He's respected the fact that I'm not going to sleep with him."

"Do you like him?"

I nod.

Mom's eyes pierce deeper. "He like you?"

I hesitate. I nod again. "I think so," I whisper.

She squeezes my hand. "Then *try*."

"I'm scared to," I admit. "Terrified."

Mom's smile makes me nervous. "Good."

I frown. "Good? Why good?"

"If you're scared, it means you got something real going on. Scarier it is, the bigger it is." She pauses for a long time. "Give the man a chance, Mack."

I shake my head, but it's doubt rather than denial. "What if he breaks my heart, and you're gone? What will I do?"

She lifts her chin high, proud. "I taught you strength, Makayla Poe. You ain't a weak-ass bitch. You're strong. *Strong*. It'll hurt. That's okay. You're strong."

I can't help crying, and she doesn't stop me this time. She's crying too. "You taught me."

"Get your big brown ass out of here, Mack."

I laugh, hug her. "Okay, okay. You need to sleep." I hug her again, hold on tight. "Mom, you have to promise you won't go anywhere without—"

She shoves me away, holds me at arm's length. "I'll go when I'm ready."

"I'll be there with you, Mom. Promise me."

"Mack, I don't want you to watch—"

"*Promise* me, Mom." I choke. "Fucking *promise*, goddamn you."

"I promise." Her eyes are steady but wet. "I promise."

"You and me, Mom. No matter what."

She smiles, and pulls me in for a hug, and then I help her get settled into her pillows, *Vanderpump Rules* reruns playing. I watch her fade to sleep, and my heart aches.

I've faced my mom's illness for years. But have I prepared myself for her death?

The drive to the airport is quick and silent, and the flight back to DC is long and even more silent.

The drive home is endless. Because, despite everything, the moment I walk into the foyer of Paxton's DC condo, I do feel like I'm home.

Paxton is waiting for me.

And he's pissed.

18

"Why didn't you tell me, Makayla?" he growls.

I stop short of him; I'm emotionally spent, and his anger is a fierce, forceful, wild thing. "Tell you what, Paxton?"

"About your mom."

I go into the kitchen, set my bag down, grab a bottle of Pellegrino from the refrigerator. Scratch that—I need something stronger. Pour a whiskey instead, and one for Paxton.

But he waves it off, and stands inches from me. "Why didn't you tell me?"

"I did tell you. I told you I was visiting my mom. I told you she has health issues."

"She's in a hospice, Makayla." He's really, *really* pissed. "You sold things to pay for her care."

I close my eyes. "John told you?"

"Yes, he did. He thought it was weird and was worried you were playing me."

"I *am* playing you, Paxton!" I shout. "She's got

advanced MS. I was drowning in bills. I couldn't keep up, even working three jobs."

"Why—didn't—you—*tell* me?" he bites out, his voice the feral crackle of a predator.

"It's not your problem."

"You're about to marry a man worth millions, into a family worth billions, without a prenup, and you don't think it pertinent to tell me your mother has a terminal illness?"

"She's my mother. She's dying. You can't do anything. I can't, no one can."

"I could have helped."

I shake my head. I can't explain it. "Paxton, you don't understand. She's all I have."

"So why not let me help?"

"Because—"

"Because you're too damn proud and stubborn to ask for help!"

I sink to the floor, finally cracking. Weeping. "She's my mother," I sob. "My mom. She worked all day every day, menial petty shitty-ass jobs so I could eat and have shoes and go to school. I dropped out to help her, but she made me go back and graduate." I snort. "By graduate, I mean get my GED. So I at least have that. Then she got sick and…it was my turn to take care of her. I promised her I'd take care of her."

"Me helping *is* taking care of her."

I can only shake my head again. "No. No. *I* have to. Me."

Paxton settles on the floor next to me. "You don't have to do it alone, Makayla."

"I do."

"You don't."

He sighs. Wraps an arm around me.

It was so hard seeing her, hearing her talk about dying, and I just can't stop myself from collapsing against him.

The light fades.

I weep, and weep, and darkness takes over.

"...Full hospice care set up. A-S-A-P. Yeah, here, in my condo. Shit, I don't know. MS, she said, basically terminal. How long? I don't know. Name is Poe. P-O-E. Harborview Nursing Home in Petoskey, Michigan. I want her here as soon as it can be arranged. Makayla will fly out to be with her for the move. Yes, thanks. Full time, round the clock. Put the nurse up somewhere in the building. If you have to buy someone out to make it happen, then do it. Make sure the nurse is the best. And if there's any kind of promising treatments, find them, get them."

I wake up to hear Paxton pacing, and talking. He sees me stir, and sits on the bed beside me.

"Thank you, Victor. Okay, goodbye." He shoves the phone in a back pocket, and stares down at me. He's a big, broad shadow in the moonlight. His eyes glitter in the dim light. "You should have told me."

"I'm sorry. It was too hard. Too scary."

"It's taken care of." He smiles. "You'll go down early next week and bring her here."

"You want my sick, cantankerous, meddling mother living with you?"

"Meddling?"

I drop my eyes. Roll over, away from him. "She made me promise to try."

"Try?" His hand rests on my shoulder.

"With you." Don't look at him—don't look at him.

"So you're not alone when she…" he trails off, unsure how to finish it.

I nod. "That. And because she could tell that I…"

"You what, Makayla?"

I finally turn over to my back, and stare up at him. I swallow my nerves and use the strength Mom taught me. "She could tell that I like you."

He grins. "You like me?" A laugh. "As in, you *like* me, like me?"

I giggle—I'm tired and my dignity is gone. A giggle is all I've got, as girly and dumb as it is. "Don't be juvenile."

"You said you like me, but *I'm* the juvenile one?"

I reach for his hand, tangle my fingers with his. "I…I care about you."

He doesn't answer for a long time. "I care about you too."

Our eyes lock. He frowns.

"This changes things," he says.

I laugh quietly. "You just arranged for my mother to come live with us."

He nods. His eyes are serious, penetrating, wild. "With *us*."

A long, tense, seething silence.

"I don't know how to do this," I whisper.

He shakes his head. Our fingers are still entwined. "Me either."

Another silence.

"Is it why you won't sleep with me?" he asks.

"Is what why?"

"The money thing. Your mom. The hospice care. Marrying me. You don't want to sleep with me so it won't feel like you are…"

"Selling myself," I finish, and then shrug. "I mean, that's part of it."

"What's the rest?"

"So I wouldn't fall for you."

"I didn't realize that that was a possibility," he says.

I laugh. "Me either. It wasn't supposed to be."

"Why couldn't you fall for me?"

"Because this is an arrangement. It's going to end. We get married, you get to where you need to be, and then we divorce. That was the agreement." I sigh. "If I started liking you, falling for you, it would hurt. And I've got enough hurt to cope with."

"How long?" he asks, his voice tender and quiet.

I shrug, knowing what he's asking. "I don't know. I think she's waiting, somehow."

"For what?"

We're in his room, I realize. In his bed. He lies down beside me, cradles me in the nook of his arm and shoulder.

"For me to…" I shrug. "Not be alone, I guess." A silence. "To know that I'm going to be okay without her."

"Will you be?"

I shake my head, sniffle. "No."

"You could…" He starts over. "You could let yourself care about me. Let me care about you." I hear him swallow hard. "It doesn't have to be an arrangement. There doesn't have to be the expiration date."

I feel my heart hammer like a kettledrum. "Paxton…" I catch my breath. "You don't want that. You said so."

"Before I understood who…who you are. What kind of person you are. How much I'd come to… to like having you around." He hesitates. "I may have changed my mind, a little."

I grin up at him. "A little, huh?"

He shrugs, endeavoring to look nonchalant, and not at all succeeding. "Yeah, a little."

"What exactly did you change your mind about?"

He exhales, and it's shaky—which is, oddly, reassuring. "You. Marriage." He's wearing his suit slacks still, and a plain white crewneck T-shirt, barefoot, casual, hair rumpled; he lies on the bed beside me, close but not presumptuously so. "Can I tell you something that may piss you off?"

I let out a small, sharp breath. "Yeah, I guess."

"You weren't supposed to be so fucking irresistible. You're so completely different from the women I normally associate with, and that was on purpose. I couldn't handle being married to those kinds of women, not even fake married, where I'd probably end up like my parents, having known but quiet affairs."

"Your parents both do that?"

He laughs. "Oh yeah. Dad's had the same mistress for twenty years—he's been with her almost as long as he's been with Mom, and I kind of feel like he's actually closer to her than he is Mom." He lifts a hand in a sort of shrug. "Mom is more complicated. Basically, she keeps a roster of like five or six guys she sleeps with. She'll see the same guy for, like, six months, a year maybe, and then she switches to the next guy. Then, once that roster of guys has aged out, she finds new ones."

"Aged out?" I echo, with a disbelieving bark of laughter.

"Yeah, she likes 'em younger—thirtyish. No more than thirty-five, no younger than twenty-five. Once they hit thirty-five, they're out, and she replaces them. Where she finds them, I don't know. Not an escort service or anything, I know that for sure because I hired a PI to check."

I frown at him. "Why? Why would you want to know if your mom is using an escort service?"

"So I know what my political opponents may find out and try to use against me." Another shrug. "Once I was sure it was nothing like that, I stopped looking. It's just your average cougar affair bullshit, a rich old lady looking for hot young studs to make her feel desired because her husband is a rich old fart who never really gave a shit about her."

I cackle in surprise. "Wow. That's harsh.

He snorts a laugh. "It's the truth."

"And you don't want that?"

He shudders. "Fuck no." Vehement, disgusted. "*Fuck* no."

"Then what *do* you want?"

A long pause. "I don't know anymore, Makayla. I really don't. If you'd asked me three months ago, I'd have said that I want to stay a bachelor. Keep my dating life private, and maybe eventually settle down with someone. I would have said that if I ever did marry someone, it probably wouldn't be love, but would be more than an arrangement. Just a marriage of...convenience, I guess. Someone I like, someone I tolerate, someone I'm at least moderately attracted to and can stand to be around. So far, I just haven't found that person." He sighs. "That's not true—I really did like Monique a lot. She was beautiful, she was classy, she was smart."

"But your mother."

He sighs, and it's a disgusted sound. "I was a coward about that. I should have fought it. I should have stood up to her better, made it more clear that her not-so low-key racism isn't okay. It's something I regret."

"Thus, me."

He shakes his head. "I don't know if that's true anymore." He turns onto his side to face me, folding his arm under his head. "Maybe that's how it started. I mean, you're not like, *black*, you know? But you're also not Caucasian."

I laugh, and it's kind of bitter. "Oh, I know. Trust me, I know."

He blinks at me. "Okay, so there's a lot of pain in that statement."

"Black mother, white father. But I grew up in a pretty rough part of Detroit, where I wasn't black enough to be accepted. My hair is curly, but it's not like my mom's, or my friends' hair. I'm dark, but not dark enough. Then, when we moved up here, I wasn't white enough to be accepted either. And most of the kids I went to school with had known each other their whole lives, so I was always the outsider." I sigh. "It was hard."

"I can't imagine."

I shrug, a small roll of my shoulder. "It is what it is." I wave at him. "Back to the important part of all this."

"Which is what?"

"What you want. From me, from this marriage arrangement we've cooked up for ourselves."

Paxton doesn't respond for a long time. When he does, his voice is quiet and soft. "You were supposed to be a safe choice." He pauses again. "This is the part I'm worried will piss you off. You were the safe choice. Someone I couldn't see myself genuinely falling for."

"Because I'm not the appropriate choice. I'm poor, biracial, uneducated, uncultured, unsophisticated." I laugh. "I'm foul-mouthed, opinionated, stubborn, independent…"

"Beautiful, funny, easy to talk to, fun to be around," Paxton continues where I trailed off. "Sexy, smart, insightful." A brief pause, just a heartbeat. "Tempting. Intoxicating."

"Intoxicating?" I ask. "What am I, cheap tequila?"

He doesn't laugh at what I meant as a joke. "No, Makayla. You're the rarest whiskey." He swallows hard. "You were supposed to be the safe bet, easy to be fake married to, easy to let go when our marriage had served its purpose."

"But?"

"But now…?" He touches my cheek, a big rough palm ghosting across my cheekbone; thumb brushing through my curls over my temple. "Now I don't know anymore. There's nothing safe or easy about you."

"Well, I'm definitely not easy," I say with a laugh.

"That's not what I meant, Makayla."

I smile at him. "I know. I'm joking."

"Are you hiding behind humor?" he asks.

I close my eyes briefly, to get away from his piercing golden gaze. "Maybe."

"Don't. This is real."

"It can't be real, Paxton. It can't be. I don't belong in your world. I can't afford to fall for you."

"Why not?"

"Because I have abandonment issues, Paxton." I smile sadly. "My father was a rich white guy, and he abandoned me. He didn't want me. He didn't want Mom. He didn't want *us*."

"Thus your ingrained, automatic disdain for me and everything I represent."

I nod. "Exactly."

"What if I didn't abandon you?"

"I don't know how to trust that. I don't know how to emotionally get past the doubt. It's a big hang-up."

"I mean, I don't know shit about getting past emotional hang-ups, because god knows I've got enough of my own, but it seems to me that they are something we'd have to deal with one step at a time. You don't just get over this stuff."

"What if you're just saying all this to get me to sleep with you?"

He laughs. "Makayla. If I just wanted you to sleep with me, I'd have seduced you already."

I frown at him. "You say that like...like if you were to decide you wanted me, it would be a fore-gone conclusion. As if you seducing me was an auto-matic thing." I laugh. "Like I'd just drop my panties for you at the first glimpse of that thousand-watt grin of yours."

He gives me that exact grin, and my heart hammers. "This one?"

I try valiantly to hide my smile. "Yes, that one."

"It's more than just the smile, Makayla."

"Oh?"

"There's a whole art to it."

"To seducing women?"

"To seducing stubborn, hard to get women." He's grinning, a cat-ate-the-canary grin.

"Is there." If he's at all observant, he'll note the ice in my tone.

"Oh yeah. I've got it down to a science."

"Do you."

"You doubt me?" Wounded, almost.

"You think, if you turned on the charm and put your moves on me, that I would sleep with you, just like that?"

"I know you're attracted to me, Makayla."

"No," I say. "You know that I'm aware that you're an attractive person. It's hard to miss, and I've never denied that you are."

He smirks at me, and my eyes follow the movement of his mouth, the set of his lips, the shift of his eyes. I'm hyperaware of everything he does, in this moment. "That's true enough, I grant you. But you're also attracted to me."

"And that means I have no control over whether I want to sleep with you. I'm physically attracted to you, so I'm just going to lose all self-control, suddenly, and throw myself at you. Like, please, take me, Paxton?"

"Not that you have no self-control. You obviously do, and a shitload of it. But you say it like throwing yourself at me is the most far-fetched notion you've ever heard."

"What pisses me off is the assumption, Paxton. You're so fucking arrogant and presumptuous. Like, *of course* I'd sleep with you—if *you* chose to sleep with me, *of course* I would. I wouldn't be able to help myself."

"So, what you're saying is, if I did this…" He leans close, and sparks dance up and down my spine, crackling over my lips—all before he makes contact—and then, his lips touch mine, and fire sings through my veins, making me shake all over, making my blood race. "It wouldn't do anything to you?"

I manage to breathe again, somehow. "Nope," I lie, popping the *P* sound.

He smirks. "I see. You didn't stop me from kissing you, I notice."

"It was okay. Decent, as far as kisses go." I'm lying through my damn teeth—it was the best damn kiss I've ever experienced, and it lasted a fraction of a second.

I wonder if he can tell.

"Just decent?" He shakes his head. "That won't do. Can I get another chance? I'm sure I can do better."

I shrug, faking nonchalance. "Sure. Knock yourself out, champ."

He laughs. He sees through my bluff, and calls me on it. "Okay. Here we go—I'm gonna kiss you so hard your panties will all but fall off of their own accord."

His grin is so cocky, so confident, so arrogant and intoxicating and infuriating—he means it. He knows damn well that he's perfectly capable of doing exactly that.

"You ready, Makayla?" He gathers me in his arms, curls me against his big hard body, his arm wrapped behind my neck and shoulders, the other hand splayed against my cheek. "Here it comes."

I have plenty of time to push him off. To wriggle out of his hold. To tell him no, don't kiss me.

I do none of these things.

What I do, irresponsibly, is tilt my face up to his, and part my lips, and close my eyes. Luxuriate in the strong warmth and protection of his arms, and fall deliriously into the wild heat of his kiss. His mouth slashes across mine, and his lips claim me. There's no buildup, no touch of lips and pause, seek, dance, play—no, this is a sudden and all-out assault. He's leaning into me, not quite on top of me but nearly, and his tongue assails the inside of my mouth and tangles with my tongue, and I have never, ever, ever even conceived of anything like this. This isn't a kiss, it's mouth-sex. Tongue fucking. An oral claim. It's a kiss that says

*YOU—ARE—**MINE.***

My body is on fire, and the only way to extinguish the flames is Paxton. Yet, the more I kiss him, the hotter the fires burn. I press my thighs together to ease the ache between them caused by this kiss. It goes on, and on. His tongue plunderers my mouth, and his fingers brush into my hair, tangling and tugging, pulling, not quite yanking but definitely exerting control over me and this kiss via my hair. He has a double handful of my hair, actually, and now he is above me, hovering over me, his big body blocking out the moon and the starlight and everything, and—where are my hands?

Oh, there they are.

Ripping at his shirt. Pushing it up, and I'm the one to break the kiss just long enough to get the opening over his head, and then I'm seeking his mouth again, demanding he give me the kiss back. And oh, he does. My hands splay on his shoulders—his skin is hot to the touch, and the muscles in his back ripple. He is devouring me—kissing me as if this kiss is required to save my life. As if to stop this kiss is to stop breathing—and honestly, that sounds feasible. I am worried if I don't get more of him, more of this kiss, more of his hard muscles and firm flesh that I will die of lack, of asphyxiation, of need.

On, and on.

Until I'm gasping for breath and he's still kissing me.

He breaks away, and he's panting. I'm gasping, and my core is aching, and my breasts feel full and heavy and my nipples are hard beneath my bra. All of me needs *more*.

"There," he whispers. "How was that?"

I don't have what it takes to play the game anymore. He kissed the attitude out of me—kissed the defiance and stubbornness right out of my system. All that's left now is pure, raw, unadulterated desire.

Manic lust.

I blink away clouds of hazy confusion—the kiss was so intoxicating that I'm not sure for a moment who I am or where I am.

"Dammit, Paxton," I whisper.

He smirks, obnoxiously cocky, damningly beautiful; the arrogant, knowing wink is just over the top. "Gotcha."

"I'm still wearing my underwear," I manage.

He lifts up, looks down at me. "You're still fully dressed, as a matter of fact."

"So, you failed." I manage to find a tiny bit of sass left somewhere deep inside. "You promised my panties would fly off on their own."

"All but," he corrects. "What I said was they'd *all but* come off on their own."

"Oh."

"Yeah," he murmurs. "Important distinction."

"Still not seduced, though," I mutter.

Lies.

I am. I'm very much seduced. I want him. God, do I want him.

"You have to admit, though—that was a damn good kiss."

I sigh. "Yes, fine, whatever. It was pretty good."

I can't say it with a straight face, though—a giggle escapes.

"I love it when you laugh like that."

I cover my mouth with my hand. "I hate it. I'm not typically a giggly type of person."

He smiles, and this one is brilliant and warm and affectionate. "That's why I love it. It's cute, and sexy."

"A stupid, annoying giggle?"

He's leaning on an elbow, and now he rolls to lever over me. "Yes. A stupid, annoying giggle. Except it's not stupid or annoying, it's adorable and endearing and real and it makes me horny as hell."

I frown. "Me giggling makes you horny?" I laugh. "Weird, but okay."

"But then, everything about you turns me on, so…"

I stare up at him, and I realize I'm stroking his back with both hands, my palms roaming his shoulders and spine—I wasn't even aware I was doing it, but now that I am I'm drunk on how amazing his skin feels under my hands, and I want more.

I hate my clothes. I want them to go away. I want to be naked with him. I want to kiss him and not stop, I want to hold him against me, skin to skin, and feel his heartbeat and I want to taste his flesh and hear him moan my name.

I've wanted him for a long time.

I've been denying it, fiercely and stubbornly ignoring it and denying it.

I can't, anymore.

He's not an asshole.

He's not just a rich, entitled, spoiled playboy with no morals or redeeming qualities.

I mean, yeah, he's rich and spoiled, and a playboy.

But he has a lot of amazing qualities.

He kisses like a god.

He has the body of a god.

I can't hold out any longer. I can't resist him anymore. I just can't.

What's more, I don't want to.

I stare up at him, and there's no more sass, no more attitude, no more stubbornness—just me and him, a man and a woman…

Falling for each other.

"Dammit," I whisper.

He winks at me. "Gotcha."

I roll my eyes and groan. "Fine. Yes, you do."

He blinks. "Wait, what?"

I reach up, wrap my hand around the back of his neck and pull him down to me. "I said you got me." I whisper, lips moving against his. "Try to keep up, Paxton."

19

H E'S ABOUT TO SAY SOMETHING ELSE, AND I'M JUST not about talking anymore. I kiss him, to shut him up.

I tangle my fingers in his hair, something I've wanted to do since I first saw him—asleep in that bed, hair mussed and splayed against the crisp white pillow. I pull his face down to mine and lift up—it starts as me kissing him, and quickly becomes something else.

Something more.

Sometimes, a kiss is just a kiss—the first time, that's what it was, Paxton kissing me to prove a point.

Other times, a kiss is something more. It's a gateway drug to the heavy stuff.

This is one of those kisses.

Lips on lips at first, my fingers in his hair, his hand planted in the mattress on either side of me. Then he lowers himself to lean on one elbow and slides his arm under my neck to support my head, and rests his body against mine—giving me a portion of his weight. I have both hands free, and I use them to explore his body. No longer just shoulders—I touch his jaw, his cheekbones; trace his spine down to the waist of his pants, up his side. He's cupping my cheek, thumb rubbing my cheekbone and temple, and then he's clutching the back of my neck and deepening the kiss.

I'm on fire.

I need him—need more.

I want him to take over—to touch me. To strip me naked and kiss me delirious and make me scream.

But I don't have the words to say that—I'm too busy kissing him, something I suddenly can't seem to get enough of, something I don't dare stop doing for fear my heart will stop. Kissing him is my lifeline, right now, and it's all there is.

But I need more.

I press my hips up, flex them against his. I feel him—there's no mistaking that he wants more, too.

His desire is a thick, hard ridge between our bodies, separated by several layers.

But all he's doing is kissing me—his fingers tangle in my hair, and his tongue thrusts into my mouth and demands my tongue, but he's making a move to push this beyond kissing.

God, do I have to do everything?

"Pax…" I murmur, sadly breaking the kiss—and I feel my heart break a little as I lose the wonder of his mouth on mine. "Too many clothes."

He smirks. God, that smirk. "Me, or you?"

I reach between us, hunt for the tab of his zipper, or anything that will get me more of him. "Both."

I find the zipper, yank it down. Fumble at the button, and then finally the trousers sag open and he lifts up and yanks them down, and he kicks them off. Black briefs, stretchy cotton molded around trim hips and a bulging erection. I reach for them, too, but he grins, and pulls away.

"Ah ah ah," he says, capturing my hands in one of his. "My turn."

I bite my lower lip. "Oh, it's your turn is it?"

"Yes," he growls. "I've been dying for this moment since I first laid eyes on you in that idiotic maid outfit."

"It's the least flattering thing I could possibly have worn."

"I know," he says. "That's why I didn't realize how fucking gorgeous you are, at first. Then I saw you on the sidewalk in those workout clothes, and holy fuck, I almost crashed."

I snort. "You did not."

"Well, no. But I fought a monster hard-on all the way to my parents' house. Those fucking shorts, and that fucking bra? Goddamn, Makayla."

I roll my eyes. "It's comfortable to lift in. I don't wear clothes like that for attention."

"No shit. That's why it's so hot. You genuinely don't seem to care who thinks what of you, and you probably don't even realize how gorgeous you are."

I pull a face at him. "I know what I look like,

Paxton." I arch an eyebrow. "You don't grow up en-
dowed like I am and not understand the effect big
boobs have on the straight male populations of the
world."

He shakes his head, his eyes not moving from mine.
"No, Makayla. That's not what I mean." He cups my
face, kisses me, and pulls away again. "You're *beautiful*."

I blink, feeling caught by sudden emotions, for
some dumb reason. "Paxton, come on."

He shakes his head again. "You're incredible,
Makayla." A smirk, then, taking some of the serious-
ness out of the situation. "Also, boobs."

I laugh, a grateful snort. "Yeah, exactly. Boobs."
I can't do serious, right now. I want him, and I don't
want it to be all emotional.

He kisses my forehead, my cheekbone. "For real,
Makayla. You're the most beautiful woman I've ever
known." His kisses descend to my throat. "I've never
been so attracted to another human being in all my
life."

I let my hands curl around his neck and the back of
his head, following his descent, kiss by kiss. "Pax…"

"I've never wanted anyone the way I want you," he
says, kissing my shoulder blade.

He glances up at me, and then returns to kissing
and talking.

"I've never *needed* anyone the way I need you." He
says this, and then kisses the hollow under my throat.

My breath is coming in shallow gasps—he's

bringing his kisses lower, now, closer to the valley of my cleavage. I'm still fully clothed; what am I even wearing? Fitted jeans, and a sleeveless button-down shirt; I'd worn plain black pumps and a light suede bomber jacket with it. Under the sleeveless cotton-blend shirt, I'm wearing one of a series of bras Julie added to my wardrobe—I had to be fitted for a bra, and discovered I've been wearing the wrong size all of my adult life, the difference in comfort is remarkable. I wanted to just get a few more sports bras, but Julie put her foot down hard on that—they didn't have to be push-up demi-cup bras or anything ridiculous, but they had to be real, actual bras.

So, I'm wearing a bra that actually supports as well as shows off my cleavage, and it is down into this display that Paxton is slowly making his way.

Nowhere near fast enough for me.

I throw my head back and gasp as he nuzzles deeper into the *V* of flesh, kissing and nipping the skin. Then, he pauses. Looks up into my eyes. Waiting. Asking if I'm going to stop him.

I bite my lip, grin, lift my chest. It's all the encouragement Paxton needs—unhurriedly, he slips open the buttons, one by one from the top down, and his gaze rakes from my eyes to my chest and back, as if he can't decide where he wants to look more. I hold still, barely breathing. It takes an eternity and barely an instant at once—and then my shirt is draping open, revealing the black silk and lace enveloping and supporting my breasts, and the expanse of mounded flesh, and Paxton loses the war to gaze adoringly into my eyes...this is unsurprising, seeing as he's faced with my nearly bared cleavage.

I sit up, and he slips the shirt off, tosses it aside. He doesn't speak, and neither do I—words are unnecessary now. I reach up behind me, unclasp my bra, let the garment hang for a moment, arms crossed in front to keep the cups in place, my eyes locked on his. And then, with a grin and a flourish, I flick the bra away across the room.

Paxton gulps audibly. "Fuck me, Makayla."

I sit on his bed, hands resting on my knees, and let him look. I'm not shy, not hesitant. I like his eyes on me; I like the desire, the awe. He just looks for a long time, nearly a minute, and then he surges forward toward me, and I stay in place, let him come to me.

I expect him to take a handful, or two, but instead he wraps me in his arms and we're pressed together, chest to chest, skin to skin, and his mouth crashes against mine, tongue slashing into my mouth. We fall backward onto the bed, Paxton on top of me, his weight crushing me beautifully. I hook my legs around his and lock my arms around his neck and kiss him frantically, desperately, and now I can't help but need him, need more, more; I delve my hands between our bodies and shove at his underwear, fingers curling inside the elastic and pulling down. He lifts his hips and I tug the stretchy black undergarment off, and he kicks them away and yes, please, god yes he's naked, beautifully nude for me, and I push him over to his back so I can just look at him. I sit up, and he crosses his arms under his head and grins, and the cocky, arrogant, *I know I'm hot* look on his face is infuriating and intoxicating at the same time.

So—fucking—gorgeous.

Broad shoulders, flat hard pecs, bulging arms, corded forearms, rippled six-pack abs, narrow hips—a smattering of dark chest hair and a happy trail to the promised land...a massive erection. Thick, long, straight, standing up against his navel, straining, veined, a plump bulbous head.

"God, Paxton," I breathe. "You're incredible."

My hands splay over his chest and rake down over his diaphragm, tracing and dancing over his abs—however he captures my wrists before I can grasp his erection.

"First things first," he says. "I need you naked. I need to see the rest of you."

I shift up to sit on my knees, unbutton my jeans and shimmy them down, flip to my butt on the mattress and yank them off, turning them inside out in the process, and then I'm clad in nothing but a pair of gray cotton hipster underwear. I begin tugging them down, but Paxton stops me.

"Please," he says, his tone formal. "Allow me."

I lie back, lift my butt off the bed, and he slowly drags the last of my clothing down, peeling the underwear off me inch by inch. When they're clear of my toes, he drops off the edge of the bed and turns to me, eyes slowly and deliberately taking me in, head to toes and again and again, pausing here and there. Breasts, hips, core.

He licks his lips, sidles over to me, eyes sparking in a blaze of arousal. "We've been dancing around this attraction for a long time, Makayla," he says, taking my calf in his hands and teasing his fingertips up to my thigh, spreading my thighs apart in the process. "I'm not sure I'm capable of holding back any longer."

"Don't," I murmur.

"No?" He bends over my legs, touching his lips to the quads of my left thigh. "You don't want to take it slow?"

I shake my head, swallowing hard as he dances kisses over my thigh, then to the other leg, then across again, inching upward with each kiss. "Slow…bad," I breathe.

He grins. "Sounds like you're getting a little bothered, Makayla."

I gather his hair in my hands and guide him where I want him—he resists my efforts to hurry him closer to my core, instead taking his time getting there kiss by kiss. I growl as he laughs, and his eyes twinkle, sparkle, and snap. Finally, his kisses land on my hipbones, one and then the other, and I'm barely breathing, fingers knotted in his hair, hips lifting—my core is questing, seeking his lips.

"Not shy about what you want, are you?" he says.

I shake my head. "Nope. Now that I've given up trying to resist you, I fucking want you, Paxton. So bad. Worse than I've ever wanted a man in my life."

"Is that so?" He says this with a smirk, kneeling between my outspread thighs, hands cradling my hips. "You want me?"

My eyes blaze, meeting his. "Don't play, Pax. You know I do. You've always known I do."

A shrug, an arched eyebrow. "I don't know, Makayla. You do play a pretty good game of hard to read." He pauses to kiss me just below my navel, then lower. And lower. I gasp, arch my hips, straining upward. "Sometimes I wondered if you even liked me as a person, much less felt attraction for me."

I play with his hair, both hands buried in it, tangling, knotting, smoothing. "That was a tactic. Trying to make myself believe I wasn't crazy about you. If I acted like I couldn't stand you as a person, it was easier to pretend I wasn't wildly attracted to you, physically."

"Did it work?"

I shrug. "For a while. Then, no. The more I got to know you, especially seeing you work at the meetings and dinners and cocktail mixers, the more I saw that there's a lot more to you than I was giving you credit for."

"And now?"

"Now?" I bite my lip, eyes on his. "Now, I just want this. I want us. I want…" I pause to fight for breath, for words. "More than I thought I wanted."

Paxton's mouth hovers over my core, his eyes on mine—golden brown, heated, aroused, hungry. "I feel like I could lose myself in you, and never come back."

"Is that good or bad?" I ask.

He huffs a laugh. "I don't even know. It's scary."

I brush a thumb over his lips. "Can we talk about this after?"

He grins. "I love the way you think."

I watch him as he lowers his mouth—but he misses my center. Instead, his lips nuzzle the tender, silk-soft, sensitive flesh just between inner thigh and the delicacy of my sex. A tongue flick, a nibbling kiss. Then the other side. I breathe rapidly, quake all over, expecting his tongue and the heat of his mouth on my sex any moment, needing it more than I've ever needed anything. I could forgo breathing to get his mouth on me. I gasp, whimper, watching him continue to tease me, lips dancing over my thighs and navel and pubis, everywhere except where I want it.

"Paxton!" I cry out. "Please."

He laughs. "God, you're sexy when you beg."

I snarl. "Quit messing around, Paxton."

He meets my eyes, smirking. "Fine. But on one condition."

I just blink at him. "Condition? Really?"

"It's an easy one." He slides up my body, and I feel his straining erection gliding and stuttering against my thigh as he hovers over me, lips centimeters from mine. "You call me Pax from now on. Just Pax."

"All the time, or when we're alone?"

"All the time. Everyone calls me Paxton." His smile is tender. "I've always been Paxton, the full name. You've called me Pax a few times, now, and I...I really like it."

I can't help but feel special. "All right...Pax." I cup his cheeks. "Now, Pax...please. *Please.*"

"Please what?" he teases.

I glare at him. "Don't."

He shifts down my body, grinning at me. "Fine. No more teasing." He comes to a halt between my thighs, and I let my legs splay apart for him.

His eyes lock onto my sex, and his eyes darken with aroused heat. "So fucking beautiful." A glance at me as he palms my belly with both hands, and then his touch grazes down, framing my core. "You know how often I've fantasized about this?"

I shake my head. "I didn't know you've fantasized about me."

He smirks. "I have. A lot. I tried not to, but I couldn't help it."

I run my hands over his arms, his shoulders, his back, touching the burly, rippling muscle. "Well, Pax, here I am, live and in person, and all for you." I gaze at him with hooded lids, expectant. "What are you going to do with me?"

"Make you scream," he murmurs. "Long, and loud."

"Prove it."

He buries his mouth against my core, tongue flicking fast against my sensitive center, the tiny nub of nerves assaulted by a frenzy of tongue-lashing licks. I cry out, unashamed, wanton—lift my hips to press hard against his mouth, and his hands curl under me, grab my ass and hold me. I rest against his hold, back arched, hips flexing. It's zero to one hundred in seconds flat, so aroused by all the teasing and needing that when he finally does lap at me with his talented tongue, I'm there in moments. Whimpering, gasping, crying out, shifting against his mouth and now I'm grinding harder and faster as his mouth works up to a quaking climax. I teeter on the edge, and then fall over and he doesn't relent, devours me through it and the orgasm is a whirlwind of heat and pressure, ripping me apart and drowning me, flinging me to heaven and splintering me to pieces. Wave after wave of ecstasy soars through me, and I am screaming, as promised, and I don't hold back, don't try to quiet myself. I don't care. I want him to know how he makes me feel, and I show him.

When I'm shaking all over and can't come any harder, can't breathe and can't stop trembling, I push him away and roll him to his back and wipe his face with my hands—his mouth and stubble and lips are gleaming with my essence. I laugh, wiping my now-smeared hand on the comforter, then leaning over him, and he doesn't hesitate to kiss me. I take my time with this kiss, taking his breath for my own, because

I'm still breathless, still shaking. He feels me shaking, and laughs through the kiss.

He stops laughing when I reach down and grasp his erection in my fist. "Ohh, fuck."

I grin at him, my head resting on my propped-up hand. "My turn."

His grin vanishes, turns to a frown of concentration. "God, Makayla. Feeling you touch me is…"

"What?" I prompt.

"Better than I'd dreamed it could feel."

I stroke his length; roll my thumb over the weeping tip. "This is as beautiful as the rest of you."

"I have a confession to make," he mutters, teeth gritted as I slowly glide my hand up and down.

"What's that?"

"I've fantasized about this too." He closes his eyes. "Touched myself, wishing it was you."

"I didn't dare," I say. "If I let myself do that, I'd have to admit I wanted you, and I was trying like hell he to keep that from happening."

"I couldn't stop it. I haven't been with anyone in a long time. Not since before we met. Well before. I'd spent most of the spring and summer working pretty much nonstop to get that bill drafted so we could put it up for a vote as soon as we reconvene." He's talking as I caress him, watching my hand move over him, and there's something bizarrely intimate about making conversation while doing something so sexual and arousing. "The party you cleaned up was to celebrate finishing the draft. Two of my colleagues who worked with me on it are Republicans, and the donkey was their way of teasing me over being a Democrat."

I nod, head still propped up on my hand, elbow planted in the mattress. "So all those strippers and hookers?"

He shakes his head, annoyed. "My friends were nagging at me for working too hard and not taking any time to date or hook up, and they figured if they brought those women in, it'd help me loosen up. I was super tense over the whole thing."

I add a twist to my hand's movement—slide up slowly, twist around the head, plunge down. "I see."

"Point is, I was…tense. It's been a long time since I've… you know. With anyone. Months—an eternity for me. And then I met you, and I was hot for you. Then I saw you on the street—and I admit I'd been driving around looking for you, hoping to find you, which seemed like a futile, stupid idea, but then I got lucky." A laugh. "And you were dressed for a workout, and I…" A sigh. "Oh god, that was it. I was gone for you."

I frown at him. "Really? Then?"

He nods. "Wanted you so bad." A pause, his hips flexing upward. "Feels fucking *so* good, Makayla. Don't stop."

I smile at him lazily. "Just try to stop me."

He breathes out, relieved, but it's shaky from arousal. "I fought my attraction to you. But then I visited you at your apartment, to ask you what I asked you, and you were in those pj's, and I got that quick little glimpse of your boob, and those shorts were so short and so tight and every time you turned around I couldn't help staring at your ass." His eyes meet mine. "The next time I was in the shower, I—I couldn't help thinking about how you looked in those pj's, that little glimpse of your boob, and your ass, and I...I..."

I grin at him. "You what, Pax?"

"I jerked it, thinking about you," he says, pausing to gasp and flex his hips. "Trying to imagine it was you touching me."

I bite my lip. "Was it good?"

"Not as good as this."

I laugh. "I hope not."

I can't take it anymore. I've been watching myself caress his huge hard length, stroking the silky, steel-hard thickness. Watching the essence weep out of the slit at the tip, watching the veins pulse, watching his monster arousal strain and slick through my fingers, and I need him. I want him. I want to taste him. I want to take him into my mouth and lick his salty essence away and make him snarl and groan and call out my name and make him need me and lose control—

I don't give him any warning, I just pounce. His eyes are closed as he lets himself drown in my touch, and when I bend over him and take him into my mouth, he flinches, gasps in shock, and then groans, lifting his hips and burying his hands in my curls, knotting his fists in my hair.

"Ohhhhh fuck, Makayla, fuck fuck fuck—" He stops breathing as I swirl my tongue, back away, and plunge deep again, and then he catches his breath and lets out a snarl of pleasure. "God*damn*, Makayla."

He flexes, drives his hips up, pushing into my mouth, pulling at my hair—not hard, just enough to show me how much he likes this and how much he wants it, needs it, and I like that hair pull. And then his movement grow shaky and uncontrolled, and I know he's close, and I wonder if he's going to let me take him all the way there.

I want to. I want to know his taste. I want to know what him losing control feels like, looks like.

But I want him inside me, too.

He answers the debate for me, via the expedient method of yanking me away at the last second and rolling to his knees with a low, primal growl. His erection is gleaming with my saliva and his essence, dripping, straining, heaving with his panting breaths. He's on his knees, and every muscle in his body is tensed, straining, his jaw is clenched, and he's breathing hoarsely.

Suddenly, playtime is over. He's a predator, and I'm his prey.

I widen my eyes, and wait.

When he has control once again, he relaxes a little—and then prowls toward me on all fours, crawling across the bed to reach me. His mouth dances up my belly, between my breasts, and then his lips latch onto my breast and his tongue sears around my nipple and I'm gasping, suddenly wild and breathless with the unexpected but oh so welcome assault, and his hand is toying with my other breast, cupping and kneading, and he switches back and forth, his mouth dancing from breast to breast, switching hands, so he always has both of my breasts. I arch my back into him, moaning at the wet sucking heat of his mouth over my nipples, which are hard, standing on end and singing with blasting intensity. I cup his head with my hands and wrap my legs around his thighs, and I feel his erection stuttering against my thigh and then nudging against my core, and I need him inside me, need, need, need.

I gather him in my hands, bring the head of him to my opening, spear his springy hardness against my throbbing center, and he moans around a mouthful of my breast.

"Condom," I gasp. "Pax, condom. Now. Please."

He growls, shifting aside to rummage in a drawer of his bedside table. Digs out a brand-new box, rips it open, tosses it aside with a string in his hand. I take the string, tear a packet free, toss the string onto the table, rip the packet open with my teeth, toss the packet aside with the condom in my fingers. Pax watches this, and his grin is pleased and humorous and aroused and complicated and passionate and wild and fierce with need.

"That was hot as fuck," he murmurs.

I grip his erection in one hand and roll the condom on with the other, and then haul him toward me, using his shaft as a handle. "Come here," I say, my voice just above a whisper. "I need you, Pax. Please."

He braces his hand beside my face, and I twist my head to the side, kiss his forearm—guide him to me. Splay my thighs open, heels digging into my buttocks to accept all of him between my legs. He's huge, hovering over me, his shoulders blocking out the room beyond, so there's only him, only us. I nestle him at my opening, and our eyes meet, a tense, fraught moment before he enters me.

"Makayla..." he whispers. "This feels like...like we're crossing into something important."

I caress his back, cup his cheek, palm his buttocks—hard, dusted with hair. "We are."

"It won't be just sex."

"It was never going to be," I say. "Especially not now."

"No, especially not now." He hesitates, still, swallowing hard. "I'm falling for you, Makayla. I've already fallen for you. I'll never want anyone but you, never want anything but this. It's scary as fuck, but it's true."

"I know," I whisper, and then grin up at him. "Are you about to tell me you love me as you go inside me?"

He grins back. "I might. How would you feel about that?"

I gasp as he flutters his hips, teasing little thrusts into me. "I...oh god, I don't know. It'd be new. I might be okay with it, but you—oh god, Pax—you never know."

He's toying with me, and himself, drawing out the moment. I'm not having it. I curl a hand around his nape and slam my lips onto his and slash my tongue against his and hook my heels around his waist and push up against him, taking him inside me in a quick hard thrust, gasping a whimper into the kiss as I'm spread apart by his thick hard length. He spears into me, fills me, and it burns so beautifully, splitting me into quaking pieces.

"Oh *fuck*, Makayla," he growls, "Jesus, woman!"

"Tell me, don't tell me—whatever," I snap. "I need you. I'm done fucking waiting."

He buries his face in my breasts, one hand cupping them and playing with him, bringing one to his mouth and he groans. "Thank fuck, oh god, thank fuck— you feel...I can't even describe how amazing you feel, Makayla."

"Perfect," I grit out. "It's perfect."

He takes over the rhythm, pushing into me, driving deep, mouthing my nipples, pinching, nipping, licking, gasping hoarsely as he moves into me. It's slow, deliberate. Gentle, but fierce. I arch my back and lock my heels around his waist, clinging to him and writhing against him and meeting him thrust for thrust.

"Pax," I moan, head thrown back, throat bared. "God, so fucking good."

He moves, driving deep in slow rough thrusts, each one starting slow and gentle in a delicate slide through my nether lips, and then as he fills me he finishes with a rough upward flick of his hips, and every time he does this some part of him slams hard and beautiful against my throbbing clit and I scream out, cling harder to him, thrust harder against him, meet his movements with my own, taking all of him and demanding more.

"Pax!" I cry, nearly weeping now with blinding ecstasy, a climax unlike any other building inside me. "More, please, more! Harder!"

He obeys—harder. Faster. His hands brace in the mattress beside my face, and he focuses on thrusting now.

"Look at me, Makayla," he snarls. "Eyes on mine."

My eyes snap open, fix on his. He's all lion, now, those big deep golden eyes primal and fierce, wild and hungry. "I'm looking, Pax."

"You feel how perfect we are together?"

I nod, gripping his flexing buttocks. "I feel it."

"You're mine, Makayla." He thrusts, eyes fixed, fierce. "*Mine.*"

I nod again, not letting go of him, pulling at his buttocks to urge him on. "Yes, Pax. I'm yours." I move with him, shaky, trembling, teetering on the edge. "And you're mine."

He rests his forehead against mine, as if hearing that took a weight off him. "Yours. All yours. Only yours," he whispers against my lips. "Never wanted that. Now I do. I want to be yours."

"Good, because you are," I murmur to him. "And I won't share you."

"You won't have to."

His lips caress mine, and then he sucks my nipple into his mouth and thrusts hard into me, and I feel him clenching, feel him shaking as he nears his edge, feel him start to lose the rhythm. I cradle his beautiful face between my breasts and wrap my thighs around his waist and hook my heels around his ass and meet him hard and fast, pumping recklessly against his hard crashing throbbing erection, and I'm crying with the wild fury of this, the emotions of it, the intensity of it, the earth-shaking, life-changing power of being joined with Paxton.

His voice is shaky, tremulous. "Makayla…" he gasps. "Mack…"

I sob. "Say my name, Pax, call me Mack again." I bite his earlobe, grinding into him. "Call me Mack while you come inside me."

I feel it. Feel him come. "Mack! Mack, oh god, Mack…" He lets go, and I hear the desperation in his growling, groaning.

His orgasm triggers mine. I come, and I come—clamping around his driving erection, spasming around him as he comes. "Pax!"

His eyes are on me. "With me, Makayla?" I've never seen such open vulnerability in a man's expression before. He's utterly shaken by this. Destroyed, as I am.

"I'm with you, Paxton," I breathe, still orgasming so hard it's difficult to form words.

He nuzzles the side of my throat, and I breathe

in his scent, feel his shoulders moving, feel the slow rough desperate slide of him through my juddering, squeezing core, feel his hard hips slam again mine, feel his powerful arms around me, sheltering me, feel his breath on my skin, feel him give me all of him—heart, soul, body, giving himself to me in way I didn't know was possible, in a way I never anticipated anyone giving himself to me.

He doesn't say it—and I'm glad. It would have been too much. I couldn't have handled that, not on top of the intensity of this.

I see it, though. It's in his melting golden-brown eyes as they meet mine, in every line of his face, in the way he goes weak and limp as our mutual climax fades, leaving us shaken and shaking.

He collapses on me, and I hold him there, heels hooked around the back of his knees, fingers tracing lazy circles on his back as he gasps against my breasts.

"Makayla," he whispers.

"Ssshhhh," I whisper, stroking his hair. "Let it be."

"Crushing you," he mutters.

I can't help but kiss his temple. "Yes. I love it."

He's buried inside me, still, and I won't let him move. "I don't want to fall asleep on you, but I just might, in about ten seconds."

I brush his hair away from his temple, scratch his back. "You can. I'd like it if you did."

He inhales deeply, breathing me in. "Never felt this way before. Not even close."

"Me either."

"Don't hurt me, Makayla," he whispers. "You're getting a part of me I've never opened up for anyone before. Scares the shit out of me."

I don't quite sob, but it's a near thing. "Same."

"Yeah?"

"Yeah," I say, laughing-sobbing-whispering.

I cradle him to me, and our breathing synchs, and his weight is a crushing burden I love more than anything, and I feel him fall asleep, and I drift off myself.

20

I WAKE ALONE IN THE BIG BED, NAKED, COLD FROM DRIED sweat, on top of the blankets, sore between my thighs and aching with a renewed need.

A soft, mournful song is being played on the piano.

I lie, listening for a few moments, and then rise, not bothering with clothing. Follow the music to the piano.

Paxton—white basketball shorts, shirtless, muscles gleaming and moving in the dim light, eyes closed, fingers moving on the keys with effortless grace. He plays a simple song, sad and slow. He leans forward, head bowing, playing with deep emotion.

I stand behind him, listening as he plays.

After a few minutes, the song ends, and his fingers come to rest on the keys, stilling.

I settle my hands on his shoulders; move to stand flush against his bare spine. He rests his head against my belly, and my hands splay now on his chest.

"That was beautiful," I whisper.

"Thanks." He doesn't move. "I composed it."

"Really?"

A nod. "I discovered piano sophomore year of high school. Sort of by accident."

"Tell me?" I ask.

He remains as he is, head against my belly, his hands covering mine over his chest. "Told you I was a troubled kid, and a troublemaker. Well, at the boarding school, I was always cutting class. I was bored stupid, and just didn't care. I was roaming the school one afternoon—I was supposed to be in math class. I came across an old grand piano in a corner of some old room. Mom had forced me to take lessons as a kid, like when I was eight or nine. I hated it then but, for some reason, I was drawn to that piano. It was dusty and out of tune, clearly forgotten. Sort of...a kindred spirits thing. I felt forgotten, you know? Sent off to live at a boarding school, no friends, no family. Like that piano." A pause. "I sat down and starting plunking at it. Seeing if I could remember anything I'd learned as a kid. A teacher heard, and came to see who it was. The teacher was Mrs. Lewis. Old as dirt, half-blind, mostly senile, but so sweet. Taught music, which was the blow-off class. No one paid attention. Well, she listened, and instead of making me go back to class, she started teaching me. I cut math class twice more, and she showed up, taught me more. Eventually, she said she'd keeping teaching me, but only if I went to math. Why, I don't know, but I did. She was nice to me in a way most adults weren't, and I guess that meant something to me. So I went to math, and met her after class.

Those lessons with Mrs. Lewis were the only thing I took seriously. Piano became an escape for me."

"I admit, it's unexpected."

He laughs. "No shit." He touches the keys with one hand. "Mom doesn't even know I play."

"Really?"

A laugh. "It's for me. You're the only one who knows."

"So you kept up with it after being sent to military school, too?"

A nod. "Yeah. I went to the dean, told him it was important to me, and that if he'd make room for me to take lessons, I'd cooperate. He had my record from the boarding school, and figured the best way to keep the peace was to go along with it. So he got me private lessons, paid for by my parents under the general expenses of the academy, and I didn't make trouble." A laugh. "I kept up with lessons through college, and graduate school. I still practice two or three times a week, sometimes more."

"Is it still the escape for you?"

He nods. "Absolutely. It's how I process things— emotions, problems, big decisions."

"What are you processing now?" I ask.

He sits forward, and I let go of him. He spins around on the bench, sees that I'm still naked, and his eyes flare, widen, heating. He captures my ass in his hands, chin on my diaphragm, eyes turned up to lock on mine. "Us."

"That's something to process?"

He nods, chin bobbling against into my belly. "Yeah." A silence. "I'm falling in love with you, Makayla. And…I don't know how to be in love. I don't know what that means, or how to do it."

I swallow hard, fingers in his hair. "Me either." I want to look away, because the honesty and vulnerability in his eyes are almost hard to see, in a man otherwise so strong and arrogant and dominant. "I'm falling in love with you too, and it scares the shit out of me."

"How did this happen, Makayla?"

I shake my head. "I don't know. I really don't."

"The thing that makes it feel…more real, I guess, is that I was falling in love with you before we slept together."

I laugh. "I know. I think I gave up the fight to not sleep with you mainly because I knew I was falling for you, and it seemed stupid to be in love with you and not sleep with you."

His hands knead my backside, caressing and exploring. "That does seem silly, doesn't it?"

I brush at his hair. Cup his cheek. "Very silly."

He blinks up at me, smirks. "Will you do something for me?"

I shrug. "Sure. What?"

"Stay here, just like this, for ten seconds."

I chuckle. "Okay, easy enough."

He leaves the bench, heading for the bedroom. "Ten seconds. Don't move."

He's as good as his word, and returns in moments, resuming his seat on the bench, hands playing with my buttocks, chin resting on my diaphragm.

"What did you do?" I ask.

He shrugs. "You'll find out soon enough."

"Fine, have your secrets, then," I say.

He stares up at me for another long moment, and then his hand slides down from my ass to my thigh, and he gently lifts and settles my left foot on the bench. He nudges my thigh away, opening me. I gasp, hiding a smile, keeping my fingers in his hair.

"Yeah?" he murmurs.

"Yes, please."

He needs no more encouragement. His tongue finds my wet center, and soon he's not just tasting me, teasing me, but lashing me to a frenzy. He holds me in place with his hands on my ass, squeezing, clutching, pulling me tighter against his mouth, and I ride his face to an orgasm I can't even breathe through, coming apart so hard under his mouth that I nearly collapse.

He reaches into his pocket and produces a condom, makes quick work of rolling it on. I wait, and then grasp him in one hand, guide him to me, nestle his thick erection at my opening, staring down at him with my lower lip caught in my teeth, heart caught in my throat, eyes welling with emotion.

I sink down on him, and we both groan at the same time.

He leans back against the piano keys, and I grip

his shoulders as he holds my ass and lifts me up. I rise on him, and he lifts, and his mouth sears against my breasts, and then he lets me fall, and I slam down hard, and his grunt is rough and hoarse.

There is no rhythm to this—it's hard, rough, fast. Uncontrolled. He grunts, and I scream. I moan, and he snarls. I whimper, and he whispers my name.

It's quick. Fresh off of one orgasm, it takes me less than half a dozen thrusts of his huge beautiful erection inside me to bring me to the cusp again, and our eyes are locked on each other, moving together, in thrall with one another. I rake my fingernails down his chest as I come, leaving eight parallel red tracks on his skin, and I growl his name in my throat again and again as I fall into pieces on top of him. He thrusts through my climax, each movement drawing clanking, tin-kling notes from the piano as his back moves against the keys. His eyes never leave mine, and I rise and fall on him through my climax and to his own—slamming harder on him to bring it out of him. To get more and more. To make him come harder and harder, until our joining is a syncopated symphony of tinkling piano keys and slapping flesh and ecstasy-lost voices.

When he comes, I feel him fill the condom, and bury his face between my breasts. I'm writhing against him until we're both sweaty again, and frantic.

Finally, we're both done, and I rest my cheek on the top of his head, and his face is still buried in my cleav-age, and I think he would live there if he could.

I lift up, pressing my breasts together around his face, laughing. "You like my boobs, I take it."

He groans, nuzzling them. "Love 'em." He replaces my hands with his, cupping them. "They're the best. Literally, the best, ever."

"Well, they're yours now."

"Not yet they aren't." He stares up at me. "I know it sounds crazy, and maybe it is, considering how we feel. But, Makayla, I don't want you to marry me for the arrangement anymore. It would've worked if we were two strangers who only sort of tolerated each other." A pause. "But now that I know we're falling in love, marrying this soon seems kind of..."

I put my fingers over his mouth. "I still want to."

A slow blink. "You do?"

I nod. "It's still crazy, and honestly crazier than it was when it was supposed to be a fake thing, and temporary. But I want to."

He sucks in a deep breath. "Would you still want it to be temporary?"

I shake my head. "No, Pax, I wouldn't."

A grin. "Funny enough, I think this will piss off Mom more than anything else could."

"So win-win all around?" I laugh. "Get married, keep your family connections, plus you get a wife who actually loves you, *and* piss off your mom."

He blinks hard. "Wife."

I choke. "Husband."

"You'll say I do?"

I nod. "And I'll mean it. It's batshit crazy, Pax. I mean, agreeing to marry you for what amounted to financial reasons was crazy enough. *Wanting* to marry you when I've known you for a matter of months is even crazier."

He rubs the tops of my thighs. "You really want to?"

I nod.

"Why?" he asks.

I shrug. "It's hard to put it into words." A pause as I think. "I've worked nonstop my whole life. Done the responsible thing. Been the breadwinner, the hardest worker in the room, the one willing to take extra shifts. I've never had a serious boyfriend because I haven't had time. I haven't been willing to let myself fall for anyone, because I couldn't handle the thought of him leaving me the way my father did, and because if I got my heart broken, I'd fall apart, and Mom needed me too much to let that happen." Another pause. "I've always done the responsible thing, the selfless thing. It's all been for her, for Mom. This would be for me. It's reckless, it's crazy, it's probably kind of stupid, but I want it. I want you. I want us. I want to do this because it's selfish."

"Does she know?"

I nod. "She told me to give you a chance. To do something for me."

"Then it's not selfish. It's taking care of yourself, for once." He smiles at me. "You just have to let me take care of you."

"You want to take care of me?" I ask.

He nods. "Very much."

"Then give me a bath, feed me, fuck me again, and then sleep with me."

A grin spreads across his face. "I think that sounds like you taking care of me."

"Exactly."

That's exactly what he does: he draws me a hot bath, and we soak together in the scalding hot water until we're sweaty, and then we rinse off in his shower.

Or, at least, it starts out like that.

What really ends up happening is I get greedy. He gets worked up in the shower, scrubbing me with a bar of soap, and I can't help but notice.

When I'm clean, I take the soap from him, lather him up starting at his shoulders, working my way down. Slowly, I scrub his chest, and then his abs, and then of course to get his thighs and ass clean, I have to go down to my knees.

I grin up at him. "I mean, since I'm down here..." I murmur.

His eyes widen. "Makayla, Jesus, you're insatiable."

I stroke him with both hands, eyes on his. "You have no idea."

I take him into my mouth, and he gulps loudly. "I think I'm getting the message."

The only way to really communicate the enormous

intensity of my reawakened sex drive is to show him, and so I do. Slowly, at first, and then more vigorously. I take him deeper, using my mouth more and my hands less, and I don't let him put me off, even though he tries to tell me I don't need to do this, he doesn't expect it, he'd rather be inside me.

I ignore him.

He cups my cheeks, forcing me to stop. "Makayla. Shit—stop. I want you. I need to be inside you."

I let him slip out of my mouth. "You are inside me," I murmur.

"Not what I meant."

"You'll get that again too." I smirk up at him, my grin teasing and arrogant. "Can't keep up, Paxton?"

I stroke him with both hands, waiting for his answer.

The water is lukewarm, but I don't care.

"I can keep up. I can take everything you have to give, and still want you again."

"Everything I have to give?" I echo.

He nods. "Everything."

"Then what I want to give you is this," I say, and plunge my mouth down around him again.

He groans, falling backward against the marble, hips tipped forward. "Fuck, Mack. Okay, okay. It feels too good to make you stop anyway."

He takes a lot longer, this time, and I'm okay with that. I take my time, hands and mouth slow and soft around his thick manhood, tasting his essence, feeling him throb and hearing him gasp. He reaches down, takes my hands in his, and we tangle fingers, and it's only my mouth now, taking him and sucking and licking and feeling him tense and throb until he's gasping helplessly.

I taste his release on my tongue, and he whispers my name raggedly through it, using every ounce of his restraint to hold still and let me take him to the end of his ecstasy.

When he's finished, I let him fall free of my mouth, and he's dangling limp, and his breathing is harsh, and the water has gone cool, I smile up at him.

"Jesus, Makayla," he gasps. I stand up, and he turns off the water.

He wraps me in a towel, and takes another for himself, and then leads me to the bedroom and I lie down, the towel around my body.

"What was that for?" he asks, sitting on the bed beside me.

I shrug. "I wanted to."

"Why?

I blush. "I saw you. In the bed at your mom's hotel. You were naked, and I was going to clean the room. You weren't entirely covered by the sheets, and…" I bite my lip. "And you were having a morning erection."

He grins. "I *knew* you'd seen something."

"Oh, I saw something all right." I groan. "It's haunted me ever since."

"Haunted you? Why?"

"Because the first thing I thought when I saw that monster cock of yours was how much fun it would be to blow a man hung like you." I can't help the grin. "I squashed the thought real fucking fast, but I thought it."

"And?" He smirks at me. "Is it everything you'd hoped it would be?"

"All that I'd hoped it would be, and more."

He leans over me, kisses me. "Now, I feed you."

The next hour or so, we chat and snack, lounging in his bed, naked but for towels—our bed, I realize.

I'm sleepy, and Paxton brings me up against his side, snuggles me close, my head on his chest. I'm still horny, still ready for more, for him, but my body has other ideas.

"I still want you," I murmur.

He laughs. "I'm not going anywhere."

I force my eyes open to meet his. "Neither am I."

I wiggle my towel off, toss it aside, and he does the same, and then he settles the thick comforter on us, and I rest my head on his chest and our fingers are tangled and I hear his heart beating under my ear, and it's all almost too much.

"Makayla, I—"

I reach up, touch his mouth. "Shush. Not yet."

He laughs past my fingers. "No?"

I shake my head sleepily. "No." I twist my face to kiss his skin where shoulder and chest meet. "Too sleepy. Too emotional. Too worn out." I gaze blearily up at him. "I'm not ready for that, yet."

He nods. "Okay. But it's true."

I nod. "I know." I kiss his chest again. "For me, too."

He sighs. "I like having you in my bed."

"Good. I'm moving in with you in the morning."

He chuckles. "You already did move in," he says. "And it is morning."

"I meant into your room." I peek at the window—dawn blushes against a gray-black sky. "Can you stay in bed with me?"

He nods. "I'll stay."

"Paxton?" I ask.

A silence. "Mmmm?"

"Thank you."

"For what?"

"What you're doing for Mom. You don't have to."

"Want to."

"Why?"

"Because I can. It's something…meaningful…that I can give you." He exhales harshly. "Stuff, no matter how expensive, doesn't seem to matter to you. It's all just stuff. This is something that means something."

I cling to him more tightly, draping myself on him. "You get me."

"I do."

I laugh. "I do."

He snickers. "Soon."

"What can I give you that's meaningful to you, Pax?"

A long silence; I wonder if he's fallen asleep without hearing my question, but then he groans, a sleepy sound of tenderness. "Already did."

"Blowjobs don't count," I say with a snort.

He shakes his head drowsily. "Not that." His eyes find mine, so sleepy. "You. Your heart. Being here. Staying here with me."

"Good," I say. "Because that's all I have to give."

"I have everything else, Mack," he murmurs. "Love, affection, tenderness...those are the only things I can't buy."

"Pax—"

He groans. "If you don't shut up and go to sleep, I'm going to say it." I close my mouth with an audible snap, and he huffs a laugh. "Good. Now sleep."

"Yes, dear," I mutter.

21

NEW YORK CITY. ONE P.M. A FLURRY OF PEOPLE buzz around me, curling, blow-drying, and putting my hair into an elaborate updo, applying makeup, doing my nails, affixing fake eyelashes.

Wedding day.

Camilla has tried to barge in at least six times, and each time she has been rebuffed by Liam and his army of bodyguards, who are being paid by Paxton rather than Camilla, and so are immune to her anger, threats, and attempted bribes.

I can hear her outside now, berating the door guards.

"—my wedding, I'm paying for it, and you damn well better let me in—"

I snicker. "How long do you think she's going to stay out there yelling?" I ask my nail technician.

She shrugs. "I have no idea." Her eyes widen. "I did her nails once. She scares the hell out of me."

I grin. "Would you believe I used to be a maid in her hotel?"

The technician stops, staring at me. "No way, really?"

I nod. "Really."

"And now you're marrying Paxton?"

I grin even more widely. "I know, right? I feel like Cinderella." I wiggle my bare foot. "Hopefully I don't turn back into a pumpkin."

She laughs. "I don't think that's how the fairy tale goes."

After an hour and a half of glam squad prep, the team leaves, and I'm alone for a blessed moment, in nothing but a thin silk dressing gown, waiting for Julie to arrive with my dress—she did some last-minute alterations to it, and she is still on the way here with it.

The door opens behind me, and I turn expecting Julie. Instead, it's Paxton. "I wanted to catch you before you put your dress on," he says.

I give him a tender smile; he's incredible in his tuxedo—he'd better be, though, considering it's a bespoke Kiton three-piece. "You look delicious," I tell him.

He kneels in front of me. "Thank you." He bites his lip. "I realized something, late last night, or early this morning."

"What's that?" I ask, touching his stubble with my fingertips.

He hesitates. "A hundred and sixteen days ago, we agreed to marry each other, as a business arrangement, more or less."

I nod. "I remember."

"And then things changed." He blinks hard. "I fell in love with you." He still hasn't said it—I won't let him. I told him I don't want him to say it until we're married.

I cup his cheek. "Save it for the vows, honey."

He shakes his head, gazing up at me earnestly, seriously, desperately. "Is this still what you want?"

"Yes, without a doubt."

"Absolute truth? You've considered it long and hard?"

I nod, wondering where he's going with this. "I barely slept last night, asking myself that. Do I want to marry him? Do I really? I've known him for four months." I bite my lip to keep the emotion at bay. "I want this, Pax."

He reaches into the inner pocket of his tuxedo, brings out a ring box. "Then I have one more question for you, Makayla." He opens it—inside is a diamond engagement ring, twin round diamonds set in delicate, intricate platinum filigree, the band encrusted with countless scintillating tiny stones, each enormous stone at least two full carats. "Will you marry me?"

I laugh, tip my head back and sniffle, reaching for Kleenex to dab at my tear-filled eyes. When I have something like control, I look at him, and I laugh. "An hour before the ceremony, you ask me."

He laughs, too, equally emotionally fraught. "I know. I just realized we'd made an agreement and just went along with my mom's plan. But I never actually asked you, and you don't have a ring, and I want this to be real, even if it is happening in the strangest way possible."

I look down at the ring. "It's incredible."

He laughs, a bark of sarcasm. "So, Makayla. Will you?"

I nod, biting my lip. "Yes," I whisper, laughing. "I will."

He holds the ring up to the light, and the brilliant gleam is blinding. "Do you want to know about this ring?"

I smile, biting my lip to keep from laughing. "There's a story?"

He nods. "Of course there is," he says, grinning, and I hear him take on his I'm-about-to-lecture voice. "The two center stones were mined in the early eighteen hundreds, and purchased by my great-great-great-grandfather at a cost that would make your eyes water even by today's standards. He kept them as family heirlooms for the next fifty years, until my great-great-grandfather had them made into two plain diamond solitaire rings. And by plain, I only mean simple, but no less beautiful. He gave them to his daughters, and they wore them as wedding rings until they both died together in a train accident in France near the turn of the century."

I stare at the diamonds. "Blood diamonds for real, then, huh?"

He smiles. "Don't worry, there's a happy ending." He traces the filigree. "So, when the wreckage was cleared and the bodies were recovered, the rings were intact, but destroyed beyond repair. My great-grandfather took the rings with the heirloom diamonds to a master jeweler in London, during the Edwardian era. The master jeweler used the diamonds to create this ring, and many years later, my great-grandfather gave it to his daughter, my grandmother. She wore it until the day she died, and left it to me in her will." He grins sheepishly. "I've had it since in a safety deposit box since she passed, ten years ago, and honestly forgot about it until this morning, when I realized I never actually asked you properly to marry me." He takes my left hand in his. "So now, my family heirloom belongs to you."

"It's too much, Paxton."

"Each diamond is a full two carats, with another carat's worth in smaller stones, set in nearly two-hundred-year-old platinum." His eyes meet mine. "I grew up staring at this ring on Grandma's finger, knowing she would give it to me. And I always wondered whom I would give it to. I'd honestly given up thinking I would find anyone worthy of wearing it."

I swallow hard. "Is it another priceless artifact, with a value of a small nation's GDP?"

He shakes his head. "You're what's priceless, Makayla. It's just a ring."

"That's been in your family in this state for over a hundred years."

"Stop arguing." He frowns at me, but there's a smile under it. "It's mine to give, and I want you to wear it."

It's so heavy on my finger, weighty in both size and age, as well as value. "Only because it was your grandmother's."

A knock on the door. "Hello? Are you decent, Makayla?" It's Julie, entering carrying a huge white dress bag over her arm.

"Yes," I call out, over Paxton's shoulder. "I'm here."

She sees Paxton kneeling in front of me, holding my hand, and her eyes immediately water. "Oh, Paxton. You asked her for real?"

Paxton nods. "I did." He stands up. "Now, you'd better get her dressed so we can get married." He indicates the dress bag. "Is that going to make Mom shit puppies?"

Julie grins wickedly. "Puppies, kittens, camels, and cows."

"Good." He leans over me, kisses me softly. "Still not saying it, but you know it."

I push him away. "Same. Now go away so I can get dressed." I smile. "You made me cry, *and* you just messed up my lipstick. The glam squad is going to kill you."

He waves a hand. "The glam squad is getting rich off this." He heads for the door. "You're beautiful."

I laugh. "I'm in a dressing gown, you goose."

He arches an eyebrow. "I'd marry you wearing that."

"I know." I bite my lip again. "It's crazy, but I know."

Julie pushes him out. "God, you two are so cute it

makes me sick." She hangs the dress on a hook on the back of the door, unzips it, and withdraws a sculpture of lace and silk. "Now *this*…oh my *god,* Makayla. This dress. You don't even know."

My eyes fill. "Don't tell me—it was his grandmother's."

She nods. "Yes." She pets the dress lovingly.

"What about the one I chose and we had altered?"

"Those were chosen by Camilla." She helps me out of my dressing gown and into the dress; I move with exquisite care, so as to not accidentally snag the lace. "This is, well…it's an antique, a priceless vintage piece."

I sigh. "Everything is a priceless antique with these people."

"Well, when you can afford literally anything, the only way to own something truly priceless is if it's an historical piece, and the deBraun family prides themselves on tradition and history." She buttons the back of the dress.

I bite my lip, holding my breath as she tucks and shoves and squeezes me into the dress. "How the— ohmygod—" I gasp as she fastens the last button, "how the hell can I fit into it? I know for a fact I'd be a giant by Edwardian standards."

Julie doesn't answer until I'm into it. Her expression makes me nervous. "We had it altered to fit you."

"It's a priceless antique," I protest.

"And it was altered by a master seamstress working

with a fashion historian, along with Vera Wang herself." A dreamy look comes over Julie's face. "What an honor that was."

I blink. "Of course," I sigh. "Paxton."

"Paxton," Julie agrees.

"Camilla really is going to shit puppies."

Julie's eyes widen. "You don't even know. She tried to get someone to alter it so she could wear it at her wedding, but the executors of the deBraun archival estate wouldn't let her." She grins. "Paxton got permission somehow, but he had to sneak it out from under his mother's nose."

I sigh and then laugh. "He's really going out of his way to rub her nose in this, isn't he?"

Julie nods, stepping back to admire me in the dress. "Very much so." She turns me around to face the mirror. "There, now look."

It's delicate, ivory from age, and if it has indeed been altered, it was done with such consummate skill that I can't tell. It's full-sleeved and the neckline is high, but the sleeves from shoulder down are sheer lace, and the neckline is a crisscross web of silk and sheer lace over my cleavage, so that while the gown bows to Edwardian notions of modesty, it's graceful and elegant and even sexy, in a demure sort of way; the silk falls to mid-thigh, where sheer silk embroidered with delicate flowers twine around my legs, the hem scalloped above my feet and draping behind me in a long train.

It's so beautiful, so elegant, and bears such personal history that I have to fight back tears.

Julie is crying, too. "I've worked for the family for a very long time, and this is my favorite moment, ever." A sniffed laugh. "At least, until Camilla sees you."

"How does he manage this stuff?" I ask.

"He's Paxton deBraun." She glances a tiny silver watch. "Speaking of which, it's time."

I swallow hard. "I'm suddenly not ready."

Julie pats me on the cheek. "Yes you are. And anyway, this part isn't for you, it's for Camilla."

"This part?" I ask.

Julie's eyes widen and she shrugs, face suddenly blank. "I just mean…" She waves a hand. "I don't know what I mean."

I hear organ music somewhere far away, and while it's not the wedding march, it's a signal that it's time for me to take my place at the doors.

I follow Julie, swallowing nerves. A young woman from the glam squad finds me and walks backward in front of me, touching up my makeup, while another fiddles with my hair, and they fuss and fuss until I huff.

"Enough," I say, trying not to snap at them out of nerves. "Thank you. I think it's fine."

They vanish, just like that, and it's me and Julie and we're gliding down a long dark hallway, and I see a pair of wide double doors, and Liam is waiting on this side of them, in a tuxedo of his own.

Liam is Paxton's best man, and he's also giving

me away—I never knew my own father, and I still haven't met Paxton's, and so Liam is the only man I know other than Paxton...and we're best of friends, after these months of being driven around by him and guarded by him and pranked by him.

He offers me his arm, and I tuck my hand around his elbow. His smile is dangerous and eager and comforting. "Ready?"

I sigh. "No." I lift my chin, steel my spine. "Yes."

"Attagirl," Liam says, in his deep, raspy soldier's voice. "Focus on Paxton, all right? Don't worry about anyone else."

"If I trip, will you catch me?" I ask, feeling wobbly on the delicate ivory heels, clutching the bouquet of white roses in a death grip.

"You know it." He eyes me. "Cold feet?"

I smile at him. "Nervous, but no. His mom is going to hate me."

"I'm not sure there's anyone she actually likes, so that's okay."

I feel a wave of melancholy. "I wish my own mom was here."

Liam is oddly silent on that, and only pats my hand. "Of course you do."

Mom has gotten worse during these last couple of weeks before the wedding—Paxton's plans to bring her to DC to live with us fell through, because she was too sick to move, and so I've made the flight out to see her nearly every day. I think seeing me learning how to be happy with Paxton has given her permission to stop fighting so hard, which is heartbreaking for me, but I can see how tired she is. I saw her last night, and she was in and out of consciousness. She saw me, kissed my cheek, told me she loved me—three squeezes of her hand.

I blink hard, push all that away.

Bum-BUM-bum-bum....

The organ is loud, and I hear a rustle of people standing up.

The doors open.

I see Pax standing at the altar, and suddenly everything is okay—the whole world narrows down to him, and only him. I don't even see the world-famous interior of St. Patrick's—just Paxton.

I'm aware of whispers as the audience sees me for the first time.

I ignore them all.

Focus on Paxton's grin.

One voice cuts through my screen: Camilla's.

"No!" Shrill, angry. "No!"

"Mother, enough," Paxton snaps.

"Not *her*!"

"Yes, Mother, her." Paxton is proud, and I've never heard such triumph in a voice before.

I manage to widen my scope of sight to take in Camilla, standing in front of me, fury crackling in her eyes.

"You!" she snarls.

I summon a polite smile. "Hi, Camilla."

She whirls on Paxton. "A hotel maid, Paxton? Really?"

Paxton's eyes go glacial, sharper than obsidian and harder than diamond. "You're embarrassing yourself, Mother."

She clicks her teeth together, and then she looks me over, and goes pale as eggshells. "Mother's gown?" Then her eyes fix on the ring on my finger. "The ring? Paxton, really? The ring?"

Paxton descends the steps and takes my hands in his, leads me past the fuming dragon that is Camilla deBraun. We stand face to face in front of the minister, pastor, reverend, priest, whatever.

"This is too much, Paxton. I won't allow it."

Paxton grins. "I've bad news for you, Mom." He gestures at the cathedral. "You put deposits down on the venue, and everything else. Guess what, Mom? I paid for it all. So, this isn't *your* wedding anymore. You planned it, and by god you did an amazing job, I must say. But it's now *my* wedding." He kisses my knuckles. "*Our* wedding."

She narrows her eyes, and she seems ready to spit on the floor out of sheer rage. "Quit pretending, Paxton."

He laughs. "Funny thing is, Mom, up until about three weeks ago, I would have been pretending." He smiles at me. "Then an odd thing happened."

Camilla eyes me, and I let every ounce of my

nascent, still-growing love for Paxton bleed through into my gaze.

"I fell in love." He laughs again. "I got engaged because you made me." He squeezes my hands three times. "I'm getting married because I love her."

Camilla huffs and whirls away, preparing to march out.

"Mom, wait," Paxton calls out, and she stops.

"*What*, Paxton?" she snaps, her voice icy and brittle.

I laugh under my breath, because all this is happening in front of a packed-out crowd of high-profile guests, the minister, and even media.

"I just wanted to thank you," he says, giving her a genuine smile, all shit-eating gleeful revenge gone, now. "If it wasn't for you, I'd have never met Makayla. So, I really do hope you stay." A thick, stifling pause. "You're the guest of honor, after all."

She bites down on her lip, sighing deeply. "You're too cruel, Paxton."

A shake of his head. "I mean it. You did this to force my hand, and I did it to get back at you, in a lot of ways—from it being Makayla, to the dress and the ring. But now, I'm doing it out of love, and all it's because of you." He leaves me at the altar, descends to stand in the middle of the aisle in front of his mother. "Stay. Please."

A tear slides down her cheek, and she has enough steel in her spine and pride in her soul that it makes her more elegant, stronger for the emotion. "My mother's dress, Paxton," she whispers.

"And Grandma's ring."

Camilla stares at him. It's a frozen tableau, not a sound to be heard—not a cough, not a sniffle, not a breath. "Truly, Paxton? It's not all some elaborate game?"

Instead of answering himself, he looks to me. "Makayla?"

"I would marry him even if he didn't have a penny to his name, and I would marry him in front of a justice of the peace, just the two of us." I catch my breath, looking around for the first time at the enormity of the gathered audience hanging on every moment of this drama. "I'd probably be happier with that, honestly," I mutter under my breath.

She stares at me, examining me, searching me, and then turns back to her son. "If this is a joke, I'll never forgive you, Paxton."

He holds her hand. "Look at me, Mom. You know me as well as anyone besides Makayla and Liam. Do I look like I'm faking this?"

He lets her search him, and it's another long, silent moment.

"Only you could pull this off," she says, summoning her pride. "Very well."

And with that, Camilla deBraun takes a seat in the first pew on the left side of the aisle, folding her hands on her lap, spine straight, head high; she is poised, elegant, and polished, as if nothing had ever happened.

Paxton returns to me, gathers my hands in his, and smiles at me. "That went well."

I huff. "Is that sarcasm?"

He shakes his head, eyes wide. "Not at all. I expected more of a blowout, honestly."

The priest/minister clears his throat meaningfully. "If that's all settled, shall we begin?"

I look out at the crowd again, and my breath hitches in my throat: I see A-list Hollywood actors, men and women whom I've grown up watching on the silver screen, and I see powerful, influential politicians looking polished and professional in thousand-dollar suits, and I see rock stars and musicians decked out in dramatic leather and dripping jewelry and tattoo ink, and I see a coalition of deBrauns in the rows behind Camilla watching with bored curiosity; both sides of the aisle are full, and not one person is here for *me*.

The only person here for me is the man I'm standing with.

I suck in a sharp, harsh, fast breath. Nod once. "I'm ready."

Paxton squeezes my hands—three times; I never told him about that, but he figured it out, watching me with my mother.

God, I miss her.

I wish she could be here.

My eyes water, and I blink hard. Paxton doesn't have to ask. "I know, Mack. It's okay."

The minister begins speaking, droning in a stentorian voice about the power of love and the weighty responsibility of marriage, and the importance of God being the center of any relationship.

I think perhaps the minister catches a whiff of Paxton's impatience, because he stumbles once, and seems to skip ahead in his prepared remarks.

Then, finally, we're led through canned, recycled vows, and I say them dutifully, even though there's so much else I wanted to say, vows I've been writing in my head for days now. But Paxton just seems to want to get through this as much as I do, because he repeats the vows without looking away from me, and then the minister asks the fated, heavy question:

"Do you, Makayla, take this man, Paxton, to be your lawfully wedded husband, now and forever, for better and for worse, till death do you part?"

I swallow hard, swallow a shaky breath, and nod. "I do," I whisper.

Holy shit. I just said I do.

Paxton answers the same question, but with no hesitation, and in a much stronger voice. He smiles as he says it, confident and proud.

We turn to face the crowd. "May I present to you Mr. and Mrs. Paxton deBraun," the minister announces, and there is a loud cheer.

Paxton raises one hand, the other holding tightly

on to mine. "Thank you for coming everyone, and please, join us at the Four Seasons at six thirty for the reception. See you all then!"

I blink at that announcement. "Six thirty?" I ask. "It's just now two."

He winks at me. "I know."

"So what are we doing for the few hours?"

"Photographs, for one thing." A long, serious look. "And something else, which you'll just have to trust me about."

I breathe carefully, searching him. Finally, I nod. "Okay, I trust you."

He smiles brightly. "Good, thank you. For now, though, we have photographs."

The next thirty minutes are spent wandering the grounds of St. Patrick's, being followed by a photographer with four cameras hanging by straps from her body, directing us to stand this way and that, pose this way, now kiss, hold it, okay good now kiss his cheek… and so on, until I'm ready to scream.

Then, finally, the photographs are done, and it's just me and Paxton alone in the church, with Liam standing at attention by the doors.

I sigh, wearily. "Well, husband—now what?"

He grins. "You're not my wife yet, actually."

I frown. "Um. I said I do, and we exchanged rings." I wiggle my ring finger at him, so the massive double diamonds glint, and the platinum wedding band behind it glistens. "I think that makes us married."

"Almost, but not quite." He smiles at me. "There's one more thing to do, yet."

I frown harder. "I've not really attended that many weddings but I think, other than the reception, we've done everything."

He just smiles even more vaguely. "Come on. I'll show you."

I sigh, nod, and tuck my hand in his arm. "Okay. Lead the way."

The way turns out to be a black Mercedes sedan, and a drive through Manhattan to a nondescript glass-and-steel high-rise in Tribeca. Instead of the penthouse suite I imagined, Liam leads the way past even the penthouse, to the roof.

A small private helicopter is waiting, engine warming up, rotors moving gently. I blink at Paxton. "A helicopter?"

He nods. "Step one."

"You're being kind of mysterious," I say, hunting his expression for a clue about what's happening.

"Just trust me, okay? This is for you."

"For me?"

He nods, a hand stuffed in his tuxedo pocket. "Yep. For you."

I sigh, and climb into the helicopter, accepting his hand as assistance for the step up. The interior is as luxurious and sleek as the inside of the fancy armored Pullman limo, the seats quilted, hand-stitched white leather with built-in footrests and massage functions and heaters and cupholders, and a cooler for champagne, and expansive views in almost three hundred and sixty degrees.

Liam and Paxton climb in, buckle, and then the rotors spin up to speed and there's a sense of weightlessness as we lift off. I hold Paxton's hand tightly, but my mind is too busy trying to figure out where we're going to be scared.

A ten-minute ride brings us to a private section of the airport, where one of the deBraun's fleet of jets waits, engines running. I'm starting to get an inkling about what we're doing, but don't dare hope.

It's a two-hour flight, which I spend restless, anxious. Despite having made this flight nearly every day for the last few weeks, it seems to take longer than ever.

Finally, we land, and the now-familiar Pullman is waiting. We make the drive from Pellston to Petoskey in record time, and when we pull up in front of an all-too-familiar nursing home, my heart seems to leap and break at the same time.

The car stops, but I don't get out. I stare at Paxton, my eyes watering. "Pax?"

"Are you ready for our *real* wedding?"

"Real wedding?"

"That scene in New York? That was for Mom, and for the media." He waves at the nursing home. "This is for us."

22

LIAM OPENS THE LIMOUSINE DOOR, HANDS ME OUT, and Paxton follows; together, him in his tux and me in the antique, heirloom wedding gown, we go inside. The hallways are so familiar, smelling antiseptic, quiet, our shoes squeaking and clicking. Heads poke out, white hair and wrinkles, eyes watching, smiles.

There is a courtyard, and it's one of the reasons Mom chose this place—her nurses bring her out to the courtyard every day unless it's raining or snowing. It's small, just a square of open space created by the lay-out of the building, filled with box shrubs and Japanese dwarf maples, some brightly colored perennials wandering in rows between stone-lined walkways. It's peaceful, quiet, and lovely.

Today, it's lovelier than ever—Pax clearly had his people work their magic: white gauzy silk is draped from tree to tree, lit with soft golden light from twinkling strands, creating a heavenly canopy. A white, rose-wreathed arch stands in the center of the courtyard.

Under the arch stands a pastor holding a leather-bound folder.

Off to one side, Mom. In a wheelchair, alert, awake, beaming. Dressed in a beautiful champagne gown, her hair in an elaborate updo, makeup perfect.

Paxton walks me to Mom. "For you, Makayla."

I blink back tears. Hug Mom. "Hi, Momma."

She grabs my hand in a fierce grip, squeezes three times. Blinks back her own tears. She wants to speak, but she can't. She doesn't need to, though—I see everything she's thinking and feeling in her eyes.

"I'm here, Mom." I laugh through tears. "Ready for this wedding?"

She squeezes my hand again, once. Smiles at me. Swallows hard, breathing deeply. "Love…you…Mack."

"I love you so much, Momma."

She extends a shaky hand to Paxton, who kneels beside her, taking her hand in both of his. "Pax…"

"I'm here, Mrs. Poe."

She gives him a long, deep, searching look. "Love… her?"

He nods, and he's moved, blinking back tears of his own. "Yes, ma'am. I do. I love Makayla very much."

A small, weak nod. "Give her…everything."

"I will. I promise."

"Break…heart…and I'll…I'll haunt you. Forever." Despite her weakness, Mom somehow manages to sound hard and threatening.

Paxton laughs. "I can't promise I won't ever hurt

her, because I'm a man and I'm an idiot. But I love her with all that I am, and I will take care of her with everything I've got."

Mom turns her attention to me. "Love him?"

I nod, brushing tears away. "I do. I really do."

"Four months, Mack. Sure?"

I laugh. "I think sometimes, love at first sight takes a while to kick in."

Mom nods, a wobbly bob of her head. Paxton's hand in one of hers, mine in the other, she presses Paxton's hand over mine, sandwiched between hers. "Bless you." Her eyes search mine, his. "Love is work. Do the work." We both nod and promise, and Mom lets us go. Juts her chin at the arch. "Get married, then."

And so, we do.

The pastor's words to Pax and me are simple, and brief. "Today is about union. It's about love. There is no audience, here, only two witnesses. Others have written with greater eloquence than I'm capable of on the topic of love and marriage, so I'll just refer you to First Corinthians, the thirteenth chapter, which many consider to be the single greatest passage on love ever written. I'm tempted to read you the whole chapter, but I won't. I'll just quote you verses four through eight, and ask you, Paxton and Makayla, to consider them every day as you embark on this journey of marriage: 'Love is patient and kind; love does not envy or boast; it is not arrogant or rude. It does not insist on its own way; it is not irritable or resentful; it does not rejoice at wrongdoing, but rejoices with the truth. Love bears all things, believes all things, hopes all things, endures all things. Love never ends.'"

He lets those verses stand in the silence, resounding in our minds.

Then, he looks to Paxton. "You have something to say, I believe."

Paxton nods, inhales slowly, holds it, and then smiles at me—it's a Paxton deBraun Special, proud and confident, arrogant, but now also leavened and softened by love. "I'm still not sure how this happened. How I managed to fall in love with you, and how you fell in love with me. I don't get it." He sighs, shakes his head. "I've been avoiding love and vulnerability my whole life, and then, right when I thought was safe, when I wasn't looking, love came and snuck up on me and...here we are. Four months to the day after I was forced into accepting an arranged marriage, here we are, marrying for real. For love."

The minister smiles at Pax. "You have vows, do you not?"

Pax laughs. "Yeah, I was getting there." He sucks in a breath, lets it out shakily. "Makayla, my vows are simple. I promise to love you as best I know how, and to spend every day learning how to be better at loving you. I promise to be open, honest, vulnerable, and faithful." A pause, a grin. "I also promise that life will never be boring."

I'm choking back tears, because it's my turn and everything I had in my mind to say has fled. "Pax..." I breathe in, steady myself. "I promise to spend the rest of our lives learning how to love you the way he—" I point at the minister, "just said love is supposed to be."

"Those are St. Paul's words, not mine," the minister says, gently correcting me with a soft smile.

"I promise to be faithful. To never give up. To forgive you when you piss me off. To be your best friend, your partner in everything. I promise I'll never stop calling you on your shit—" I glance at the minister. "Ooops, sorry. Your crap."

He just grins. "I'm not offended, and I don't think God is either. He loves everyone, even potty mouths."

I laugh through tears. "Good. Anyway. And I also promise that life with me will never, ever be boring."

This time, it's meaningful, deeply and personally intentional and moving, when I say the words.

"Do you, Makayla Poe, take this man, Paxton deBraun, to be your lawfully and spiritually wedded husband, for better or worse, for richer or poorer, in sickness and in health, till death do you part?"

I sniffle, squeeze both of his hands three times. "I do."

"And do you, Paxton deBraun, take this woman, Makayla Poe, to be your lawfully and spiritually wedded wife, for better or worse, for richer or poorer, in sickness and in health, till death do you part?"

He inhales deeply, smiling at me with the full force

of his bright, dominant, forceful, beautiful personality. "I do."

"Then, by the power vested in me by the state of Michigan, and, more importantly, by God the Father, God the Son, and God the Holy Spirit, I now pronounce you man and wife." He pauses, hesitating with a grin. "You may kiss—"

Paxton's got that part down, his lips on mine, hot and searching and demanding.

"I guess you know," the minister says.

I laugh even as Paxton kisses me breathless.

It is in no way a kiss appropriate for a wedding, but I don't care, and neither does Paxton. It's a kiss that speaks the words he's still learning how to voice, that I'm still learning how to hear. It's a kiss that encompasses the wild, insane, reckless way we fell in love.

It's a kiss that speaks of our future.

When the kiss finally ends, Paxton is still holding me in his arms, bent over backward in a deep dip, his hand on the back of my head, the other at my back, his lips brushing mine.

"Can I say it now?" he whispers.

I laugh, nod. "Yes," I breathe. "You can say it now."

He kisses me again, briefly. His eyes twinkle, sparkle, dance. "I love you, Makayla."

To hear those words, meant with such sweet, soul-deep sincerity, breaks my heart into a million pieces, tangles the pieces and twines them and braids them and weaves them into the pieces which make up Paxton, and reforms me into a new whole, one with Paxton, in a way I would never have considered possible, until now.

"I love you, Paxton." He lifts me upright, and I can finally breathe again. "Now what?"

"Now we spend a few minutes with your mom, and then we fly back to Manhattan for the reception, and then from there we fly to the Seychelles, where my wedding gift to you awaits."

"The where, and your what?" I blink at him. "My what?"

"Tropical islands off the coast of Africa." He grins. "You're gonna freak out, so I'm not going to tell you."

"Paxton deBraun, I swear, if you bought me an entire island or something, I'm going to…" I laugh, sigh, and shake my head. "Well, I'll just tell you that I hope you plan on helping me fill it with kids."

He smirks. "It's not a whole island."

I sigh in relief. "Oh, good."

"Just most of one."

"Paxton."

He eyes me warily. "When you say fill it with kids, though…how many are you thinking, and how soon?"

I just grin. "I don't know. Half a dozen at least. And…soon."

"I feel like we should've discussed this before now."

I laugh. "I'm teasing, mostly." I pat his chest. "I do want kids someday, though."

Mom takes my hand, squeezes. I give her my attention, and she's glowing. "I could probably...hang on for...a few more...years...for a...a grandbaby."

I kneel beside her and hug her as tightly as I dare. "You better."

"Happy?" she asks, smiling up at me.

"Beyond happy, Mom." I kiss her cheek. "Thank you."

"For?"

"Making me give him a chance. I wouldn't have, otherwise."

"Love is...worth the risk." She brings my hands to her lips, kisses my knuckles. "Besides...he's cute."

I grin up at Paxton. "Hear that, honey? Mom thinks you're cute."

He has produced, from somewhere, three champagne flutes, and a bottle of champagne—which, knowing him probably cost more than this entire building. He pops the cork, pours bubbly champagne into the three flutes, and hands them to us. Mom holds hers carefully, in both hands, and we toast.

"To you, Mrs. Poe—for encouraging your daughter give a man like me a chance."

Mom smiles, shakes her head, and summons her strength. "To you two, and to love—may it last forever." She sips, a tiny, token sip, and then rests the flute on her lap.

She's tired, I can tell.

We spend a few more minutes with her, and then

she's falling asleep, and I hold her, hug her, kiss her cheek, and promise to come see her soon.

Two hours later, we're back in Manhattan, celebrating with a bunch of people we don't know. Or, I don't. Paxton seems to, but he's never far from my side, introducing me to people as his wife, beaming with pride.

The celebration goes late into the night, but at some point well past midnight, Paxton spirits me away from the reception and into the helicopter once more— it takes us to the airport again, and this time to a much larger jet—his father's executive whatever monstrosity. I'm half asleep by this point, and take little notice of what it looks like. I'm content to let Paxton sweep me off my feet, literally, and carry me into a bedroom, lay me on the bed, help me out of my dress and into a big soft T-shirt of his, and he cradles me in his arms as the jet takes off and whisks us away somewhere remote.

I don't care where we go—I'm where I want to be.

Epilogue

Eight years later

I'M STANDING IN THE COLD, BUNDLED UP IN A THICK, warm, but fashionable jacket. It's January 20, and I'm watching my husband swear an oath.

"...And will to the best of my ability, preserve, protect and defend the Constitution of the United States." He's nervous, I can tell—who wouldn't be? He's proud, though, and eager, and excited, and fearful.

Beside me, on my right, is our eldest son, Jackson, seven, with his father's golden eyes and dark hair, and my dark skin and fiery attitude. To my left is our daughter, Cambria, five, fair-skinned like her father but with my curly black hair and my eyes, with her father's confidence and self-assured arrogance.

Camilla watches from beside Cambria—that's an oddity, Camilla and Cambria. Camilla fell in love with Jackson, being so much like Paxton as he is. But it was Cambria who truly changed Camilla, and not just because she was named in honor of her grandmother.

Something about Cambria just...changed Camilla. Sweetened her, softened her. They're holding hands, right now, actually, and while my relationship with Camilla is sometimes still awkward and tense, seeing the way she is with my daughter is enough.

They both have elements which remind me of Mom; Jackson has her smile, and Cambria has her laugh. My chest tightens whenever I think about Mom—she passed a couple years ago. She hung on so she could meet her grandchildren, kiss them, bless them, and it means the world to me that Mom got to meet my babies.

Paxton removes his hand from the Bible, shoots me a cocky grin and a wink that says *Hey, baby—guess who just got sworn in as president.*

I couldn't be more proud of him. He campaigned on a promise of bringing together the divisive political scene, and even in the process of running for president began the work of uniting politicians from both sides as only Paxton could—the election was a landslide of record-breaking proportions, with voters from all walks of life coming out to put their faith in Paxton and his promises of unity, healing, and progress.

God knows he's accomplished those things in his own life—repairing and improving his relationship with his mother, especially since the birth of Cambria, and making inroads into a relationship with his father, who is mostly retired now. Paxton did end up taking over his father's company, but restructured it to run it to only need his input a few times a year, and with most of the profits going into a family trust for our kids and eventual grandkids.

The rest of the ceremony is a blur, and I have eyes only for my husband.

Eight years, two kids, and a stupid amount of money later, and my husband is still shooting me those cocky, cheesy winks, and I'm still falling for them.

When we finally get a moment alone, he curls an arm low around my hips and kisses the shell of my ear. "Well, Madam First Lady. How do you feel?"

"Proud of you," I whisper, kissing the corner of his mouth. "And more in love than ever."

Paxton laughs. "Not bad for an arranged fake marriage between people who knew each other barely four months, right?"

"Yeah," I agree. "Not bad." I lean up to whisper in his ear. "Now, let's get the rest of this nonsense over with. I need to show my husband, the president of the United States, exactly how proud of him I really am."

If we weren't obligated to attend the rest of the festivities and celebrations, I think he would have swept me off to the nearest empty bedroom right then and there…

And I would have let him.

But he'll be worth the wait, today and always.

The End

Visit me at my website: **www.jasindawilder.com**
Email me: **jasindawilder@gmail.com**

If you enjoyed this book, you can help others enjoy it as well by recommending it to friends and family, or by mentioning it in reading and discussion groups and online forums. You can also review it on the site from which you purchased it. But, whether you recommend it to anyone else or not, thank you *so much* for taking the time to read my book! Your support means the world to me!

My other titles:

The Preacher's Son:
Unbound
Unleashed
Unbroken

Biker Billionaire:
Wild Ride

Big Girls Do It:
Better (#1), Wetter (#2), Wilder (#3), On Top (#4)
Married (#5)
On Christmas (#5.5)
Pregnant (#6)
Boxed Set

Rock Stars Do It:
Harder
Dirty
Forever
Boxed Set

From the world of *Big Girls* and *Rock Stars*:
Big Love Abroad

Delilah's Diary:
A Sexy Journey
La Vita Sexy
A Sexy Surrender

The Falling Series:
Falling Into You
Falling Into Us
Falling Under
Falling Away
Falling for Colton

The Ever Trilogy:
Forever & Always
After Forever
Saving Forever

The world of *Alpha*:
Alpha
Beta
Omega
Harris: Alpha One Security Book 1
Thresh: Alpha One Security Book 2
Duke: Alpha One Security Book 3
Puck: Alpha One Security Book 4

The world of Stripped:
Stripped
Trashed

The world of *Wounded*:
Wounded
Captured

The Houri Legends:
Jack and Djinn
Djinn and Tonic

The Madame X Series:
Madame X
Exposed
Exiled

The Black Room
(With Jade London):
Door One

Door Two

Door Three

Door Four

Door Five

Door Six

Door Seven

Door Eight

Deleted Door

The One Series
The Long Way Home

Where the Heart Is

There's No Place Like Home

Badd Brothers:
Badd Motherf*cker

Badd Ass

Badd to the Bone

Good Girl Gone Badd

Badd Luck

Badd Mojo

Big Badd Wolf

Badd Boy

Badd Kitty

Badd Business

Badd Medicine

Dad Bod Contracting:

Hammered

Drilled

Nailed

Screwed

Fifty States of Love

Pregnant in Pennsylvania

Cowboy in Colorado

Married in Michigan

Standalone titles:

Yours

Non-Fiction titles:

You Can Do It

You Can Do It: Strength

You Can Do It: Fasting

Jack Wilder Titles:

The Missionary

JJ Wilder Titles:

Ark

To be informed of new releases, special offers, and other Jasinda news, sign up for Jasinda's email newsletter.

Made in the USA
Middletown, DE
06 July 2021

43701078R00220